SOAP AND WATER

Camille Nelson

IBSN: 979-8-218-09203-0 (Paperback)
Printed in the United States of America

Editing by Katherine Pelz and Janet Robbins Rosenberg

Cover by Jason McNeil

Special thanks to Karen, MJ, and RJ for your insights and inspirations.

CONTENTS

PROLOGUE

Rain. The soft pitter-patter of drizzle accompanies a glorious overcast sky. The endless beat in New York's Greenwich Village sags a bit due to the lazy feel of the day, but the ever-present energy remains as foot traffickers bustle with a certain lagged pep, commuting in a mixture of designer raincoats, hoodies, and ponchos to protect themselves from the lukewarm precipitation. We picked such a perfect day for this, the weather matching the mood to a tee.

I decide to get there early. I knew she would be late, but I still decide to arrive before our agreed-upon time. Maybe I need time to get my thoughts together; maybe I need time to relax, to settle the rolling tree trunk in my stomach.

Just beyond our meeting place, a few brightly colored magazines sporting beautiful models on their covers catch my eye, and I stop for a closer inspection. I take in the vibrant and artful canvases of the various fashion, lifestyle, and musical periodicals with new eyes, with a curiosity and awareness I'd never recognized before. Everything around me is tingling. Are these nerves? I can even feel several instances of subconscious inquisition from women, and some men, as they hip and hop toward their final destinations. I feel like a superhero; like I have intimate, innate powers. I've felt this way before. She must be close.

As I skim the litany of chiseled jawbones and gaunt waistlines, I notice a caption on one of the model-laden glossies that reads, "The Unspoken Fling. Do You Ever Tell Your Significant Other? Page 69." Immediately after, I hear her voice, turn, and see her.

***

The subway slows to a growling stop, the doors open, and I immediately ignore my advice as I shoot out of the tin sardine box like a cannon and leap up the slippery staircase, landing swiftly yet carefully on every other stair.

It feels like I'm climbing to heaven. The physical exertion, the anticipation, and the anxiety that are operating inside of me all at once have put me in a state of dizzied euphoria. By the time I get to the top of the stairs, I feel like I am floating. When I stop, my body keeps going, floating over everyone and everything, even the rain. It's terrifying. It feels like I am going to just float away and vanish into the cosmos.

I start to panic. I attempt to grasp at whatever is around me, to try to get grounded, to try to gain my sea legs again, but it is impossible. The ether has me, and I am on my way to another place.

It's only when I see him that my soul comes crashing back down to Earth. Admittedly, I am glad to be back, back home.

Feels like I haven't seen him in ages. He is different, but the same. He has the same confidence and coolness in his stance, as if he'd lived a former life as a sultan, and his eyes can still light up a dark, dank subway tunnel.

Finally feeling my feet underneath me again, I take a deep breath, then begin my approach. As I move in closer, I follow the raindrops as they splash down on his smooth, chocolate skin and trickle down to his chin and fingertips, only to be released back to the atmosphere ever so briefly before nurturing this new world. My mouth longs to catch those rebirthed droplets before they reach the ground. To taste him again, to be fertilized by his essence one more time; that's remained on my mind since last laying eyes on him. And there he is, reading a magazine, being pelted with Earth's tears. What a magnificent sight!

I watch him for what seems like an eternity. Then, when I muster up enough moxie, I feel my mouth speak. "Searching for something new, Mr. Booker?"

When my eyes finally take her all in, I can see that she is awkward, self-conscious, and absolutely radiant. She is all of the things I had come to know about her, and it is still an intoxicating, delightful mix. She is the perfect concoction of unpronounced sex appeal and unfocused magnetism. If she wanted to, she could take over the world, she just doesn't know how. She stands there with a smile that could block traffic.

"You're late, Ms. Lamberty," I said.

She gasps, then looks at her watch. "I'm not late!"

"We said three thirty. It's going on three forty-five."

"Okay, so we'll be fashionably late. Fashionably late is good. Just think, for the first time in your life, you'll finally be considered fashionable. I know you've been trying and everything, with the silk shirts and all, but this time it's a sure thing!"

I employ my best faux frown and try to think of a snappy comeback, but my mind goes blank—plus, she was right.

"Whatever," I say as I flash my trademark smile, the left corner of my mouth curled higher than the right.

"You'll be in! You'll finally get to sit at the cool table . . ."

"I got it, I got it, damn you." I laugh, happily conceding defeat.

We begin to stroll through the sloppy puddles and waves of wet villagers. He seems to know where he's going, so I faithfully follow his lead. I step where he steps.

"So how've you been?" he asks.

"Ugh! Finally went back to work on Tuesday. Third shift. Brody gets up to go to work at like seven and I don't get up until like two, so we never see each other. It sucks. You?"

"Just finished a production of *Richard the Third*. I'm taking a few weeks before I start looking again, just to chill for a bit," he says.

"Wish I could do that."

"To be honest, I really don't have time to take a break. Toni and I planned a trip to Seychelles this fall, so I need to constantly be pulling in some dough."

"You can always go back to the stroll!"

He laughs from his gut, and I reciprocate. This is familiar, and we recognize it. It was almost like the last six months of total silence hadn't happened, like we've picked up right where we'd left off . . . before the incident.

"Things never change with you, do they?" he says.

"You know I still have to give you grief. That much hasn't changed."

"Anything else stay the same?"

I feel the goose bumps begin to surface on my arms as my tongue lies dormant in my mouth. He lingers awhile, but then pushes on when he sees I'm not going to give him an answer. I'm not sure if he can tell that I desperately want to respond, but I'm just not able to do so.

As we continue to push our way through the damp dankness, we seem to acknowledge each other and the silent attraction that is beginning to simmer between us. This too is familiar.

I can smell the wet concrete as we proceed through the puddles and posh purveyors of designer handbags and silk scarves. The stinging scent adds weight to the sensory satisfaction I am experiencing just being next to him again. The inhaled sulfur burns the back of my throat—a necessary discomfort to keep me tethered to reality. I secretly thank the pain for preventing me from falling completely back down the rabbit hole.

I watch him lead me through the soft, wet jungle of bodies and buildings as if he is a hero, leading me toward safety. He pridefully clears a path for me, and I relish walking in his shadow. We both seem so comfortable in our roles, and naturally fall into them. Even the people we pass pay their respects to us as we display a type of deference that mimics a royal couple making their way through a smattering of their subjects. This couple has power. This couple has panache. This couple is not a couple.

We continue our trek until we reach a quaint Greek restaurant with Greek lettering on its signage. The rain starts to pick up as we step under the restaurant's awning and snap our umbrellas closed. He pulls the heavy oak door open for me, and I enter. I can feel his eyes running down my back and landing on my ass as I walk past him. Automatically, I put an extra hitch in my switch. Not purposefully; it is just a natural, spellbinding reflex brought on by his attention. I am presently aware of the danger in this, the danger I am walking into. Admittedly, I am scared, but I continue to walk through the terror, hoping he won't notice how frightened I am as he follows me inside, his eyes still on me, and my body still organically reacting to his astute study of my body.

The smell of freshly baked bread and the sweet sounds of Miles Davis's "All Blues" soothe my suffering, and the elegant, yet not fancy enough to be off-putting decor helps me ease into the space with more grace than I think I possess at the moment. The atmosphere is breezy and inviting, a perfect place to welcome two wet patrons from the summer splash. We approach the hostesses station and are greeted by three lovely ladies.

"Table for two?" the most attractive hostess says.

He nods, and the hostess walks us to a table situated next to a large window. Heavy rain begins to pelt against the transparent pane as we are seated across from each other. An awkward tension fills the space between us, then migrates to my chest. It feels tight. I am situated squarely in front of him, and it makes me uneasy. I can't look at him, so I admire the water-splashed design on the window left by the constant precipitation.

The silence lingers for what seems like a day. I figure he won't talk first, so I decide to break the ice. I gather all the breath I can in my lungs and say, "Thank you for coming. The way we left it, it was . . . incomplete."

"Yeah. Incomplete." His voice is timid and soft. It barely reaches me, like he's talking to himself. I still can't look at him.

Just then, my attention is drawn from the window by a busboy approaching the table with a silver water pitcher in his hand. The busboy tips the pitcher toward my glass, and I follow the thick stream of fluid as it leaves its housing and purposefully splashes into my glass, leaving small ice chips dancing with delight on the surface.

As the busboy moves to fill his glass, my eyes happen to lift and meet with his, and my ravenous mind immediately springs into action:

I am outside, standing in an alleyway between two residential buildings. I can hear the conversations from the several apartment windows above, but they're too high up for me to see inside. It's cold. I can feel the frostiness on my skin, and I can see my breath as I stand in solitude, waiting for something to happen.

Suddenly, I am forcefully pressed against a brick wall, my face sliding against the cold, hard surface. I am being smothered by a figure who aggressively fondles my breasts and kisses the back of my neck. His breath is hot and so are his lips. His kisses feel like dollops of heated wax being strategically placed on one of my most sensitive spots. They send a shudder up my spine, and sensations to my pleasure points. My heavy breathing and staccato moans indicate my bottomless pleasure. I turn my head to face my Adonis. It's him.

He reaches around to the front of my waist, lifts my miniskirt, slides his fingers under my panties, and begins to warm my clit. As I saturate his fingers, I take in his scent. It's a devilish mixture of fragranced and natural musk, something akin to what he would smell like after a day at the office. The smell expands my appetite and entices me to gorge on him like I would my favorite meal.

When I can't take it anymore, I turn to face him, and slide my panties to my ankles. Simultaneously, he unzips his pants and slides them and his boxers just past his butt. He hoists me against the wall, enters me, and begins to feverishly thrust. My panties swing and dangle off one of my elevated legs as we move with each other's lust. Our sex is fat, swollen by brutal and ballistic maneuvers. Both of our pants and moans fill the shallow alleyway, turning the cramped space into an intimate opera hall, capturing a chaotic symphony of unbridled ecstasy.

As the busboy pours into his glass, a small rebellious drop lifts and falls onto the table, near my hand. This subtle nudge from physics is just enough to awaken me from my daydream. Now fully aware, I notice that we are still eye-locked.

Hello again, stranger.

I force my eyes toward the table, grab my glass, take a sip, and reaffix my focus onto the fascinating exterior waterworks. A familiar rouge becomes present in my cheeks as the waiter lights a flame on the single small romantic table candle.

I am convinced that the danger I felt earlier is now a very real thing, and all of the nervousness and angst I experienced while trudging to get here was well warranted. What have I gotten myself back into? I keep my gaze locked on that glorious pane, and watch the rushing water sweep trash down the wide New York gutters,

washing the soiled streets clean.

1

I stared at the bright rays shining through my cracked bathroom windowpane as if I were studying a Monet. The small blemish acted as a prism; it bent the intense light and created a beautiful rainbow of colors on the white tile floors. I loved looking at that phenomenon and how the light that formed the spectacle shot through the crack like an effervescent beam. The concept of the scattered light entertained me to no end almost every morning until the elevated sounds from the bustling Upper West Side street below my apartment began to slip through the crack in the window and reverberate against the walls. That always seemed to jar me back to reality.

I walked through the candied spectacle while fidgeting with my hair and my stomach in knots. I was on the clock again, and time was moving too fast . . . again.

I landed in front of the medicine cabinet mirror, haphazardly folding and flipping my hair with my hand, to no avail.

Today of all days, you want to be unruly.

On top of that, we were situated in the icy crevice of the cruelest part of winter; thus, I was completely devoid of pigmentation. I hated my complexion during that time of year. I literally looked like a piece of chalk, or at best, and with some industrial-type contouring, a vampire, or some other gestation from the crypt. When I reached the brim of my disgust, I simply let go of the creative hair knot and let it fall limply over my face, hoping to cover God's mistake.

As I blew the bangs from my eyes, I noticed my charming fiancé, standing behind me in the mirror's reflection. He was holding our pet cat, and I instantly fell in love all over again.

"Misty wanted to wish you luck," he said. The sleeve of his blue-and-white plaid pajamas dangled back and forth as he petted the cat's fluffy mane.

"You know, Brody, it's bad luck to wish me luck."

Brody lifted the cat toward his right ear, oh so close to the sexiest version of bedhead I'd ever seen, and pretended that he heard something. "Oh! Wait a minute. What did you say?" He listened for a bit, nodded, then commented, "Excuse her. She says break a leg." His smile was so warm it melted my kneecaps.

I approached them with my drunken-like gait and rubbed noses with Misty, her cold, wet protrusion not being enough to derail my affection. "Aww. Thank you, Misty. You're my wuvy dovey wuvy."

After that embrace, it was back to business. I was now officially running behind schedule and had to get moving. I turned back to the mirror and resumed untangling the cluttered mess my hair had become.

"You know, she's going to be crying for you all day," Brody stated.

"I'm sure she'll get over it."

"What about me?"

I turned and faced him. The light of the sun had soaked the left side of his face, and his rare, fashion model–type jawline was accented by a slender shadow running just underneath it. Even in his blue-and-white plaid pj's, which were frayed at the bottom and had holes in the crotch area, it was as handsome as I had ever seen him. How lucky was I to be engaged to this awesome specimen of a man! I loved him with all that I had, with more than I had, and I absolutely could not wait to be his wife.

"You're going to cry when I'm gone?" I sincerely asked.

"The tears have already started to well up . . . well, maybe it's because I'm becoming allergic to cat fur, but that's just too much of a coincidence!"

"You're an ass!" I said as I turned back toward the mirror.

Through the reflection I watched him put down the cat and move in close behind me. I felt first his breath, then his lips tickle the back of my neck. He inhaled my scent, a mixture of soap and lavender.

"But I will miss you very, very much," he said as he kissed me on the neck.

"Oh my God," I oozed as the goose bumps began to sprout. This was a love I'd always wanted, but could never grasp.

"I'll miss you too," I responded as I continued to fidget.

I could tell Brody was getting frustrated by my displeasure with my appearance and was becoming more and more perturbed that his efforts weren't having a lasting effect. I didn't like disappointing him, but he had to realize that that was me. I'll never be satisfied with my appearance, never. Even though we'd been together for a while, he still hadn't learned to accept this unquenchable quirk of mine, and I wasn't quite sure how to get him to understand. It wasn't a deal breaker, but I did worry from time to time about how much of an impact this would have on our future.

Eventually, he gently took me by the hands, lowered them down to my side, and requested that I look into his deep, brown eyes. Just that easily, just that quickly, all of my chaos melted away. It happened to me every time. I don't know how he did it, but I absolutely loved it when he made time stop for me. He was a magician.

"Don't worry. I'm sure you'll be perfect," he said.

"What if I don't get along with anyone?"

"Believe me. Everyone will love you. I do."

He handed me a small, red, forked-tongued hair clip. I smiled, took the doodad, and situated it in the back of my hair, creating a flatteringly simple style. Finally, I was content, and Brody was the reason once again.

With his beautiful sun-kissed reflection staring at me through the mirror, I said, "And I love you," before I saluted my savior by turning and giving him a passionate kiss.

2

Struggling and out of breath, I hustled toward a golden revolving door attached to a beautiful, monstrous skyscraper in Midtown Manhattan. I tried to zip through the circular entrapment, but there was an elderly woman trying to shuffle her way through the entryway as best she could. When the elderly woman finally cleared the revolving door, I pushed with all my might, thrusted myself out of the cylinder case, and rushed toward a set of golden elevators at the end of the long corridor.

I repeatedly pounded on the UP button until it almost cracked. Finally, I heard the *ding* and the doors welcomed my entry. I stepped in, pressed the button for the fifth floor, then leaned back against the wall to catch my breath. The soothing elevator music immediately began to calm my frenetic disposition, and the doors began to slowly close. However, before they were completely shut, I heard a voice careening down the hallway.

"Hold the elevator!" the female voice said assertively.

I hesitated for a moment, evaluating my needs versus this stranger's, but eventually I succumbed to my inner good samaritan and pressed the OPEN DOOR button. I could hear the footsteps of the person approaching as I held the button down, keeping the elevator doors ajar.

"I've got it!" I confirmed.

Even with the verbal confirmation and me feeling like I'd been holding the doors open for an eternity, the rhythm of the approaching footsteps never broke their cadence—slow, deliberate. The *click-clack* on the marble floor was harsh, like the person was wearing sharp, expensive steel heels. When the footsteps finally reached the lip of the elevator, a beautiful young-looking woman outfitted in the trendiest designer fashions entered.

"Thanks," she said dryly.

I completed an internal eye roll, then finally pressed the illuminated fifth-floor button so the doors could close. Another voice chimed out asking us to hold the door; however, we both allowed the door to shut on the desperate approacher.

The woman in the elevator with me was interesting. I watched her as she whisked her multicolored head wrap off and flipped her dark, luscious hair. Her full body of hair along with her mammoth-sized midnight shades made her look like a Hollywood starlet. Her perfume was also divine, sweet, regal-smelling, and applied with the perfect touch of grace. Even the elegant scarf she was wearing, tied like a blossomed rose, spoke to her elegance and attention to detail. She resembled a very young-looking Jackie O, and it turned my stomach. She was the type I've always felt the most uncomfortable around: the confident ones who knew exactly how to wear themselves, so much so that I began to secretly worship and resent their personas. I continued my envious stare as the elevator lifted to its zenith.

When the bell dinged and the doors opened, she exited the crude transport first, and I followed behind, almost like it was custom. We continued to walk down a long hallway equipped with several wooden doors on each side of the walkway. Each door had a sign with the name of a well-known play or musical on it. We passed by doors that read OLEANNA, THE ODD COUPLE, and THE PHANTOM OF THE OPERA. Several pianos pumping out show tunes as well as the accompanying vocalists could be heard behind those closed doors. I held my breath each time Jackie O passed by one of the rooms.

We continued past A RAISIN IN THE SUN, and HAIRSPRAY, and I stopped as the starlet approached the last door in the hallway. As she read the sign on the door and entered, I let out a deep grunt and slumped my shoulders. *It just had to be that room, didn't it? It just had to be.* I slowly approached the door and read the sign: ROMEO AND JULIET. I leaned my head against the door's cold, hard, wooden frame for a moment, took a deep breath, then entered the room.

The room was very open, wide, and spacious. The stark white paint on the walls made it seem bigger than it was, and the large dusty windows provided a sense of depth and history to the space. There was a certain coolness to the room that led one to believe the thermostat was set to a below-average temperature on purpose. In the center of the room sat a long, square table. Nine people were seated at the table, all with blue folders in front of them—including the beautiful woman from the elevator. All nine turned toward me as I entered, almost as if I were an intruder. I could tell that I'd interrupted the current conversation and that my cheeks were turning red.

"I'm sorry. Am I late?" I asked.

A stone-faced man who must be the stage manager answered, "We were just getting started. Have a seat."

Great, already fucking up. Nice first impression, Anne.

I timidly approached the table, took off my coat, then sat in the only available seat, next to Jackie O.

Once I was seated, the stage manager picked up where he left off. "As I was saying, my name is Trent Cornelius, and I will be your stage manager for this tour. A little background on me: Originally from North Carolina. Came to New York to make it as an actor, didn't work out, now I'm stage managing. Simple as that. This is my fifth tour, and each time I close a tour I say, 'That's the last one. No more tours for me.' But what can I say? Theater is crack." He smiled. Trent's observation was met with confirming smirks and head nods.

"Now, how 'bout we go around the table? Tell us about yourselves, briefly."

Oh crap, I hate this. I've always dreaded introductions, especially introductions in front of a group. I was certainly not afraid to be in the spotlight when encompassing a character, but I absolutely loathed showcasing myself, especially when I was forced to do so. I took a few deep breaths to calm the panic that was beginning to tighten my chest.

Trent gestured to his left. A portly, scruffy-looking man in his early twenties leaned forward and answered in a heavy Brooklyn accent, "Joey Drivus. Actor. I, along with Christian, did this tour two years ago. Don't ask me why I'm doing it again."

We all laughed. Joey even chuckled a bit.

"And what role will you be playing?" Trent asked.

"Oh! Ah . . . I lucked up and got the Romeo gig this year."

A few of us gasped with our eyes. This was clearly going to be an unorthodox retelling of the classic tragedy if he was to don the mantle of the most famous Montague.

"Moving on," Trent said as he gestured to the long-haired, heavyset man sitting next to Joey, outfitted in gothic apparel.

"Hi, guys. My name is Christian. Like Joey said, I too was on this tour two years ago. I don't know about you, Joey, but I had a great time when we last went on the road," Christian said.

Joey cut his eyes and sucked his teeth at him.

"I thought it was great. Maybe it was just me," Christian responded.

"It was just you."

"Oh. Well, I'm excited to be here again and can't wait to work with you guys," Christian said with a pleasant smile on his face.

Jesus. Has everyone done this tour before? Am I the only newbie? The vise grip on my insides compressed even further.

The person next to Christian, a young, attractive redhead with a raspy, low-pitched voice, leaned forward. She spoke through a thick, sultry Southern twang. "Hey, y'all. I'm Sally Sutherford. Originally from Texas. Been up here for 'bout two years. After graduation, I kinda dibble-dabbled in all kinds of plays and productions. Some of 'em was kinda out there a little, but none of 'em was Shakespeare. Been kinda afraid of the Bard, but I figure I'd rather face 'im while I'm young, know what I mean?"

"Say it, sister," Jackie O answered.

"But what can I say, I'm excited, I'm scared, I'm ready to work, and I look forward to gettin' to know y'all," Sally said.

I exhaled a sigh of relief. My young age and inexperience were always a sense of trepidation for me when starting a new show. I typically was billed as the ingénue, and that carried a lot of weight and responsibility. All eyes on me. I had enough swirling around in my head here at the beginning, and I didn't need a shred more of anything extra added to my plate. Hearing Sally's experience, I knew at least at minimum I wasn't the ingenue. Even more than that, I'd been in a few Shakespearian tours and was on my way to becoming a master of his works. I gained an ever-so-slight bump in confidence from having this little edge on Sally, and I sank into my seat a bit, a little more relaxed. *Maybe group introductions aren't all so bad!*

A tattooed young man outfitted in a Def Leppard T-shirt leaned forward. As he moved, he snorted a globule of snot into his throat, hacked, swallowed the loogie, then cleared his throat before he spoke through his gravel-based voice box. "Ah . . . yeah. I'm Johnathon. I, ah . . . this is my first acting gig. I'm actually the lead singer of a band. We're normally on our own tour this time of year, but I decided that this was something I wanted to do, so I'm taking some time off from the road to do this."

"Wow. That's pretty cool," Sally said.

"Yeah. So I know I'm in the midst of professionals here, so just bear with me as we go through this. I'm a hard worker and a quick learner. Shakespeare is important shit, and I promise not to fuck it up."

As we "professionals" silently shifted and twitched in our seats in reaction to Johnathon calling Shakespeare's precious work "shit," the man next to him broke the tension with his Latino accent.

"Hello, everyone. I am Salvador Elison Herrara. I am twenty-six years old, and this is my second tour with this company too. Different play, same company. Former marine. My tour of duty lasted for four years. Afterward, I decided to leave to pursue acting full-time."

"That's some leap," Sally stated.

"What did you say?" Salvador asked.

"I said that's a big leap. You going from being in a position of power in the army to being an actor, a profession with very little power, relatively speaking, at least at our level in our careers."

"First off, I am a marine. I was not in the army. There's a big difference. Second, there's less power than you think in the armed forces. You're under orders. There's no freedom. With acting, there's tons of freedom and tons of power in that freedom. Actors are some of the most powerful people on the planet, missy! Maybe you'll learn to own your craft as you get a bit older . . ."—"

"She didn't mean anything by it, Sal. She was just complementing you on your dedication to your craft," Jackie O interjected.

Salvador was swelling as Jackie O put her hand on top of his, rubbed it for reassurance, and whispered, "Cool it." After a moment, the fire began to slowly dissipate from Salvador's eyes.

"I didn't mean anything by it. Really," Sally said.

"At any rate, I've never regretted my decision to pursue my dream, and I'm just glad to have the opportunity to play again," Salvador calmly stated.

"Thank you, Salvador. Thank you. Let's keep moving," Trent commanded.

The next man had his hair styled in an immaculate set of thick cornrows, and his manicured hands made flamboyant gestures as he spoke. "Well, I'm not a real soldier, but I did play a gentleman of the armed forces in *A Soldier's Story* last fall. I must say that's the closest I'll get to a battlefield, and I definitely do not regret that decision. My ass'll be hiding right behind you, Salvador, if it goes down."

"I gotcha covered, buddy," Salvador responded.

"Seems like I've been in this business forever; twelve years, but it's moved so fast. The years just seem to fly by with all the ups and downs. One thing about me, I'm really a grouch in the mornings if I don't get my coffee fix, so if you see me looking cross-eyed as we're setting up the stage, just leave me alone till around lunchtime. I most likely will have tamed the beast by then and returned to my natural charming self."

With a flourish, he chuckled, then eased back into his seat. Before he's settled, however, he abruptly jolts himself forward and speaks.

"Oh! I'm Leroy by the way. Leroy Perkins."

He chuckled again and leaned back into his seat as the gentleman next to him leaned forward.

"Hey, everybody, I'm Todd Booker . . ."

Whoa. It was the first time I was getting a really good look at this guy, and he was gorgeous. The nerves that had been swimming in my stomach since I woke up this morning began to transition into a violent breaststroke, pounding and slapping at whatever was in there. Everything about him spoke to my primal instincts: the way he talked with his masculine hands, the way his lips curled as he talked, the slight flaw in his nose, which made it look a little crooked. He looked like a rugged bad boy, but spoke like a scholar—the best of both worlds. My body temperature rose infinitely just from watching him speak.

". . . born and raised in Ohio. Been out here for three years. Love it. Absolutely love it. Gotta love a place where you can get a daily fix of the arts, you know? This is my first tour, so I'm eager to learn the ropes and get out there."

"Believe me, you'll learn the ropes quickly enough, buddy," Christian said.

"Yeah. In about the fourth month, I guarantee you'll be eager to get back home!" Joey said.

"I doubt it, but we'll see," Todd responded.

Jackie O adjusted her colossal shades, leaned forward, and said, "I'm Molly Hapsburg, born and raised right here in Manhattan, and I don't think I'll ever leave. Been doing this a long time. Long time. Tenth tour."

"Holy cow!" Sally commented.

"Been doing shows since I was fourteen," Molly stated.

Knew it as soon as I saw her. Incredible. Should make it a point to get to know her a bit. Could learn a lot from this one. Hope she's nice.

"Sooo, you're saying you're not excited to go out for the hundredth time?" Salvador asked.

"Of course I am. I was excited when our old tour went out, Sal, but once you get over the initial rush, it's kind of the same ol', same ol'. No offense to you guys."

"None taken. And finally . . ." Trent said as he gestured to me. Almost simultaneously, I lost my breath as my body rejected the natural impulse to inhale. I sat quietly for a few moments, struggling silently as the rest of the room waited for my response. All of the eyes on me felt like searing nickels on my skin.

Oh shit, oh shit, oh shit! BREATHE! BREATHE, GODDAMMIT!

Slowly, oxygen began to float into my collapsed lungs, filling up just enough for me to get a few short breaths in before I began to speak. In real time, this sequence probably felt short, unnoticeable. To me, it felt like forever.

"Hi, guys. First, let me apologize for being late. Just got off to a horrible start this morning. Won't happen again. I'm Anne. Anne Lamberty. I haven't been acting long. A couple of years, but I'm totally in love when I'm doing it, even though I don't know what I'm doing most of the time."

I felt a giggle slip out, and I noticed that my castmates didn't giggle back.

Shit.

"Just . . . ah . . . ready to learn and ready for the experience," I concluded.

"Thank you Anne. Thank you," Trent says as he checked his watch. "I'm sure we're all eager and excited to dive into things, but since our director is running late . . ."

The door violently swung open and in walked a slim, balding man in his mid-forties. He had a slight sashay about him.

"Speak of the devil, your director, Vincent Chicago, ladies and gentleman!" Trent said as he applauded. The rest of us followed Trent's lead and began to collectively applaud for our new leader.

Vincent laughed, then said, "Why are you applauding? I haven't done anything, for Christ's sake. Relax. Sorry I'm late. It's crazy out there. Well, I must say it's good to see you all again! I think I met all of you at the casting, did I not? Yes, I'm pretty sure I auditioned all of you, but if we weren't formally introduced, hello, I'm Vincent, and I'm here to try and put together a show that will be professional, brisk, and most of all, shockingly taboo. I'm sure some of you are saying, 'Shockingly taboo? This is *Romeo and Juliet*! It's love, romantic prose, and whatnot.' That's exactly right, but I cast each and every one of you because I thought you could bring something different to the roles: something primal, something vulgar, something never before seen in Shakespeare. Barring the language, he gives us so much freedom to create our own characters with our own idiosyncrasies, sicknesses, and perversions no matter what's on the page. We will take those liberties and stretch them as far as we can. That's what he would want: for us to do something with his work, not simply just to perform it. This will not be your mother's and father's Shakespeare. It will be yours."

We were all inspired. Everyone around the table had newfound light in their eyes. Vincent took a breath, then looked at Christian and asked, "How was it? Better than last time?"

"Identical," Christian responded.

"Identical?" Vincent asked.

"Identical," Joey chimed in.

"Oh well, so much for being creative. Well, then . . ." Vincent said as he took out his blue folder and plopped it on the table, ". . . shall we?"

Vincent flipped open his folder, and we followed suit. "*Romeo and Juliet*, Act One, Scene One . . ." Vincent proclaimed as he began to read the opening stage directions. Like professionals, we took his cue, climbed into the skin of our characters, and launched into a spirited read-through of the material. All of us had a blast performing a work of the world's greatest playwright, even if it was just a table read.

Even with the blocking restrictions, we took great pleasure in acting out scenes at the table, interacting and sharing moments with each other, and breathing original, spicy life into the text. It was like our eagerness to explore this text out loud and with each other had been pressurized for many, many months and it had now exploded into a colorful, combustible powder keg of expression.

While everyone was buried in their script as they followed along during the reading, I detected a certain panache coming from Todd as he delivered his lines. His energy and flair were so inviting that I looked up from my script, and realized that Todd had already memorized his lines and was delivering them as a fully realized, albeit seated, character. I was instantly amazed and inspired that he was already off book, and conjured immediate respect for him and his preparedness. Even with my limited experience, I knew real dedication and talent when I saw it, and it was bouncing off of the walls in his case. This was a true thespian. A professional. A sexy-ass professional.

Throughout the reading, Vincent provided subtle direction, and both we and Trent scribbled notes onto our scripts. Once all was said and done, each of our individual scripts resembled an artist's sketchbook, with markings, drawn arrows, circles, rectangles, and bright, florescent-colored highlighted areas all over the pages.

When the reading was complete, everyone in the room was pleased, but spent. The chemistry we just witnessed indicated that we had something special, but we also knew we had a lot of work to do.

Vincent looked proud of himself. I imagined he was patting himself on the back for executing yet another wonderful casting job. He stood before the table and said, "Good work today, guys. Go home, relax, take everything in, and be ready to get on your feet tomorrow."

"Tomorrow's call will be eight o' clock, ladies and gentlemen. See you in the morning," Trent said as he stood and began to fold up the extra chairs in the room and stack them against the wall.

Our weary company began to disburse, so I began to pack my bag. As I did, Todd approached.

"That's mine," he said.

When our eyes met for the first time, I couldn't speak. Once again, I was out of oxygen. It was his eyes. For years I had been lauded for my eyes. Many men, and women for that matter, had gasped and swooned over my eyes, almost to the point where I thought it was a running joke. Never quite understood what people saw in them that made them react that way. Well, after looking into Todd's, I thought I may have had an idea.

When I finally caught my breath, I was uncontrollably giddy. I felt like I'd just taken a large toke from a thick Jamaican joint. I felt a giggle spasm coming on, so I tried to mask it by employing a lower vocal register, but it didn't work.

"I'm yours? Excuse me?" I said as my voice cracked.

"No. No," he said as he pointed to the blue folder sticking out of my bag. "That's mine."

Light-headed, I looked at my possessions and realized that I had inadvertently placed Todd's script into my bag.

"Oh God. I'm so sorry. I guess it was near mine," I said as I handed his script back to him. When he accepted the script, I could feel my face flushing.

"Yeah, yeah, yeah. Trying to get me in trouble on day one, huh?"

I gasped. "How dare you! Accusing me of malice! I would do nothing of the kind. Not to people I barely know."

"Ha! So what you're saying is that I should keep both eyes open once I get to know you?"

"Well, I would hope you would always keep both eyes open unless you're sleeping. Or unless you're some kind of pirate or something."

"Well, quiet as it's kept, it does seem like I'm always chasing the booty."

"Impressive! Boy, did Mr. Chicago know what he was doing when he selected this cast or what? A brash, crass individual like yourself to play the most timid, least threatening Montague, Benvolio. He hit that one right on the head!"

"That's nothing. Wait till you see me after a few drinks. I'm like the male version of Cardi B on steroids. Talk about impressive!"

"Can't wait for that. Promise to work your inner Cardi into the show at some point?"

He held up two fingers and said, "Scout's honor."

I laughed. "Do you lie to everyone you meet?"

"Just to people I barely know," he said as he smiled and walked toward the exit.

I smiled as well as I watched him exit. I could tell that it was a different smile, a strange smile, one I hadn't felt before. I took inventory of that but didn't dwell on it, resumed gathering my things, then left for the day.

3

Steam and the strong, piercing smell of lavender filled the area. I've always loved lavender. It reminded me of my mother's home. It was a scent I could get lost in, one that provided me with a type of comfort I rarely felt from any other source.

The sound of water slapping against acrylic invaded my ears. Well, that, along with a softly played version of "When the Music's Over" by the Doors creeping from my small Bluetooth speaker. I loved the Doors as much as I loved lavender. Both made the atmosphere serene, with a slight charge of electricity and ripe danger.

I could barely see my slender, sleek figure as it was saturated in the dense fog. I enjoyed the perforated streams of water as they ran down my back and over my head. I turned to face the active showerhead, leaned against the wall, and watched the moisture bead up on the inside of the sweaty shower door. The humidified design on the frosted glass was beautiful. I admired the dripped tracks and trails the shower's tears had created; a road map to nowhere left by the fantastic waterworks.

As the song settled into its third stanza, with the haunting organ and faithful bass line taking center stage, my thoughts started to wander over the happenings of the day. I glazed over my tardiness, the crazy commute, the diva in the elevator, the lively read-through, and . . . those eyes. Those eyes, those deep, dark chasms, gave me pause. Just thinking about them sent my equilibrium into a tailspin, as if I'd taken a leap off of a towering mountain.

I leaned against the slippery shower wall to counteract the dizziness, all the while thinking about the man behind those eyes. He had been on my mind since we parted, and I realized that I felt

strange thinking about another man this much, a man I barely knew.

My fiancé was in the other room, for Christ's sake. What type of

woman was I, allowing my thoughts to be stolen like this? I felt like I

was wrong, and started to condemn myself. Yes, indeed he was

attractive, but so what? I'd seen attractive men before—hell, I'd

walked past attractive men all day that day, and ignored a handful of

catcalls from them, just like every day. Why the hell was I stuck on

this one?

Get a grip. Snap out of it.

Even with my conscience attacking me, my thoughts of Todd

lingered. I couldn't help it. I wondered what he thought of me. Was I

pretty enough for him? Did I hold his attention as much as he held

mine? Was he intrigued by me? I had no clue. I only knew three

things: he was handsome, he was charming, and his eyes could

conquer the world's problems.

Now, as if in a trance, I felt my hand start to glide across my

damp breasts. They were smooth, warm, and heavy from the steam.

My hand continued to travel down my slick skin to the front of them, where I gently tugged at my nipples and cupped my areolas as the steam in the room thickened. I was extra sensitive there, and my hand did nothing but exacerbate the sensitivity. After a few seconds, it was almost as if I could feel every drop of fine precipitation in the room landing on them; millions of microscopic pellets of liquid, bursting simultaneously on my nipples. I'd felt that type of acute stimulation before, but tonight, the intensity was magnified one hundredfold.

I closed my eyes as my hand slid down my wet stomach, and in between my glistening thighs. I grazed my sensitive spot with my middle finger, and my clitoris jumped and swelled as if to announce its presence. I slid two fingers past my passion pearl and entered myself, stroking my G-spot. As I inhaled, I could taste the lavender in the room, and I became supremely relaxed. All of my tension, inhibitions, and worries seemed to evaporate, and I gave myself permission to let go.

The steamy, wet covering of the shower only intensified my pleasure as I continued to fondle myself. It felt as if the entire room was soaked. I slipped two fingers out of my soaking, aching cavity, then placed my middle finger back on my clitoris. I applied a little pressure, and began to rub small, controlled circles on my fleshy lobe. I used my other hand to tease and tickle my nipples and before long, everything started to work together like a finely tuned symphony, and I was its conductor.

I was getting close. I purposefully morphed my vocal confirmations into deeply exhaled breaths, short, barely audible moans and sensual sighs, which also added fuel to my libido. Just one thought about those eyes, and I'd go over the edge. Instead, I thought of what I already had, resisting the temptation to venture into the unknown. As the pressure built, I continued my boycott, staunchly and steadfastly thinking only of my loved one. I guess you could've considered me a rebel with a cause: on a mission to prove to myself that I was in control, that those eyes had no control over me. It was going to take more than a three-minute conversation to warrant prime positioning in my fantasies.

The more I got worked up, the more my lust intensified for Todd. It got to a point where the ferocity of my urges shocked and subtly frightened me, adding even more sensations to the building heap.

Once again, I forced my fiancé into my mind in order to counterbalance the heavy weight this intriguing stranger had placed on my psyche, so maybe, hopefully, I could remind myself of where my real pleasure derived. I tried to fight all with all that I had in me, but nothing could derail that train as I began to feel the familiar pre-rumble, and the rumble was robust, bigger than I'd experienced in a while. This too frightened me.

I gripped the shower bar for balance, then suddenly, a hard knock at the door jarred me from my daydream.

"Hey! Let's go, honey, we're going to be late!" Brody yelled.

Even though I was distracted, I continued with my mission and reached success with an average explosion, the intensity clearly affected by the interruption. I bit my lip through the shock wave.

"Honey?"

Hungover, I drowsily made my way to the water dial and turned it off.

"Okay, okay. I'm coming," I replied.

I rested my head against the shower wall for a minute, spent. Once the aftershocks wore off, I took inventory of the sinking pit I felt in my stomach. *What the fuck was that? I can't believe that just happened.*

I placed my head in my hands for a few moments and let the wet, wrinkly protuberances comfort and soothe my face. *What the fuck is wrong with me?*

The last of the water exited the shower, causing the drain to gurgle. Slowly, I slid my face up through my fingers, and let my hands run under my chin and down my neck, chest, and stomach. The sinking pit I once felt had subsided, but was still definitely there.

Eventually, I exited the shower and wrapped myself in a towel. I cleared the foggy residue from the bathroom mirror, then looked myself in the eye for a moment.

Those eyes, those fucking eyes . . .

I frowned and shook my head, then grabbed my toothbrush, lubed it with a small line of toothpaste, and began to brush my teeth.

4

Several dinner guests, my fiancé, and I sat in a sprawling living room, enjoying a lavish cheese and wine spread accompanied with various sliced meats. The light and engaging atmosphere was accented by a touch of Dave Brubeck's "Blue Rondo à la Turk" being played softly in the background. The warm vibe supported the long, tested friendships in the room and would have made a stranger feel like an outsider. It was a closed love fest, an affectionate assembly at its best, spread over polished, hand-detailed hardwood floors.

Brody and I engaged in the free-flowing social commentary, as Michelle Bodney, hostess of the party and owner of the lavish Upper East Side apartment, led the discussion.

". . . so all I'm saying is that we should have a say in whether or not we want to pay taxes. That's all."

"Please excuse my wife. She knocked her head against one of the cabinets last week. I think it's had some lasting effects," Tom Bodney, Michelle's meek yet extra-friendly husband, responded.

"I've had these feelings before we even met, honey."

"I was trying to give you a way out, but— . . ."

"I don't need a way out— . . ."

"Giving citizens the option to not pay their taxes? That's crazy!"

Mike Jameson, WASPy Republican and longtime friend of Tom, chimed in with, "Who's gonna fix the potholes on my block? Who's gonna repair the tunnels and bridges?"

"More important, how are the sports arenas going to be built?" Brody asked.

"Two words. Private contractors," Michelle responded.

Lisa Unez, a beautiful, confident, thirty-eight-year-old single mother of two, interjected with, "You're nuts. The private sector? People can barely support themselves these days. Sports arenas and potholes aside, what about public assistance? You guys know I would have been dead in the water right after Brian and Mindy were born without that help."

"How are the twins?" I blurted out to Lisa as a desperate attempt to change the subject. I felt myself falling back into the familiar space of feeling inadequate and not being able to contribute to the conversation due to the subject matter being over my head. "I miss them. You should've brought them along," I continued.

"And have them destroy Michelle's newly waxed floors?" Lisa responded.

Michelle interjected, "No, they would not mess up Michelle's hardwood floors. But they could have beat up the carpeted floors upstairs with Gabriel. He would've loved the company. He keeps saying, 'Ma. Can I have a brother?' It's so cute."

"What do you think about Gabriel getting a sidekick? Should I be on the lookout for a shower invite?" I asked Michelle.

Michelle and Tom looked at each other and seemed at a loss for words. Tom tenderly took Michelle's hand then spoke, "We have been trying with no luck just yet, but soon."

Awkward silence filled the room for a moment as Michelle and Tom shifted in their seats. The guests noticed the uneasiness of the couple, and I immediately felt guilty. I felt a river of blood rushing to my cheeks.

Nice one, Lamberty. Way to put them on the spot. Your public personal interrogation technique remains flawless.

"Well, just know that second one comes out much easier than the first," said Lisa, snapping the downward spiral.

"Really?" Michelle inquired.

"I mean, one came right after the other for me, but yeah, it was a cakewalk. I almost fell asleep."

"No way!" I reacted.

"Yup! The nurses had to keep nudging me because I was nodding off."

"Probably was the drugs," Brody jested.

"Ha! Not a chance mister. Okay, maybe it was the drugs, but you can't deny the finished product!" Lisa stated as the group of old friends shared a laugh. She reached over, touched my hand, and said, "When it's your time, honey, embrace the morphine. Become friends with it. Worship it! It will guide you through to the end."

"Thought that was my job," Brody said.

"Your job? You have no job! This will be all your fault! You will be to blame. The best thing you can do is smile and keep your mouth shut as she swears at you and bites down on your knuckles!" Lisa exclaimed.

"Are you two planning on having a little one?" Michelle asked Brody.

"It's in our future, but the timing has to be right."

In the middle of the conversation, my mind wandered back to my favorite toy when I was a little girl: a brown-haired, brown-eyed doll named Kristina. I'd dress my slim, plastic companion in pretty little dresses, and style her hair for hours until it started to fall out. Kristina would cuddle and sleep with me every night, and talk to me when I had a bad day and needed to be comforted.

For me, Kristina was the closest I'd gotten to having a daughter to date. While I'd been ready for motherhood for some time, I'd always been very careful about who I'd ultimately choose to be the father of my children, as I was committed to rearing a healthy, disease-free child in a complete, two-parent family. Thus, I'd been very picky when it came to my sexual partners, and outside of committed, monogamous relationships, I always practiced safe sex. I'd never been pregnant, and never considered becoming pregnant with anyone except Brody.

"I'll tell you a secret. The timing's never right. Even when you think you have it all together, there'll be something you missed. Plus, she's got that clock you have to worry about. How old are you? Twenty-two? Twenty-three?" Lisa asked me.

"Twenty-six."

Lisa noticeably gasped. "The time is now, sweetie, while you're young,"

"I know, I know. I really want kids. I really do. Things just have to be right, that's all," I said as I made eye contact with Brody.

"Things like what?" Lisa asked.

Brody replied, "We're not financially ready. It'll take me a little more time to pass the bar, and Anne . . . well, Anne . . . We're just really not where we'd like to be in our careers yet. Let's keep it at that." He continued to try to make eyes with me, but I looked away. Once again, I was placed in the inadequacy corner. Self-doubt crept in and flopped on my back like a two-ton potato sack as it always does, and as always, the weight was unbearable.

"Once we get some headway in that department, we'll start giving it some heavy consideration," Brody continued.

"You've got a better chance at winning the lotto than having your careers put you in the position to be totally financially ready for a child. Twenty-six. Prime time. There's some good things happening down there at twenty-six. The fallopians are greased just right. The good, supple eggs are floating through there. You wait too long, and those tubes'll become jagged, snagging and breaking all the good eggs. Now, only the hard, rigid eggs can pass through. You know what kind of babies come from those? Psychos, rapists, and corrupt politicians!" Lisa said as the group erupted with laughter. "No, seriously. You guys should begin talking this up now, because whether you like it or not, you two are on the clock.”

“Thank you for your candid insight, Lisa. Now can we stop talking about tubes, eggs, and rapists? It’s not sitting well with the cheese and meat platter,” Brody said.

As the guests began to engage themselves in another topic of discussion, I solemnly sank into my chair, trying to hit the bottom.

***

The night was uneasy, unsettled. I couldn’t seem to relax as I reviewed my script under a dim lamp in my cramped one-bedroom apartment in East Harlem. The apartment was cold and creaky, as the super hadn’t turned on the building’s radiators just yet; still a few weeks away. It was an atrocity to say the least, since temperatures had sunk below freezing outside for at least the second week in a row. The space heaters selectively placed throughout my small apartment did very little to thaw the literal icebox.

The chilly domicile got even chillier as my live-in girlfriend, Toni Baker, entered alongside an icy blast of air. She looked worn, almost as if her once-beautiful appearance had been stolen from her by hard living.

"Hey, babe," I greeted. No response. I only heard the sounds of Toni shuffling exhaustedly to the kitchen, dropping her keys on the counter, then lumbering into the bedroom. "I made dinner," I followed up.

"Already ate," she yelled from the bedroom.

"At the office?"

"We stopped and got drinks afterward. Drinks led to appetizers, appetizers led to dinner, and ya know."

"Did you want to try and catch a show later— . . ."

The bedroom door slammed shut. The deafening impact slapped my skin and lingered as the sound echoed throughout the hollow home. The sting seemed to be in concert with the sound, both slowly subsiding simultaneously. When pain-free, I found my comfort in my only solace: my work. I dove back into my script, and received the warmth I'd been seeking.

***

By this time, the small dinner party had morphed into a minor mixer. The liquor was flowing, the once-soft music had been elevated, and the vibe settled into a mature groove. As such, the guests naturally segregated themselves into two intimate groups; Michelle, Tom, and I were conversing in the living room while Lisa and Brody remained engaged in a nearby hallway. Everyone spoke through slightly slurred speech as the buzz had become contagious.

Tom had just finished up one of his raucous stories, and Michelle and I were laughing hysterically.

". . . I tell ya, I've never seen anybody move so fast!" Tom said.

"Well, you didn't have a choice, did you, Michelle?" I asked.

"I was running out of options! It was either me or him. He spilled his cup of gazpacho all over me as I knocked him away from the cab door. Ruined a perfectly good blouse, by the way," Michelle responded.

"At least you got the cab!" I said.

"Yes! That sale only comes twice a year. I had to be there when the store opened!" Michelle stated.

"I've always known you to be vicious when it comes to fashion, but come on!" I said.

"I don't know my own strength. I must've had the 'coffee with kick' that day," Michelle said with a wink. I immediately stopped laughing. *Oh fuck. Here we go.*

"Oh, okay, so now you pass the buck to me?" I asked.

"The 'coffee with the kick' girl! That's you?" Tom asked.

"That's me. It's the commercial that won't die. I did that four years ago, and they're still playing it! I haven't received one red cent of residuals yet."

"Screw the residuals! I'd just be happy to be known as 'the coffee girl,'" Michelle said.

"Yeah, well, the coffee lost its kick about three years ago. I need to find something else I can be known for."

"Well, now you can be known for playing the enchanting Nurse on Shakespeare's biggest stage," Tom said.

"Enchanting? More like goofy. And it's not a big stage production at all. The cast has been severely stripped-down, and we'll be doing the show for high schoolers the majority of the time. That being said, we're probably going to perform on some of the smallest stages imaginable. I heard the last time this group went out, they had to perform in a horse's stable."

"Eeeew," Michelle reacted.

"Who cares. What you're doing is still pretty heavy stuff. Some people shy away from that kind of work," Tom stated.

"I'm sorry, but I'd shy away from manure dodging too," Michelle said.

"I'm not talking about that. I'm talking about Shakespeare. A lot of people are afraid to even touch the text, much less perform it. You should be commended," Tom said as he placed an encouraging hand on my shoulder.

"I don't know. I agree with you to some extent, and don't get me wrong, it is about the work, and I love the work, it's just that . . . I don't know . . . I don't know if I'll do the role justice."

I could see Michelle noticing my mood shift. She had now realized what Tom had been trying to accomplish during this conversation and decided to contribute as well. "Come on now. You're a wonderful actress," she said supportively.

"That's why this is the first job I've booked in four years?"

"Baby steps, kid. Gotta take baby steps. This tour'll do you some good," Tom responded.

"That's just the thing. I mean, I'm excited that I have an acting gig, and I'm excited about being able to tour across the country, but . . . I don't know. Something's still missing."

"If performing the work of the greatest playwright in history is not fulfilling you as an actress, what else is there?" Michelle asked.

"Exactly," I say as I slump my shoulders. I grab my wineglass off of the table and begin to get up. "I need another drink."

"There's another bottle at the bottom of the fridge. Bottle opener's in the drawer on the right," Tom advised.

As I exited the living room, I could hear Tom and Michelle exhaling their annoyance as it sank in that their quiet mission had crashed and burned, with only the flaky, charred ashes of failure remaining in the atmosphere. The mood had indeed changed on that side of the room.

I entered the kitchen, opened the refrigerator, and located the chilled bottle of wine, a 2010 Santa Margherita Pinot Grigio. I took the bottle out of the fridge, set it on the counter, opened the right-side drawer, and searched for the wine bottle opener.

The drawer's stainless steel contents were immaculately positioned, each fork, spoon, and knife had its place; each spatula in its own secure cove. However, the space for the wine bottle opener was vacant.

"Can't find the opener, Tommy."

"Oh! Damn me. Check in the long cabinet."

I moved to the long cabinet and opened its doors. Nearby, Brody and Lisa were having quiet dialogue in an adjacent hallway, and I was now just an earshot away from their confidential conversation. Unintentionally, my focus slowly shifted from the search to my silent eavesdrop.

"It's just that you are perfect. You have strength, courage, you will yourself out of situations. That's so respectable. That's what I need," Brody said.

"You have to be patient, Brody. I wasn't always like this. Circumstances force people to be who they need to be. Just be patient. A couple more years, and you'll see the growth in her," Lisa responded.

"I've been waiting for growth for five years already!" Brody stated. I could hear the frustration in his voice. It was disappointing to say the least.

"Maturity is a process, Brody. If you don't fertilize the soil, you'll never grow fruit. You have to nurture her. For a woman, the twenties can be very cumbersome. She's trying to figure things out, find her place, and you being there will help a great deal," Lisa advised.

"I just don't know how much longer I'm supposed to wait for her to get through this. I need a woman, not a confused girl who doesn't know who she is and can't handle her own problems and insecurities," Brody said.

WHAM! I slammed the cabinet doors shut, then hurled my wineglass toward Brody. The flying flask landed and smashed on the hallway wall, near Brody's head. The noise and action jarred all of the guests out of their discussions. I could feel them watching in shock as I stormed out of the apartment with Brody sappily stumbling after me.

***

I'd just finished taking a shower and was drying off. The bathroom was filled with steam, fogging up the mirrors and humidifying the small space of solace. I took a minute to think about what was waiting for me just outside the bathroom door. I was exhausted mentally, and I hated the fact that in this rare moment of domesticated peace, those invasive, corruptible thoughts had invaded my mind. I'd worked hard all day, I had earned this moment, and I had every right to spend it uninterrupted. Not on that day. Not on any day.

As I wrapped myself in a towel, Toni entered naked and emotionless. She walked straight for me, not stopping until our lips met. She kissed me hard, with intent. I heard her longing in her strong exhales.

I had been here before. Toni was like a light switch: sometimes she was on, sometimes she was off. There was no middle ground. I had to work with the ebbs and flows of her and ride the wave once the machine was turned on or I'd never get a chance to surf. So in those moments of spontaneous passion, I always obliged. Even though I felt like a piece of meat the majority of the time, I was okay with it, because, hell, I was surfing.

I leaned in to kiss her back, but before I could, she snatched the towel from my waist and aggressively gripped my swelling manhood. She squeezed and stroked me during our lip-lock, and I began to converse back to her through my increased breathing. When the tempo and pitch of my pants signaled my readiness, Toni hopped onto the sink, spread her legs, and teasingly invited me in.

The steam in the room shifted as I approached with vigor, hoisting her legs onto my shoulders and gripping her tightly by the waist as I attempted to align myself by shifting my hips. I slid my swollen head up and down her pleasure point, making her moan and gyrate even more. My huge, tight mushroom felt like a smooth, spongy boulder on her small delicate pearl, but the contrast in size only added to the pleasurable friction. Slowly, methodically, I started to beat my fat head on her clit like a drum. She pulsed to the beat, almost as if her entire body was feeling the weight and strike of my thick stick—an intensely stimulating percussion for both of us, it seemed.

I could feel that she was ready, as my head became saturated in her secretion. When I pushed in the tip, we both felt the searing warmth of each other, and for a brief second, I remembered what our love once felt like: tingly, spicy, and filled with bursting heat. But before I could fully dive into the electric pool, she pushed me away, and forced my head down to her cavity.

As if trained, I obediently filled her with my tongue. I sucked, licked, and flicked her sour-tasting clit while rubbing and caressing the intimate grooves on her G-spot. My tickle seemed to have ignited a familiar fire. Her breathing had turned into a staccato symphony.

Her moans and gasps for air filled the room as I buried my entire face into her dirty muff, and she twitched and jerked her approval of my methods. Her approval, and the strong smell of sweaty, enclosed-all-day vagina mixed with the airy soap in the room turned me on. I was rock solid and could explode from one single sexy caress from her, but the only touch I felt from her was an aggressive grip to the back of my head, holding me in place, and pushing my face deeper, deeper into her tender pocket.

I could see her secretions trickling onto the outside of her labia and running like a stream down the sides of them, lubricating her inner thighs. The warm wetness felt good on the side of my face, her slippery thighs sliding up and down my cheeks each time she squirmed. I was committed to my craft so much so that I continued until I almost drowned, until she was satisfied. When she erupted, she nearly cracked a nearby mirror with her fist as I envisioned all the aggression, stress, and frustration that filled her day shooting from her body like a cannon. The mirror made a deep squeaking sound as her hand slid down its surface as if it itself was satisfied, moaning its pleasure as it came.

Once the aftershocks subsided, she hopped down from the sink and left without speaking a word. I watched in agony as her beautiful, naked, unpenetrated body strolled away from me with a drowsy, quenched sashay.

Left at the altar once again with a throbbing dick, I was forced to relieve myself if I was to get any peace. I used her slippery cum on my hand as lube in an effort to feign some sort of physical connection with my girlfriend. It was a cold, rote release, one that left me only remotely satisfied. After I cleaned up my mess, I hopped back in the shower and began my cleansing ritual all over again, except this time I added this latest episode to the growing list of unfavorable occurrences in my current situation with Toni, something that all the water in the Hudson River wouldn't be able to wash away.

Once I finished, I dried off and slipped into my pajamas. I inhaled one last breath of the misty vapor, and exited the bathroom, which opened into the bedroom. The room was dim, with only one small lamp providing illumination. Toni, on her side of the bed with her legs tucked under the covers, was sitting up and reading a book underneath the light of the lamp. She looked totally content and at peace. Instead of disturbing that peace, and the peace of the apartment for that matter, I didn't bring up what just transpired. I never did. I was just trying to get through another day at sea without making too many waves or capsizing.

"How's the novel coming?" I asked.

"It's coming," Toni flatly responded.

"Is that like the fourth book in the series?"

"Fifth."

"Fifth? Damn. They haven't solved the case yet?"

"It's a long series, Todd."

"You're telling me. I saw somebody reading installment fifteen on my way to rehearsal this morning. Fifteen!"

"So you can see, I've got a long way to go."

I recognized the slight tension in her voice, but decided to try to spark another round of initiation anyway. "This tour I'm working on should be pretty interesting. This kind of thing can get taxing, you know: shows day in and day out, moving on to the next location, life on the road. Everyone's nice and professional, but we're all just so different. They're really trying to break some traditions with this one. It's like they threw a group of talented misfits together and said, 'Here. Perfect what's already been perfected!' I think we'll be okay, though. We have the caliber of people to do well, but it'll definitely be something unique. Hopefully, I won't push too hard and try to make something out of nothing. I've just got to simply let it come to me. It's got to come out of me and not from me. I have to own it. I have to live it."

I turned to see that Toni hadn't been listening, as she was completely engaged in her book.

"Toni!"

She slammed her book on the bed.

"Can you please?" she said.

"Can I please what?"

"Shut up! Can't you see I'm trying to read?"

I digested her venom, and Toni resumed her reading. This scenario had played out on many a night, each time a little different, but the result always remained the same. That night, however, I was at my limit, and was determined to pick at this scab until the wound was completely exposed.

"Is something wrong?" I asked. Toni sighed loudly, and continued to focus on her book. "I mean, because if I did something wrong, I have no clue what it is," I continued.

That did something. I knew it would. She put her book down and said, "You haven't done anything, and nothing's wrong, okay?" She then raised her book back into place, just over her eyes, so she was out of view.

Unfortunately for her, I wasn't nearly done. In fact, I hadn't even gotten started.

I called her name. "Toni." She ignored me. "Toni!" I yelled. She slammed the book onto the bed again.

"WHAT?" she yelled back.

"You've been giving me the stiff lip all month. What's the problem?"

"I told you already . . ."

"Fuck what you told me! We both agreed that we were going to work on this relationship, and now it's like you're bailing out."

"I'm still here, aren't I?"

She started to raise the book over her eyes again, but before she could, I snatched it from her and rifled it across the room. "Talk to me, dammit!" I said.

"What do you want me to say?"

"I want you to tell me what's up your ass!"

"I keep telling you there's nothing— . . ."

"Bullshit! What is it? Are you not happy anymore?"

"No."

"Are you sure?"

"Yes."

"I don't know. This feels very familiar, though."

"What do you mean, 'familiar'?"

I paused and sighed. I could see the road I was about to venture onto, and I dreaded it. However, I knew I was going to have to tread lightly here if I was going to get to my desired destination: the truth. I looked away from her and asked, "Is there somebody else?"

"No."

I paused again.

"Are you sure, Toni?"

"No, goddammit, no. There's no one else."

I looked at her like I was trying to see the truth beneath her skin. Unfortunately, I still hadn't managed to master that skill. On top of that, Toni was a master of deception. She knew the exact gestures, facial expressions, and responses to confidently cover her sneakiness. She'd been honing them for a lifetime, and by the time she'd met me she had the status of wizard.

"Okay, so what's the problem, then?"

"I keep telling you there is no problem. This has just been a long month. You know I'm working extra hours on the job because of the conversion, Mom is on my back for what we're going to do with Dad, and I'm weighing whether or not to get certified so I can be eligible for that promotion we spoke about. There's a lot on me right now."

"Okay, okay . . ."

"And when I have some time to just chill and relax, that's really all I want to do. Has nothing to do with you, honey. Sometimes

I just want to read my book, and be silent for a while. I know that's selfish, and I know I've been selfish in other ways, but just know I'm doing what I can to stay afloat, to stay sane. I haven't gone anywhere, baby. I'm still here with you, I just need you to be patient with me as I work through all of this crap that's going on in my life right now."

"All right, I got you. Sorry if I was pressing you."

"Nah, it's okay, it's fine," she said as she reached over and hugged me. We kissed. It was a kiss that was as tender as one of the several we had just after we'd first declared our love for one another. Hadn't had a kiss like that in what seemed like ages.

"Now, can I please get back to my novel? You always want to have these discussions at the best parts!"

"Sure, fine. Go on ahead back to your reading. I'll leave you alone."

I kissed her again, and it actually started to develop into something. We both were responding to each other like we hadn't in a while. It wasn't just raw lust; this time there was a thread between the actions. It felt like honor, respect, caring; it felt like love.

Before we got too hot and heavy, she broke away from my grasp and hopped toward the bathroom.

"Too much water," she said.

"I'll still be here when you come back."

She smiled and disappeared behind the door, leaving it cracked open a smidgen.

As I heard her starting to urinate, her phone lit up and chimed simultaneously. It was nearby, but just out of reach, and just far enough away for me not to be able to make out what was on the display screen. As Toni's trickle continued, curiosity attacked me like a bear. It walloped me over the head with doubt, suspicion, and anxiety, but I fought back. I resisted the urge to investigate by throwing in a full dosage of the good times and love that Toni and I had shared over the years, the love we'd just experienced with each other, and the very recent reassurances from her that everything was fine.

I stood my ground all the way to the end of Toni's stream. The last few drops fell, the toilet flushed, and water in the faucet began to run. As I heard Toni washing her hands, the bear came back with an uppercut I didn't see coming. The impact made me feel the searing hurt and pain from her last betrayal, one she vowed she would never repeat, with an apology I'd never fully accepted. The last betrayal was a misstep, according to her, something out of character for her, and I believed her, mostly. But that pain—that pain lasted even after the forgiveness and reacceptance of her back into my life. That pain remained under the surface for the years of good times, happiness, and love we'd shared for the remainder of our relationship, until that very moment. The bear's uppercut had brought that feeling of insurmountable hurt back to me, and it felt like I'd been hit by a two-hundred-pound bag of cubed ice.

All of the air was sucked out of my lungs, and I began to have a small panic attack. My chest felt tight, and I could feel myself starting to sweat. As I looked at the still-out-of-reach phone, I heard Toni sloshing around the water for the final time, then the water shut off. As I heard the floorboards in the bathroom shift, marking her movement to her hand towel, I knew I had to strike right then if I was going to slay the beast that had me on the ropes and almost down for the count.

Quickly, I darted across the bed, grabbed her phone, fumbled with it a bit due to my sweaty palms, and found a way to press the home button even though my fingers were shaking like mad. When I read the notification, I immediately began to calm down. My anxiety subsided, my sweats ceased, and I became eerily calm, almost numb.

I placed the phone back in its original spot and scooted back over to my original position just as Toni exited the bathroom and struck a sexy pose.

"Oh, you're still here," she said.

"Still here."

"Well, what should we do now?"

"I got a couple of ideas."

With that, Toni, walked over to me, pushed me down on the bed, and began to kiss me on my neck. Aggressively, I grabbed her by her hair, sat up, and flipped us both over so that I was on top. I began to choke her and whisper nasty, demeaning things into her ear, things she loves to hear, and, true to form, it produced the desired effect. She became wetter than the ocean.

When I entered her, it was like I blacked out. I couldn't feel anything, nor could I hear anything. I knew I was saying things, and she was responding in kind, but I couldn't hear our interaction. My vision was blurred as well. All I could see clearly was what was affixed permanently in my mind's eye: the notification I'd seen on her phone. A message from Darryl: "You make it home okay, baby?"

Nonetheless, I kept pounding away, numb, lifeless, soulless, until I came, then damn near fainted from exhaustion.

KO.

****

I walked briskly through the cold night air, crying hysterically, arms folded. Brody jogged frantically behind, trying to catch up to me. I was doing my best to outpace him, but I knew my efforts would soon be futile. We were both having tremendous difficulty with our equilibriums, so that was buying me some time.

The Upper East Side streets were quiet. In the city that never slept, this area seemed to have a rare immunity to the moniker. The only sounds heard on the long avenues were what was emitting from our sloppy struggle.

"Anne . . . Anne, come on . . . Will you wait a sec!" Brody yelled.

Just get there. Just get there.

We crossed from east to west without me relenting one bit. I continued to power walk away from Brody as best as I could, my smoky breath snaking around my head like a ghost in the night air, and Brody continued to struggle with keeping pace. Eventually, he gave up. He let me walk ahead, but kept me in his sights as he trailed behind. This trot continued for several streets and avenues.

When I finally reached our building's door, I quickly unlocked it, entered, and let the door close behind me. A few seconds later, Brody followed suit.

Just get there. Just get there.

I ran into the bedroom as I continued my everlasting sob. Brody followed behind and said, "Dammit, Anne, you're overreacting." I tuned him out and headed for the closet. I started slamming my clothes, hangers and all, into a large suitcase.

Brody embraced me from behind. "I wish you would let me explain," he pleaded.

I aggressively pushed him away. "No! No! No explanation necessary. I understood every word!"

"What you heard was out of context . . ."

"You've done enough. Don't you dare insult my intelligence too!"

"Honey, look. I probably had a little too much to drink . . ."

"Truth serum, Brody. Truth serum!" I screamed at the top of my lungs.

"Listen, baby . . ."

"No, you listen! I'm sorry I can't be your perfect little woman who handles her perfect little problems perfectly. I'd always thought you accepted me for who I was, flaws and all, but I guess I was wrong." I slammed the suitcase shut. "I'll call you when I grow up." I snatched the suitcase from the bed and began to exit.

Brody stood firmly in the doorway and said, "Whoa, whoa, whoa. Where are you going?"

"Get the fuck outta the way . . ."

"We need to talk about . . ."

"Fuck talking. Now move!"

"I'm not going anywhere until you calm down and hear me out."

"I've already heard what you have to say. NOW I WANT YOU TO MOVE!" I said as I began to ram myself into him. "MOVE, MOVE, MOVE, MOVE, MOVE!" On my final thrust, I vomited all over him.

"Ahh! Jesus!" Brody yelled.

Embarrassed, yet determined, I wiped my mouth and moved past him. I had to get out. The walls were caving in on me, and the pasty acidity in my mouth led me to believe that my digestive system wasn't finished with me just yet. To shake the risk of further shame and making more of a literal and figurative mess, I needed an escape. I quickly hustled through the living room and exited.

Just get there. Keep going, and get there.

Just as soon as I was outside, I tripped and fell on a sheet of ice, badly scraping my knee and popping my suitcase open, spilling my clothes everywhere. Blood began to pool, then flow down my knee as I scrambled to gather my clothes and shove them back into my suitcase. I clicked the suitcase closed, stood up, then began to limp away from my apartment.

Gotta get there. I've gotta get there.

Even though it was eternally quiet on the streets, it felt as if all eyes were on me again. Everyone knew about the fight Brody and I had had, everyone had heard our conversation, everyone had seen me lose my lunch, everyone knew Brody thought I was inadequate. My enflamed self-consciousness brought added heat to every pore on my body, and made my legs turn into gelatin. I could feel myself slipping away, slipping into the abyss.

Gotta keep going. Got to get away.

My intensified weeping slowly began to falter with each step.

Got to be happy.

Eventually, I collapsed on the sidewalk.

5

I could feel the morning sun pouring onto my pillow as I emerged from a surprisingly peaceful slumber. Street murmur spilled through a nearby open window, providing the required white noise for a Manhattanite. After a few extra moments in my safe coma, my closed eyes slowly pulled apart.

First thing I saw was the cracked ceiling, the paint chipping near the corners. Then I felt it: a sharp striking pain in my brain, remnants from the previous night's libations. I moaned and placed my hand on my forehead. *Never again. Never again.*

The door slowly swung open and Brody entered with a small food platter stacked with several pieces of toast, a bottle of ginger ale, and two aspirin. "Hi. Figured you'd need this. I did," he said.

As I repositioned my body, I grimaced and reached for my knee. Brody sat the tray near the bed, then sat down. "It's gonna be sore for a while. I took a look at it and bandaged it up last night," he continued. I pulled back the covers, confirmed his admission, then privately admonished myself for being so irresponsible, and for being such a klutz.

"Listen, I'm sorry for what you heard last night. I didn't mean it. Really. Things have been crazy at work, and I needed to vent. I know, what a subject to vent on, I know. I just needed to let go of some frustration, that's all. It didn't mean anything. I still love you and want to be with you," Brody said as he reached out his hand and touched me on my shoulder. He rested it there, most likely hoping, praying for reciprocity.

I limply rolled my head away from him, toward the clock. "Fuck," I said through a sigh. I periodically inhaled through my gnashed teeth as I struggled to get out of bed and began to get dressed.

"I . . . I think that if we could just talk about this . . ." Brody said as he attempted to help me up. I refused his assistance, grabbed my toothbrush, and began to limp toward the bathroom.

"I'm late," I said stonily as I walked into the tiled haven, turned on the water, and began to brush my teeth, all the while supremely aware that Brody was just outside the door, waiting for my return. I brushed for an extended period of time, almost until my gums bled. When I spat out the last amount of spearmint foam, I reloaded my brush with paste and dove in again. I breathed a sigh of relief when Brody finally lifted the breakfast tray from the bed and walked out of the room. As soon as he did, I spat, rinsed, and rushed into the bedroom to put on my clothes. I quickly got dressed and ran out of the room.

As I flew to the front door, I shot past Brody, who was sitting at the dining room table, sorrowfully eating the breakfast from the tray.

***

I entered the room in a burst of wind, and I immediately regretted it.

Idiot! You know they're rehearsing, why would you do that?

The room was sweaty, rank, and filled with hot breath. I could tell there was some serious work being done in this space, and all of the participants were razor focused on the goings-on, until my dramatic entrance, that is.

I stood frozen while Vincent, Todd, Joey, and Johnathon, fully engaged in thespian fisticuffs before I entered, cut their eyes at me from the center of the room. Trent and the remaining cast members sitting on the outskirts of the room did the same.

"Quietly go through your warm-up. I'm working on your scene next," Vincent barked at me.

As I began to limp to an empty coat hanger, Vincent noticed my uncommon gait. "Are you all right?" He asked.

Great. This is just fucking great.

"I'm fine, just a little stiff. I'll be okay," I responded as I continued to hobble. I could tell he wasn't buying it.

"What happened?" he asked.

"Oh, just me being clumsy, that's all. I'll be fine, really."

"I'm not worried about you, darling. I'm worried about the masquerade scene I have to rehearse this afternoon with a lame Nurse!"

"I . . . I'm sorr— . . ."

"Get through your warm-up and be ready to work when I call you!"

Vincent went back to working with the male threesome. I caught eyes with some of the cast members as I dropped my bag and felt that most uncomfortable heat again. I took off my coat and sincerely mouthed the word *sorry* to them. Most looked on me with soft eyes, but Molly rolled her eyes and shook her head in disgust. The heat increased.

Christ. I don't know if I can do this anymore.

***

As the morning began to expire, Vincent directed the rest of the cast through a strenuous rendition of the masquerade scene. I sat against the wall, dejected, writing notes as Vincent choreographed.

"Now, remember, everything's in the hips; one, two, stop, one, two, stop. You want everybody to want you, but more important, you want to piss Daddy off, so really give it to them. Sexy thrusts, sexy thrusts!" Vincent says to Molly as he demonstrates the swivels and pelvic pumps he's requesting. "Okay, now, when Romeo enters the scene with his two comrades, we have to have him as far away from Tybalt as possible. So as they enter up right, we'll have Tybalt down left dancing and chatting with the frisky Nurse when she's able to move appropriately," he pointedly commented toward me. I forced a conceding smile as I continued to jot down notes through an inferno of emotions and self-consciousness.

As if by rote, Vincent took a look at his watch and said, "Let's pick up after lunch, people. Trent?"

"Ladies and gentlemen, you have an hour. Please be back and ready to go at two," Trent bellowed.

The rest of the cast exhaled a sigh of relief as they dispersed to their personal belongings. Joey, Christian, Salvador and Molly grabbed their coats and exited the room together. The rest of us revealed our bag lunches, scattered ourselves across the room, sat on the floor, and began to dissect our treasured paper sacks. After the rustling settled, an uncomfortable silence filled the room as we quietly chewed our food and occasionally glanced at each other.

Sally, sitting near Leroy, unconsciously asserted herself. "This has been pretty intense, huh?"

"Unfortunately, this is standard procedure. It'll get worse before it gets better," Leroy responded.

"I knew it wasn't gonna be a cakewalk, but I didn't expect it to kick up so fast. It's only the second day!"

"Well, we only have a month to get this whole thing together. They'll bleed us for the first three weeks, then once we pretty much have it down, they'll ease up a bit."

Johnathon then scooted himself within earshot of the talkative twosome.

"Three weeks of this?" Sally asked Leroy.

"Give or take a few days," Leroy responded.

"Hoo boy!" Sally exhaled.

"Hey. Will we have longer breaks during that last week of rehearsal?" Johnathon interjected.

"Depends on how well we've grasped the show," Leroy answered.

"Would be nice to have a longer lunch. Get some other stuff done," Sally commented.

"My band and I have a meeting with a record label during that last week of rehearsal. I have to be there," Johnathon said.

"Then go. Like Leroy said, we should be on our *p*s and *q*s where the show's concerned by then, so I don't see no harm in it," Sally suggested.

"Talk it over with Vincent early. Today if you can. The earlier the better. I thought you'd given that life up," Leroy said.

"Technically, I've given it up. I've stopped touring, I'm not writing or playing every day, but I don't think I'll ever be able to shake it. It's inborn," Johnathon stated.

"I know what you mean. I've tried to quit this profession at least twenty times. Just keeps calling me back. I try to ignore it, but it never works. It just keeps nagging me until I give in," Leroy confessed.

"Love's submission!" Todd yelled across the room, revealing his long-distance eavesdropping.

"What?" Leroy asked.

"What you described is called 'love's submission.' It's this theory that says that we are all controlled by the things we love the most. No matter the circumstances, no matter how hard we try to resist, our most passionate vices will always dominate our psyche. Each time we try to impose our will on these passions, we lose. We're forced into submission because during the time we're trying to control these inspirations with our minds, they actually become deep physical needs. Physical cravings. We must live them out or it will feel as though we have never lived. 'Love's submission,'" Todd responded.

"Damn," Leroy said.

So eloquent. So intelligent. So precise. "Whose theory is that?" I yelled across the room.

"Some philosopher. Heard it at a seminar," Todd answered.

"That's pretty deep, dude," Johnathon replied.

"I've never heard it before, but it's true. You've gotta do what's in your heart or you'll just be miserable," Sally stated.

"Too bad what's in ours doesn't pay much!" I said, generating hefty laughter from my audience.

"The crap in my heart barely covers my rent!" Johnathon said.

Leroy pointed at his feet and admits, "Mine covered these sneakers. That's it!"

Joey and Christian reentered the room amongst the laughter. Each was carrying a white bag with Chinese lettering on it. Molly and Salvador entered right behind them, both eating ice cream sundaes.

"What did we miss?" Christian asked.

"Just talking about how our glorious profession lucratively compensates the up-and-coming talent," Sally answered.

"Yeah, it's been determined that we're working for sneaker money," I said.

"Oh yeah. That's a given. Last year it cost me money to do a tour like this. Prime example of doing it for the love. I'd strongly advise against that approach," Molly said as she affectionately touched me on my arm.

With Molly warming up to me, it felt like a great opportunity to check the temperature of the group and make amends for my misstep this morning.

Okay, Anne, put on the face, turn on the charm, and get these people back on your side.

I stood and walked toward the rest of my fast-chattering colleagues.

"Hey, guys? I was waiting for everyone to get back so I could apologize for my tardiness this morning. I said yesterday that it wouldn't happen again, but I just had a horrible night last night, woke up with a hangover . . ."

"No sweat, Anne. I've been there. As has most of the cast, I'm sure," Leroy said.

"Too many times to remember," Johnathon responded.

"Oh yeah," Joey agreed.

"I'm notorious for it. I'm surprised I haven't been in your shoes yet. That day's coming," Salvador admitted.

"I'm really sorry, guys," I lamented.

"Don't worry about it, missy," Sally said.

"Not a big deal," Christian agreed.

"Yeah. It's cool," Todd said.

Whew!

"Just don't lie to us anymore," Molly stated.

Shit.

The mood in the room shifted. It's as if a black hole has opened and it is rapidly sucking all of the good vibes and forgiveness into its belly. I was thrown for a loop and visibly shaken.

"If you say you're not going to do something, don't do it. Just a general rule of thumb for people who work on a team," Molly continued.

"Molly," Salvador said as he softly grabbed Molly's hand.

Molly seemed to take the hint. "Just don't let it happen again, okay? We all have to do our part in making this company run as smoothly as possible. When one isn't here or can't rehearse, it affects all of us. All I'm saying is be considerate of your castmates. That's all."

All eyes fell on me, putting me in the spotlight once again as everyone awaited my response.

She's right. Of course she's right; she's the veteran on this tour. She's done this time and time again. She's a professional, they're all professionals, and what am I? A newbie who can't even make it to rehearsal on time. I'm the weakest link on this tour and all of them know it. That's why they're all staring at me, waiting for me to acknowledge my green behavior and commit here and now to acting like a professional from here on out. I'm not ready. Should've never auditioned for this play. I can't do this.

"I'll try," I responded.

Molly then broke free of Salvador's grip and walked away while the rest of the castmates resumed their jovial conversations as if nothing had happened.

***

After the exchange with Molly, I watched Anne seclude herself from the group. She shriveled into a dark corner of the room and stared out the window as she nibbled on her sandwich. I wanted to go to her to tell her not to sweat it. I could tell she was affected, but she really didn't have to be. We all had her back because as a cast, we have to stick together. Accountability is one thing, but it was too early to start throwing daggers, especially in front of the rest of the cast. No need to mentally break one another down as it was going to be mentally tough enough on its own. Molly was out of line, and I wanted to let Anne know that, to hopefully build her back up a bit.

Just as my thoughts locked in on my observations, Leroy interrupted my flow by drawing me into another conversation. Just like that, my brief interest in Anne's psyche was forgotten, and I quickly moved on to the happenings elsewhere in the engaging room.

6

I opened the door to my apartment and immediately stopped in my tracks. The whole place was decked out in sweeping romantic flair. Fresh flowers peppered the front room, candlelight illuminated the exquisitely set dining room table, and soft music played in the background. An exquisite aroma invaded my nostrils: beef Wellington. I knew this version by heart. My intuition was confirmed when I spotted Brody in the kitchen busily putting the final touches on his specialty cuisine. He frantically checked his propped-up iPad with the recipe to ensure perfection, as I'm certain he was aiming for it to be one of his finest creations.

His dinner selection had sentimental value, as this was what we both ordered on our first date, and it was our favorite meal, when prepared properly. A surprising commonality, no doubt, but our overall love for cuisine had always been a magnetizing force in our relationship. Domestic wars had been fought and emotional truces had been agreed upon over our dining sessions. Given recent events, this one felt important. This one felt necessary. I knew it, and I'm sure he did as well.

Nonetheless, I entered totally blind to the atmosphere Brody created. I dropped my bag at the door and began to walk toward the dining table.

Brody lovingly approached and said, "Care to join me?"

My stride remained constant. As I passed by the table, I dropped a thick stack of mail onto it, extinguishing one of the alluring candlelights. I proceeded to my room and slammed the door shut with all intentions of not opening that door again until the new day's sunlight crept past the horizon.

I took a seat on the bed and hung my head. I could still hear the soft music seeping under the crack of my door. I just wasn't ready to face it, to face him. Still too early, still too raw. I'd be a mess if I were to talk to him; needed to be stronger.

***

Finally night's blanket solidly shrouded the area. I slid into my most comfortable pajamas, lay on my bed, and began writing in my journal. Brody had since left the apartment, my cold shoulder freezing him out into the chilly winter air. I thought about my current stance with Brody and wondered if I was being too harsh, if maybe I'd added a couple more imaginary hurtful words to his diatribe the other night that would explain my stern response. My thoughts didn't linger too long before I remembered the sharp sting felt by what I'd heard directly from his mouth, and a strong sense of justification overwhelmed me. *This man has hurt me more than he could ever know.*

I knew what I was doing was completely fair and warranted. I felt strong in my realization, one of the few times that I'd taken control of my situation over the past few days, and taken something for myself: time. Time to come to grips with my new reality, time to heal. I was proud of putting myself first, and standing firm until I was whole enough to consider giving pieces of myself away again.

That being said, loneliness had become a permanent resident within me since the incident at the party. Brody and I had always been in constant communication, another staple of our relationship, and I'd relied on him for my happiness in the past. I'd allowed him to be responsible for how I saw the world and how the world affected me. Now that I'd shut him out, there was a deep, longing void and a supreme sense of disorientation in me. I needed to feel whole again, or at least closer to whole than I did at that time.

Desperate for interaction, I closed my journal, reluctantly picked up the telephone, and begin to dial. I waited with dreaded anticipation as the phone rang. I almost lost my breath when I heard the answering click.

"Hello?"

"Hi, Mom," I said.

"Hey, sweetheart."

"You sleep?" I asked.

"Oh no. We're just lying here catching an old *Golden Girls* rerun. I'm surprised you called."

"It's Tuesday, Mom."

"Is it? Guess I lost track of the days. Maureen, Ted, and Conner have been wearing me out since they've been here."

Oh fuck . . .

"Crap! I was supposed to wish Conner a happy birthday yesterday, wasn't I?"

"Maureen waited for your call . . ."

Fuck me!

"Oh geez . . ."

"Don't worry. I covered for you. Told her you were studying for the bar."

"Why did you tell her that? There's no way she's going to believe that!"

"Why wouldn't she believe it? You've always had what it takes to be a lawyer."

Here we go. Will she ever let this go?

I sighed and grunted. "We've been over this, Mom. I'm an actress. I won't be taking the bar, filing through legal briefs, or preparing for depositions. The closest I'll get to being a lawyer is playing one on TV," I said.

"Well, I and the rest of the family'll be holding our breath for your *Law & Order* debut. That way we'll at least have a glimpse at what you could have been . . ."

"Mom . . ."

"I know, I know. That's just what I believe you were born to be. I can't help it. So do you want to talk to Maureen now or— . . ."

"No. I called to talk to you."

"What about? You still have money for food, yes?"

"Of course I do . . ."

"You haven't gotten kicked out of your apartment, have you?"

"No, Mom. Everything's fine that way. I can take care of myself."

"Then what is it, my darling?"

"Brody and I had a fight last night."

I could hear the sigh through the phone.

"Anne, how many times . . ."

"Just hear me out before you say anything, okay?" I interjected.

"Why should I? It's always the same thing. You and Brody are out somewhere, the waitress looks at Brody as she takes his order, you think she's hitting on him, you get upset and throw one of your patented temper tantrums. Did I hit the nail on the head?"

"No. Not even close."

"Really, Anne. It's time to start growing up and taking care of your own problems. You've had your issues with jealousy all your life and you refuse to this day to acknowledge them!"

"It's not that, Mom. I heard Brody saying some awful . . . —"

"You want me to confirm that your jealousy was justified, but I won't. Not until you work out your own insecurities. That's the only way the problem can get solved, honey. You have to do it yourself. Time to grow up, Anne. The family's waiting on you."

I remained silent as I heard Mom release a disappointed exhale again. "So, did you want to speak to Conner now? He's dying to hear from his favorite aunt."

"Yeah. Sure. Put him on."

I heard Mom put the phone down. Her voice began to lose its volume as she moved away from the receiver.

"Just a minute, sweetheart. Conner! Conner! There's my big boy, there he is! Wanna talk to your auntie? Yeah? Wanna talk to your auntie? . . ."

Mom's childlike babble continued as I waited sorrowfully for my two-year-old nephew to answer. After a moment, I could hear him speaking mindless drivel into the phone. My heart warmed, and I smiled when I heard his voice.

"Happy birthday, Conner."

I lingered for a while, then touched the END CALL button on my phone, my smile quickly sinking into the permanent worry lines in my face.

✳✳✳

I walked through the night-lit Harlem streets exhausted. On my way home from a long day, I typically could conduct energy from the salsa and raggaeton music I would hear blasting from the apartment windows down the blocks. "Suavemente" generally could throw me into a tizzy. There have been many times when I'd dance all the way home after just hearing the chorus whiff past my ear, the drums and bass line staying locked in my head for the duration of my journey. Not that night. I could barely lift my legs to walk, much less do any type of intricate salsa steps on the two, the only way I know how.

I damn near collapsed at the sight of the steps to my apartment when I reached them. I started to ascend but stopped midway. My hesitation lingered as I observed the living room lights glimmering from my unit's window.

Toni.

Just hearing her name in my brain sapped the rest of my energy out of me. Slowly, I descended the staircase and walked away from my dwelling.

7

Rehearsal was grueling. In general, rehearsal was a grind, but today seemed to be more intense than usual. This was our third consecutive week of intense practice on our craft, and the productive wear and tear was starting to show up in the work. I thought we needed a break, but it wasn't up to me. The schedule was tight, and we were going to be on the road soon, so the producers and Vincent were mashing the gas.

A weary Todd, Johnathon, and Sally were center stage, while the rest of us observed an active Vincent engaging with his collaborators.

"This exchange sets up the whole thing," Vincent said to Sally. "It's like you're saying 'fuck you' to him, his whole family, his whole world! By the end of this scene you should have bitten your thumb so much that you don't have one to bite!"

He then turned his attention to Johnathon and said, "And you're like, I'm not going to let this chick bite her thumb at me and get away with it! Not only is she a Capulet, but she's a woman as well! You'll surely lose the respect of your comrades if news of this gets back home. You've got to stand up for yourself now! You guys are in the market square; you've got spectators all around. You can't let it leak that you've been punked! The same goes for you," Vincent said to Todd. "Yeah, you were trying to keep the peace, but she's pushing you now. Pushing you past the point of no return! Then she says that one word that sets you off, 'coward.' In front of all the people in the square, she calls you a coward! That's worse than what she's done to your good friend here. She's insulted your manhood, your honor, and she's a woman at that! You hear that word and you go ape shit! Kind of like a mental patient at Bellevue. This is not the peaceful, jovial Benvolio we know and love. This is an animal, one like we've never seen before, one that will not stop until you have her pretty little head on a pole!"

Todd and Johnathon are taken back by Vincent's ferocity. He was an animal, and he was clearly devouring this heavenly text like it was his prey.

Shifting gears like a pro, Vincent sweetly turned to Sally and said, "Now do you see the beauty in casting Tybalt as a woman? Nothing can get under a man's skin better than a woman can. And when she gets under there, she's a bitch to get back out. And you are that bitch. The tormentor of men's souls. You have the power to bring out the worst in them, and you want to push those buttons. You want to manipulate your little puppets until they do something that can't be taken back. Use your prowess, use your cunning, use what we men wish we had, that treasured intuition, to get what you want! Females, what a delectable species."

Trent, who had been sitting near the rear of the room, stood and got Vincent's attention. "Ah, Vincent?" he said as he pointed to his watch.

Vincent turned and looked at the clock behind him. Five thirty p.m. With a mixture of satisfaction and disappointment, Vincent turned to us and said, "It seems that playtime is over, ladies and gentlemen. Please come prepared to run through the entire play on our feet tomorrow once before our dress rehearsal. Marie, our fabulous queen of wardrobe, will be here with the costumes around one thirty; our dress will be at two thirty. Please keep your lunches short and sweet; in fact, I suggest you bring your lunches tomorrow to save time. I still want to go over the tomb scene and the scene at the Friar's after Tybalt's death before the dress, so again, be diligent on your lunch break. Just a reminder, Kevin, the choreographer, will be coming back in on Thursday to stage our last two combat scenes." He looked to Trent and asked, "We'll have knee pads for them, right?"

"Check," Trent replied.

"So you will have knee pads this time. Are there any questions?" Vincent asked. We were exhausted. We couldn't ask any questions if we tried. "How are you guys holding up?"

Silence.

"That well, huh? Let me tell you a secret. The one thing I've learned about this business is that you've got to have some serious stamina if you want to succeed. The ones that last are the ones who have stamina. Take care of yourselves, stay healthy, and get rest, get rest, get rest, get rest," he said as he repeatedly nudged Todd with his foot.

Todd chuckled and replied, "You got it, Coach."

"You promise? You look like shit. I need all of you here."

"And you'll have it. I promise."

"Okay, then. Until tomorrow," Vincent said as he turned to gather his belongings.

"Ladies and gentlemen, before you pack up your things, could you all gather back here for a moment? We need to make some decisions on a few things," Trent said.

Vincent exited gleefully as we moaned and congregated around Trent.

"Thank you for your diligence, thank you for your professionalism, thank you for a full three weeks of rehearsal. We are now at the point of our journey where we must decide on tour duties."

"Tour duties?" Sally asked.

"We all sign up for different chores while we're on tour. Somebody has to keep the van clean, somebody'll be in charge of bringing the light kit onto the stage, mic batteries have to be changed out, and other stuff like that," Leroy responded.

"Bingo!" Trent replied.

"Didn't think it was going to be all fun and games, did ya?" Molly said.

"As a matter of fact, I did," Sally replied through a laugh.

An annoyed Trent broke up the side chitchat with, "Excuse me. Thank you." He shuffled and flipped through a few pages attached to a clipboard, read their contents, and continued, "We have a few extra positions open this year. All of them paid, of course . . ."

Joey whispered to Christian, "Hope they increased the pay rate this year."

"Yeah, this company had a banner year last year. We deserve a pay raise," Christian whispered back.

"As it looks, the rates have remained the same as last year," Trent commented, still entrenched in the papers on his clipboard. Christian, Joey, Salvador, Leroy, and Molly let out a collective moan.

"Hey, take it up with management. I'm just the messenger. At any rate, we need to sign ourselves up for these positions. This year, we need a fight captain for the combat scenes, a dance captain for the masquerade scene, a person in charge of lights, a person in charge of the sound equipment, someone to take care of the travel van's maintenance and cleaning, someone for wardrobe duties, and three people to build and break down the set. One person can have two positions, but everyone must hold at least one position. Do we have any volunteers?" Trent asked.

"I have no problem being fight captain if no one else wants it," Salvador stated.

"This is staged combat, Sal. Not the hand-to-hand, grenade-launching, bayonet-poking kind of combat you learned in the service," Molly jabbed.

"I'm quite sure I can scale it back for the production, honey. Take it easy," Salvador responded.

"Anyone have an objection to Sal's request?" Trent asked. We remained silent, and Trent confirmed the new appointment with, "Ladies and gentlemen, please salute our new fight captain." We applauded our approval.

"I might as well sign up for dance captain. I've been training since I was five," Sally said.

"Sounds like a match to me. Anyone disagree?" Trent asked. He paused for a few seconds of prolonged silence, then responded with, "You're hired, kid. Who's next?"

"Which duty pays the most this year? Is it still wardrobe?" Joey asked.

Trent quickly flipped through the rate sheets and said, "Yes, wardrobe still has the biggest payout."

My spine elongated. *Ooh. I'm all for that. Extra money will make this whole thing make sense. It'll give me a reason to stick this out.*

"The bosses upstairs have taken into account the hassle it can be to handle the wardrobe duties. Not only are you loading and unloading those heavy costumes, you'll also be required to launder each item; with some of them being hand wash only. Management knows this can be a daunting task especially during the times when we'll be getting off the road late at night and the laundry has to be done for the next day; it can be a pain. Therefore, they've decided to accommodate you. Sound appetizing to any of you?" Christian, Todd, Molly, and I raised our hands and began to nominate ourselves. "Typical," Trent replied.

"I did wardrobe last time I was out on tour. I know what it's all about. I can show the other person the ropes," Christian stated.

"Thank you for volunteering your leadership, but we'll need to take a more diplomatic approach in this situation, I'm afraid," Trent said to Christian. "Let's see. All four of you really want this position? We have plenty more slots that need to be filled. Slots that pay pretty well," Trent said.

Unfortunately, we were unable to hide our indifference to Trent's pleads for open-mindedness. It was all over our faces.

"I'm getting married this fall and would really appreciate it if you guys would allow me to get wardrobe this year. I really need the cash," Christian pleaded.

"So do I," said Molly.

"So do I," said Todd.

"Yeah, so do I," I said.

"Ladies and gentlemen, I don't want to get into this type of stalemate. We all need extra money these days, so I don't want to put you in the position of giving up more money on the behalf of someone else. We'll simply let fate decide," Trent stated. He then tore a blank sheet of paper from his clipboard and ripped it into five pieces. He handed a piece of paper to each of us, the wardrobe "nominees," and kept the last piece for himself. He shielded the paper as he wrote something on its surface.

"I just wrote a number between one and ten, sound familiar? The two closest to the number will handle wardrobe. Good luck," he said.

The wardrobe nominees stared at Trent and his piece of paper as if we were trying to physically read the magical digit that would boost our financial fortunes. Eventually, we scribbled our submissions onto our ballots with confidence and handed them to Trent.

Please let me get this. This will make it right. Please let me get this.

In an air of full suspense, Trent flipped his piece of paper over and showed it to us.

"Three is the number, ladies and gentlemen. Three is the number," he confirmed.

Yes! Thank you! Finally some good fortune!

Christian immediately let out a large sigh as Trent unfolded all the pieces of paper. He discarded all but two pieces of paper in his hand. He held them for a few seconds as he studied the results.

"Interesting," he said.

Interesting? What's interesting?

"What is it?" Todd asked.

"Looks like two of you wrote down the magic number," Trent replied.

Of course. Of course there's a fucking tie! Again, thank you! Shit.

"Who's still in the running?" Molly inquired.

"Todd and Anne," Trent answered.

"This sucks," Christian stated.

You could say that twice.

"We'll flip a coin between you two . . ." Trent said as he reaches into his pocket.

"Wait a sec. How do you guys feel about splitting the duties in half?" Leroy asked.

"In half?" I said.

"Wardrobe is a pretty big job. Might be better if two people worked on it. That's what we did on my last tour, and it worked fine," Leroy suggested.

"Will we get the same pay?" Todd asked.

"I can check on it, but I'd imagine so," Trent said.

"That's fine with me," I stated.

"I can do that," Todd confirmed.

"There you have it! Say hello to your newly appointed laundry czars, Todd and Anne! Now, anybody have an itch to cover any of these other duties?" Trent asked as he jotted Todd's and my name down on his clipboard.

So I'm paired with Mr. Happy. That actually is interesting. Hope I can control myself with this fucking guy. What am I saying? Of course I can! He had me out of my own head the first week, but I've calmed down since then. A little infatuation here and there, a few sparks, but I've held it together nicely since that initial meeting. I've got this. I've been able to carve out a nice working relationship with him, so I'll be fine. It's still pretty early, though. I wonder if we'll be able to continue to work well together or if we'll get to a point where we'll dread going to work every day. None of it matters at this point, I guess. Time to celebrate! I'm in the money, honey! I just won the fucking lottery! Woo-hoo!

8

It was a chilly afternoon. Icicles were clumped up on the outside of the rehearsal room windows, and the steamed radiator inside the room continued to occasionally knock and growl. The activity in the room didn't match the frigid surroundings, as we had just completed an intense dress rehearsal, and were changing out of our costumes while Vincent huddled with the "money"—the bright-eyed, pink-faced producers of the show.

The room was hot and sweaty, yet full of accomplishment. A good-natured vibe of progress ran through the workhorses in the space as we suspected we might be on to something special, something groundbreaking. The dress rehearsal couldn't have been executed any better, and everyone in the room knew it.

The entire cast was giddy. We chatted and joked with one another, and celebrated our achievement and our newfound bond. The energy mimicked the end of a Friday school day, and I was caught in the wave. Even though things hadn't improved at home, this was the highest I'd felt in a while. I took it all in and relished the feeling, soaking up every last piece of the spirited ambiance.

As I hung my costume on the wardrobe rack, Molly approached me holding an armful of soiled garments. "Where do you want us to put these?" she asked.

"What do you mean? What are those?" I responded.

"You're on wardrobe, right?"

"Right."

"This is my laundry from the show."

"But I thought . . ."

"Doesn't matter if it was a dress rehearsal. It's time for laundry."

I paused, thinking for a place to stack the dirty laundry.

"You know what? I'll just leave 'em here." Molly said as she dropped the garments on the floor. "I'm sure you'll figure out what to do with them. Thanks," she concluded as she skipped away.

Bitch.

Todd, who'd witnessed the entire transaction, approached me with a laundry bag draped over his shoulder. "Just got this from Trent." He presented the bag and continued, "Now they'll have a home."

I picked up Molly's discarded clothes and started to put them in the bag. "Great. Now all we have to do is pick up the other homeless victims scattered around back here and we'll be— . . ."

"Put those back where they were," he said.

I reluctantly dropped the clothes back on the floor.

Todd then wheeled the wardrobe rack to the center of the room, and said with his most powerful stage voice, "Excuse me! Excuse me, my fellow castmates!

Love hearing him like this. His voice is so strong, so commanding. Makes me weak.

"Please be kind enough to place your laundry in this nice bag Trent has graciously provided for us. I'll hang the bag here, on the end of the clothing rack. This is where it'll be each laundry day. Just pitch your soiled items in, and we'll take care of them. Any items not in this bag will not get laundered." He then walked over to the crumpled pile of Molly's clothes on the floor and continued, "For example, whosever these are will get left here if they're not in the bag when we do our laundry run, feel me?"

All the actors except Molly responded affirmatively.

"Good," Todd responded. He wheeled the rack back over to me, then whispered, "Now we wait."

He is so damn sexy!

As the other cast members resumed their bustle, Todd and I looked out the corners of our eyes and caught Molly standing completely still, staring at the pile of clothes she'd left on the floor. "Wait for it," he whispered.

Molly began to take a step toward her soiled garments, but stopped herself short.

"Wait for it."

With a flip of her hair, Molly composed herself and began to take long, confident strides toward the steaming heap. She snatched them off the ground and shoved them into the laundry bag with rebellious force. I smiled to myself. Todd graciously turned to Molly and said, "Thanks for helping us out, Molly. I really appreciate it."

With another flip of her hair, Molly turned and ostrich-walked back in the direction she came. "No problem," she said flatly without turning around.

"Thanks!" I shouted as Molly continued her trot without a response.

I covered my delighted laugh with my hands so it didn't carry. "Ha! I enjoyed that," I said to Todd.

"I got a little something out of that too," he replied.

"Are you always this cut-and-dried? I mean, I need to know since we're going to be doing laundry together. I've gotta know when you say there's no more quarters, there's really no quarters!"

"Yeah, I pretty much say how I feel. In a few selective words, you'll get my drift."

"That's refreshing."

"Are you making fun of me?"

"No, no, not at all. Seriously. It's refreshing to be around someone who's not going to bullshit you. Someone who won't sugarcoat what's on his mind. Never figured you for a straight shooter, you being so quiet and all."

"I'm not really."

"You throw caution to the wind more than I do."

"I meant I'm not quiet. Not at all, really. And I bet you're a lot more adventurous than you think you are," Todd responded.

"I was referencing that caution-to-the-wind stuff to you being able to speak your mind openly and freely. I'm the opposite. I'm too cerebral. It makes me hold my tongue in certain situations. On the other hand, my mouth's probably the only place on my body where I can apply the brakes. My psychic has classified me as being a free spirit in the body and mind, but not the mouth."

"Nothing happening in the oral department, huh?"

"Well . . . sometimes . . . ya know . . . when I get a craving. Let's just say my fiancé and I have a special shorthand when it hits," I said seductively. *Whoa, tiger! Where is this newfound spunk coming from? Totally uncalled-for and inappropriate, Lamberty. Reel it in.*

"Ha! I bet you don't put the brakes on that mouth in those situations!" Todd responded, making me blush.

"In those situations, I wouldn't dare!" I said. *I said reel it in, dammit! Stop this!*

Thankfully, the tone of the conversation melted away. However, we couldn't seem to stop smiling coyly at each other as we continued to organize the clothing rack.

***

The heavy activity presented earlier in the room had dramatically subsided as the producers and the majority of the cast had gone home. Vincent and Trent talked over the next day's schedule as Todd and I lugged two moderately filled laundry bags from the backstage area.

"So how are we going to do this?" Todd asked.

"Well, the nearest laundromat is about four stops uptown," I replied.

"This little bit of laundry isn't worth the trip uptown. Do you have machines in your building?"

"No."

"I'll tell you what. There's only a couple of hand-washable items in here. Why don't you take those home, get those clean, and I'll take the rest of the load to the machines in my building," Todd suggested.

"That's too much."

"No, it isn't. It's actually easier than heading uptown."

"But I wanna do my part. We should split the workload in half. I'll find a laundromat near my place."

"Don't worry about it. I'll do this this time, and you'll just owe me, that's all," Todd said slyly.

"Owe you? Oh God!"

"Don't worry, it won't be anything painful. But one day, I will ask you for a favor."

Uh, no. It would not be a good thing to do any type of favors for you, Mr. Sexy Man. No, indeed.

"Can't I just reimburse you for the quarters?"

"Nope."

I groan. "What kind of favor?" I asked.

"Patience. It will all be revealed when I come for you."

"Look at me. First day on the job and already in debt."

"Not all debt is bad. There's good debt too."

"Owing someone something is never a good thing, but I will say the offer is tempting."

"The reason my offer sounds so tempting is because you need the rest. I can tell from rehearsal," Todd said as he lifted the bags of laundry. "I got what you need right here. Stop resisting and let me take care of it. You can return the favor later," he continued.

I contemplated. Owing this sexy stranger this early in our interaction felt like a dangerous proposition; however, it admittedly excited me. As I pondered, my eyes completed a once-over on Todd as if they were on autopilot, then landed on his hands: bulky, veiny symbols of stoned strength. I imagined his grip to be as unforgiving as a vise, but his caress to be as gentle as sheepskin. My mind, my eyes' most willing companion, forced me to recall his tight, ripped biceps and bulging forearms as he lifted and corralled the heavy human-sized bags of wardrobe earlier in the day. I imagined that I was one of those bags, with Todd lifting and tossing my body over his shoulder like I was his possession.

I want to be manhandled. I want him to manhandle me.

As soon as I thought it, I immediately condemned the thought. Look but don't touch; fantasize, but always self-condemn: a code I'd lived by since I'd hit puberty.

Masking my arousal sparked by this man, this interesting, intriguing man was becoming an art, and I was becoming a master. I quickly muted my internal glow and responded, "Okay. But if it gets to be too much for you, I want you to promise that you'll call me."

Todd laughed softly. Even that had a pull on me.

"I promise," he replied.

"You have my number?" I ask.

"Yes. You have mine?"

"Yep."

"I'm sure I'll need you at some point. Stay by the phone," Todd said.

"It won't leave my side," I responded as we gathered our belongings and exited the room.

***

The laundry room in the bowels of that old, dusty apartment building was like a tomb. Cobwebs littered the ceiling corners, and multilegged parasites inhabited the crevices in the cracked cement. It was a cold, dark, bleach-smelling coffin for creatures of the night.

There were only four machines in the room, two quarter-operated washers, two quarter-operated dryers, and both were on their last legs. One of the rickety drying machines was in full permanent press mode, clanking and rumbling like a disturbed spirit, trying to make its way back to the land of the living.

I entered this icy cement block out of breath. Lugging the laundry bag home had turned out to be more tedious than I'd originally thought, but I was still generally in a positive mood, basking in the afterglow of my latest engagement with Anne. Her spirit and soft strength tickled me. I knew she was more than met the eye, and the fact that I'd recognized that energized me. I felt as though I had my sights on an undiscovered treasure, a bounty I hadn't even defined yet. The thought of peeling this onion and discovering what was inside granted me with a much-needed infusion of warmth and electricity.

I turned on the light, climbed down the stairs to the base of the room, plopped the deceivingly heavy bag on the floor, and leaned against the activated washing machine. As I began to relax and catch my breath, my solitude was interrupted by an unwanted voice. "Well, hello."

I turned and saw Toni standing at the top of the stairs, empty laundry basket in hand. I didn't hear the traditional whine of the door opening due to the smash and crash of what I assumed to be her garments in the drying machine. I silently looked at her for a moment, then turned and began to unload the dirty laundry from my gargantuan bag.

"Have you started a new job or something? Working on a new project I don't know about?" Toni asked as she descended the staircase. I continued to quietly separate the clothes, hoping, praying that this stain was washed away as I knew if it wasn't, it was only going to spread. "I just ask because your hours have been very different lately. You won't answer my calls; you won't respond to my texts," Toni continued as she dropped the empty laundry basket to the floor.

I turned on the water to the washer and activated the machine. After a second or two, I reopened the washer, squeezed a small amount of liquid detergent into its cavern, and closed the lid. "Where have you been?" she asked. I continued to ignore Toni's words as I let the water run for a few seconds, then commenced to load the washer with the filthy clothes. "So now I get the silent treatment?" she continued.

I slammed the washer lid closed and turned to face Toni, finally acknowledging her. In her eyes, I saw the light switch from yellow to green, and I could tell that she was about to mash the gas. "What the fuck is going on, Todd?"

"You tell me."

"Tell you what?"

"Tell me about Darryl."

She hesitated. "What about him? I work with him at the office; you've seen him at the Christmas parties. What?"

"You were with him the other night. After work."

"Yeah, we went out for a few drinks, so what?"

"You made it seem like it was a group of you all that got dinner, like your team went out after work, grabbed a bite, had some drinks. But nah, it was just you and Darryl hunh? Okay, what did you two do afterward?"

"What do you mean?"

"After dinner, what did you two do?"

"I went home. I assume he did too. Where's all this coming from? Darryl is a colleague, Todd. There's nothing going on here."

"All your colleagues call you 'baby'?"

She hesitated again. I filled the silence with, "Darryl was worried if his baby got home all right. You hit him back to let him know his baby was safe and sound later that night? While lying next to me?"

"You went through my phone?"

"He checked up on you while you were in the bathroom. The phone was right there, so. I keep telling you to put a lock on it."

"You went through my muthafuckin' phone!"

"Don't make that the issue, Toni. What the fuck you got goin' on with Darryl?"

"I told you Darryl and I just work together. That's it! I can't control what he writes. We haven't done anything with each other. I haven't done anything wrong."

"Yet."

"Get the fuck outta here, 'yet.' Okay, okay, Mr. 007 phone spy, did you get a chance to look at all of the messages between Darryl and I? Did you check the entire thread?" She took her phone out and attempted to hand it to me. "Go ahead. Take a look at it, and tell me when you find me texting something inappropriate to him. Find where I'm in the wrong."

"You sure you want me to do that, Toni?"

"Go ahead! You'll find some interaction, yes. I'm not a robot. There may even be some soft flirting in there, but I never cross the line, and I specifically tell him I'm with someone. I can't help it if he's got something else in mind."

"You could stay the fuck away from it. You could not entertain it."

"I'm not entertaining it! We met to discuss a part of the conversion over a meal and drinks, that's it."

"You think I'm a sucka, don't you? I'm no sucka, you know. You think I am, but I'm not. Never was. I've always seen right through the bullshit. You try to be sneaky and conceal what you're doing, and act like you're all innocent, but I know what's going on, always have. I'll try to ask you to come clean with me, to tell me the truth and all can be worked out, but you never tell me the full story. Somehow, you always seem to tell me just enough so I won't assume anything. You'll always leave something out. Something that keeps you from revealing the kind of person you really are. You and I both know what that is, but we'll never say it, will we? We'll just continue to think the truth while you'll keep saying meaningless *I love you*s, and I'll continue to read the messages that tell me otherwise."

Toni gasped. She seemed taken aback by my frankness, and for the first time in a long time, I could see the respect in her eyes. "Like I said, I'm no fool. You'd be surprised to know what I know," I continued.

"If you claim to know so much, if I've been fuckin' around on you all this time, why did you stay with me? If I was doing all this stuff, why are you still here?" she asked.

"Simple adjustment of the heart, baby. I learned not to give it all to you a long time ago, when I first started suspecting shit. Yeah, you've had a portion of me, but you haven't had all of me since the first time you fucked up. You admitted that one to me, and I give you credit for that, but you haven't had my whole heart since then, and you'll never have it all again. That's how I'm still able to be here, because I just don't care as much."

"So you don't care about us now? So I could just go out there and do anything, and you wouldn't give a fuck about it?"

"I mean, I've known who you are for a while now, so I'm pretty much numb to you and what you do. From the beginning, you told me I gave you all that you needed, that you had no reason to go get anything from anyone else, right?"

"Oh, give me a fuckin' break, Todd . . ."

"Right?"

"Yeah, okay, sure. Right, I said it."

"So even with you being fully satisfied, you still stepped out. You had no reason to, but you did, and that fucked me up. It fucked us up. Your greed changed our relationship, and it hasn't been the same since. But even before the first time, though, I knew there was potential for this. I knew you liked to party, I knew you liked to flirt, and that anything could happen when you got some liquor in you; I knew that from the start, but I still fucked with you. I knew what you were, but I accepted it because I couldn't deny the bond we had. The bond made me think we could still have something good. I guess I also hoped you'd recognize a real one when you got one, but like I said, in the back of my mind I knew what I was getting into when we started, so I really have no one to blame but myself."

"You are so full of shit, Todd. You know I wasn't out there planning to step out on you. Yeah, you gave me all I needed, but fuck, I'm human. I get turned on by other people. That's not going to stop no matter how satisfied I am with you. I also make mistakes, just like the rest of us, you included. But don't trivialize this whole thing by making it about drinking and partying. That has nothing to do with it. Sure, you can blame yourself for having a part in what our relationship has become, but not for deciding to still fuck with me after knowing 'what I am' or whatever you're calling it. Blame yourself for being insecure."

"My insecurities have nothing to do with this. If anything, my insecurities have been validated by what you've done and what you continue to do!"

"All that you're accusing me of has been brought about by your insecurities, Todd! You've always thought I was cheating. Even before the first time. If I was texting, if I went to the store, if I wore something sexy to a party, if I danced with someone, I was accused of fucking someone else, and it truly wasn't the case! So when someone came around I had a history with, yes, I fucked up, but you pushed me there. And you continue to push me, so I say why not flirt, you think I'm doing worse anyway, so fuck it. I still maintain that I don't cross the line, I haven't since the first time, but you won't believe me. Should have never told you about the first time . . ."

"See, that's the problem! That's the philosophical problem right there! You think the issue is that you *told* me. The issue is that you did it! You should've never done it! And you blaming this shit on me is bullshit. I didn't fuck anyone else. You did! You fucked this up, not me!"

"I'm not saying I didn't make a mistake, Todd. I did, and I've apologized for that. But you contributed to it. You can't say that you didn't. And if you think I've been playing you all this time, why wouldn't you act like you gave a damn? You're just going to go along with it and let me play you? If I was doing you so wrong, you should've checked my behavior."

"I shouldn't have to check you. We're in a relationship. Shouldn't have to force you to be faithful."

At that point, I was broken inside because I knew she was right. I should have checked her. I should have stood up for myself and asserted my worth. I didn't have to take what I believed she was doing to me, and I allowed it to happen by deadening my expectations and spunk for the relationship. I vowed right then and there to never let something like that get away from me again. Hindsight was indeed 20/20.

"You're right, Todd. I shouldn't have to be forced, and again, it was never my intention to get caught up like that when I was unfaithful. I know that hurt you and probably still does to this day. I know this, and I wish I could take all of it back, but I can't. Just know that since then, I have been faithful to you. You are the only person I have been with; you are the only person I want to be with. That mistake in the past had nothing to do with you or my love for you. I loved you then, and I still love you now. I wouldn't do anything to bring that type of hurt back on you again, trust and believe that. I love you, baby, and even with all that has happened, I know deep down, a part of you still loves me too."

I remained silent as I was thrown off balance from her acuteness. She was always a sharp woman, perceptive, observant. Her ability to see through the bullshit was one of the qualities that had drawn me to her. She was my superhero with X-ray vision, and now those superpowers had been turned against me, exposing my closely guarded hand.

"You know what we've been through, and you know we're meant to be together. That's why you've stayed. That's why you couldn't walk away so easily. I know in my heart you're the person I'm supposed to be with, and I know you feel the same," she stated.

The last statement hit me right where it hurt, like acid being pumped into my veins. "How can I love you when I can't trust you?!" I exploded.

She moved in close, looked directly into my eyes, and said, "Give it time, my love. That's all we have. Give it time."

I angrily watched as Toni wiped away a few tears, swiped up her laundry basket, and ascended to the top of the stairs. She paused just before she reached the door. With her back to me, she said, "I'm willing to do what's necessary to get your whole heart again, Todd, but you've got to start trusting me. I can't wait forever," then slowly exited. Seemed like it took a lifetime for the door to close behind her.

I stood still for a moment, with her last statement still echoing in the chamber. I slammed my hand on top of the washer in disgust. What a mess she'd made. Hell, what a mess *we'd* made. Once again, she'd turned her transgressions into an equal playing field. It was something only she could do with such bravado and confidence, another unique talent of hers that I'd always found repulsive.

I was so turned off from the episode that I kicked a large dent into the spinning drying machine, popping open its door and freeing a few of Toni's undergarments. I fumed as I stared at the limp, lifeless panties and bras I used to have such reverence for, lying on the soiled surface. That's what my desires and aspirations with Toni had turned into, a sprucely cleaned delicate, perched upon solid, unforgiving filth.

As I seethed, my phone began to ring. I picked up the phone and breathed hard into the receiver a few times before answering, "Yeah."

"Todd?"

"Who is it?"

"It's Anne."

My mood immediately lightened. A sunshine-filled sensation washed over me like a wave. "Anne? Hey."

"Hey. Just wanted to see how it's going."

"It's going."

"Had my phone by my side all night."

"Yeah right."

"I did! And it didn't ring once!"

"You sure? I could've called while you were in the shower or something."

"Positive. I brought the phone into the shower with me! I wouldn't hang my partner out to dry like that. Get it? Hung out to dry?" Anne jested.

"I got it."

"A little laundry humor there."

"Thanks for the effort, but . . ."

"I know. I know. I'll do better next time."

"So I guess you didn't need me after all, huh?" Anne asked.

"Uh . . . yeah," I respond.

"Yeah, you needed me, or . . ."

"Yeah, I handled it on my own. Not a big deal."

"Because you know I'm just a phone call away if . . ."

"It's not a big deal. I've got it. I wouldn't have you traipsing out here at one in the morning to help me fold a load of socks. Why are you up so late by the way?" I asked.

"Couldn't sleep. Lotta things on my mind."

"So you thought you'd call and bug me."

"I figured you'd still be sifting through the soot. Was I right?"

"Yeah. Still sifting."

We shared a moment of silence. All that was heard were the busy laundry machines. It was starting to feel uncomfortable.

"Still there?" Anne asked.

"Yeah. Uh . . . listen. Let me put this next load in so I can get to sleep at a reasonable hour. Don't need Vincent commenting on the bloodshot eyes again," I said.

"Good point. Guess I'll take another crack at counting sheep."

"Do you know the trick to making that work?"

"No. What?"

"Only count the evens. You'll go to sleep faster. It's something about dealing with even numbers that relaxes the brain."

"Really?"

"Oh yeah. Also, make the sheep multicolored fluorescent, and when they jump over the fence, make 'em say, 'shrimp sushi!'"

"Fuck you!"

"Good luck with that, okay?" I replied.

"Whatever. Hope you're washing till the wee hours of the morning,"

"That's something I can only hope for. See you tomorrow."

"Tomorrow," Anne said as the call disconnected.

I exhaled the few remaining folds of tension from my spat with Toni. All was clear, back to equilibrium. Now, grateful to be back on rhythm and balanced, I placed another load in the open washer and started a new cycle.

9

A flurry of activity was underway backstage. We had just finished another dress rehearsal and were in the middle of our customary end-of-day hustle and bustle. We ripped and ran around each other, stripped our clothes off, threw some to the ground, and hung the others on racks. Mic tape was being torn from hairy flesh, and the accompanying lavalier microphones were being disassembled and placed back in their cushiony cases.

The fast and furious action slowed a tad when we heard Trent's baritone voice booming through the wings. "Thank you, ladies and gentlemen, for a good run. Please be prompt in your changes as Vincent would like to have a word with you before we disperse. Thank you.”

Leroy, the person in charge of stowing the electrical equipment in the show, dropped the last electrical wire into a large metal case, closed it, and yelled, “Good run, guys!”

Joey, coughing and sounding severely stuffed up, responded, “Thank God. I’m glad that’s over. Sorry if I sprayed a couple of you guys out there. Can’t seem to shake this cold.”

“I’m sure taking your shirt off and twirling it around at the concert last night didn’t help,” Christian replied.

“What can I say? I was moved,” Joey said. He then turned to Johnathon, gave him a man slap on the shoulder, and said to him, “You rocked last night, man.”

“Thanks, dude. Thought we overdid it on a couple of songs, but whatever,” Johnathon commented.

“Are you kidding? You guys let us have it! Seriously, I was moved by what you guys did up there. Truly moved,” Joey said.

“You were moving something for sure,” Sally chimed in.

"Excuse me, my lady, but are you commenting on my dancing?" Joey asked.

"For a moment there I thought I was transported into *Saturday Night Fever*!" Sally responded.

"I thought I saw someone striking a pose on the dance floor. One finger in the air . . . that was you?" Johnathon asked.

"Ha! You did have the Travolta thing down pat. You lost me when you took the shirt off, though," Leroy said.

"Didn't need that visual," said Johnathon.

"The shirt should've stayed on," said Christian.

"Could've kept the shirt," Sally said.

"I'm sorry, okay? I thought I could freely express myself with you guys. Next time I'll know I can't give my all. I'll have to hold some of the Joemeister back," Joey responded.

"Aww. Don't hold back the Joemeister! We like the Joemeister. Just keep the shirt on," Sally said. Joey gave her a look, and she continued with, "We're just looking out for your best interest. Can't have our Romeo being sick, can we?"

Joey wasn't buying it, and Sally could tell. She quickly made eye contact with Christian, Leroy, and Johnathon, searching for support.

"Oh! Yeah! Health! Your health is what's important to us man. Gotta have you well for the show," Christian said.

"It'll be best for you and us," Johnathon said.

Leroy snickered and said, "Yeah . . . we need you in tip-top shape."

"See!" Sally commented to Joey.

"Oh . . . all right," Joey replied, the nervous tension melting from his shoulders. With the awkwardness subsided, we all eased back into our day-ending routine for a few quiet seconds. All of which was interrupted when Christian blurted out, "Just next time, give us a warning if you're going to unleash Chewbacca on the public," as he pointed to Joey's hairy chest.

Leroy, Sally, Christian, and Johnathon erupted with laughter. Eventually, Joey gave in and joined them with a genuine full belly laugh. His was the lengthiest of the group.

"That's all right, honey. Don't let it bother ya. I'll fix you some homemade chicken noodle soup for your cold," Sally said to Joey.

"I'd like that. Thanks," Joey responded as he cracked a smile. Sally smiled back, and suddenly, the room felt ten degrees warmer.

However, even as things warm up, there was a stiff chill in close proximity as Molly and I were getting dressed nearby. Although shunned from the start, I was still eager to get into Molly's good graces. I'd never had someone just plain not like me for no apparent reason, so this was new territory for me, and I wasn't sure how to handle this catastrophe. The situation made me uneasy, like a thick, flat, noodle-like worm in my stomach. It had to be expurgated.

"Good run out there today," I said to Molly.

No response.

"I thought the scene when you have it out with Capulet was really powerful today," I continued.

Molly pulled her sweater over her head and commenced to flip and primp her hair without comment.

I relent as I felt the stinging frost from Molly's shoulder once again.

Unbelievable. This chick really is a piece of work. That's it. I'm done. She doesn't want to talk to me? Fine. We can make that happen.

I took a seat on the floor and began to put on my shoes. As I skillfully began to manipulate the laces, my eyes happened to land on a wall mirror that had become newly visible from my new position on the floor. In the reflection, I captured one condensed second of spectacular magnificence, a frontal view of Todd, covered only by his boxer briefs as he was pulling up his pants. I witnessed the moment before his delectable smorgasbord was eclipsed by a stiff layer of denim.

Oh shit. Oh . . . shit! I can't look at this. I shouldn't.

In that brief moment, I inspected every hair on his toned, tight thighs. I followed a thick, protruding vein up his inner thigh to the snug leg elastic attached to his boxer briefs. I worked my way up the black cotton undergarment and watched it stretch and swell as Todd shifted his body. As Todd lifted his pants past the three-quarter level, my eyes swooped downward to ingest the wonderful brooding bulge that anchored my discovery. The waistband of the boxer briefs seemed to dip from the weight of his majestic gift. My focus was so intense, I noticed the ripple of its glutinous side vein as blood pulsated its way through the passageway, continuously nursing and feeding the plump organ.

I shuddered.

I could feel drool starting to well up on the surface of my bottom lip as Todd got his pants to his waistline, tightened his belt, and walked away from the mirror. Before he walked out of the reflection, I caught a glimpse of his high, athletically firm buttocks. I breathed deep and closed my eyes for a moment . . .

I've never had it this bad. I am so turned on right now it's ridiculous! I can honestly say that I don't think I've ever been so physically attracted to anyone else, and that includes Brody, and that's shameful! I barely know anything about him, but maybe that's part of it. Maybe that's the fantasy. That's fine. Maybe I should fantasize about him. Hell, it's not hurting anybody, and it's natural, for Christ's sake! We're human beings! We have urges! Plus, I'm sure Brody has had plenty of women he's fantasized over and whatnot. Wouldn't be wrong for me to do it either. In fact, it's healthy for me to do so. Just as long as I keep it in my mind, I'm golden. One thing I can say for sure is that I've never felt like this before. It's like he has some sort of power over me, coaxing me, wooing me. Now all I want to do is stare at his crotch. Jesus, I bet his dick is magnificent! I can't get the print of it out of my mind. Its shape, the way it was just sitting there, thick, heavy, bulky, like a tree trunk. I'd have to flex my muscle just to hold it in my hand. I wonder how it feels, how it tastes . . .

Suddenly, I'm awakened by . . .

"Hey."

I slowly opened my eyes and saw Todd standing in front of me, shirtless. I was out of breath. I had to inhale a few times just to be able to respond. "Hey," I said.

"Did you hear?"

Oh my God. Did he hear me? He couldn't have heard me, could he?

"What? What? Did I hear what?" I responded as I glanced at Todd's chiseled chest.

"I forgot to hang up the items that were supposed to be air-dried last night . . ."

I made brief eye contact, then as if on autopilot, my eyes automatically made their way down his torso. His abdominals were ambassadors of congruency.

Goddamn, what are you doing to me?

". . . and all of Molly's shirts were still wet. She had to do the entire performance in wet blouses! . . ."

My eyes began to travel back down to his glorious crotch, but I stopped myself by closing my eyes, shaking my head, and quietly moaning.

Nope! Stop it, Lamberty. You know where this is going.

". . . I told her it was an accident, but she wouldn't listen. Now she blames both of us for deliberately trying to sabotage her!" Todd said.

It took all of my willpower to not completely fall into the belly of the lust trap standing before me, and I was shocked to realize that willpower alone was not going to be enough for me to resist. Thus, I dug deeper and relied on whatever was left of my moral compass and my eternal devotion to my fiancé to finally compose myself and get back to equilibrium.

It was a battle I almost lost, as I was down to my final reserves, but it was one that I needed to win.

"I guess I can't handle this thing on my own. Guess I need you after all," Todd said. Exhausted from my internal gymnastics, all I could muster was a simple smile.

Leroy entered the area holding his costume and hung it on a nearby clothing rack.

"What happened last night?" he said as he approached Todd and I. "We were looking for you at John's concert."

"Oh! The concert . . . yeah . . . well . . . you know, we had laundry duty last night and . . . uh . . . it ran a little long," Todd said. He and Leroy looked at me for confirmation.

"Yes . . . a little long," I stated.

"Sorry we couldn't make it. I'll . . . I'll go apologize to Johnathon," Todd said as he began to walk toward Johnathon. When I was alone, Leroy looked at me cockeyed.

"What?" I asked.

"You guys could've made it out last night; between loads," Leroy said.

"Hey, those are the sacrifices we have to make in order to stay clean, right?"

"I guess."

"We took on these assignments willingly. We knew what we were getting into, what we would have to give up," I said.

"Did you really?"

I pondered for a moment, then answered, "No. Not at all."

Leroy chuckled while I sprouted a conflicted smile.

The comfort of night had always enriched me. Its dark blanket seemed to act as a restoration chamber for me, healing my wounds, resuscitating my spirit, and calming my soul. The best things that have ever happened to me occurred post-nightfall. This was when I was at my best, this is when my mind was the clearest.

On that crisp night, I was in my apartment, situating some of my personal items in a suitcase. My bed looked like a war zone: sheets flipped back; sweaters, underwear, socks, and shoe boxes littered about. Nirvana blasted through my speakers as that attempt to corral my personal items had become more than a packing ritual; it was a therapy session.

As I worked my way through, a framed picture of Brody and I sitting on my nightstand caught my eye. I picked the picture up and studied it for a moment. Something was different about the picture. The two people in it looked the same, every hair, every article of clothing was in place as it had always been, but still, something was different. Maybe what was different was how I felt when I looked at these two young lovers, clasped in each other's arms. Maybe the feeling I once had while viewing this pic had faded or was now buried deep within me, in a space that I couldn't access anymore. I wasn't sure what it was, but I knew something had changed.

My moment of reflection was interrupted by a simultaneous soft knock and opening of my door. Brody entered and said hello. I flipped the picture face down on the bed and resumed packing with my back to him. Brody watched me continue to ignore him for a painfully long moment.

"We can't continue to do this. I know you're leaving, but we can't . . . We're not going to make it if we're not communicating.

Please talk to me. I don't want our last night to end with us not speaking to each other," Brody said as I continued to methodically pack in silence. He told me he wished things were different, that he'd never said what he did. He told me however this ended up, if we eventually stayed together or wound up breaking up, he'd always love me. My silence continued.

In the quiet, I could feel Brody taking another painfully long stare at me. When I didn't respond, he eventually exited. As soon as I was alone, the tempo of my movements slowed to a crawl, then stopped. Tears began to well up in my eyes as I sunk to my bed and silently wept next to the overturned picture.

***

Mornings invigorated me, especially the morning sun. The fact that I was born on a sunny Sunday morning might have had something to do with that, but I'd never admit it. I'd always been quite taken at the opportunity for a new start, and each new morning provided that opportunity to me. The sun could be optional, but the strength I wielded from a fresh day's rays couldn't be denied. When touched, I felt like a solar-powered superhero, ready to start a new journey toward conquering the world. Nothing could stop me once I was lit on fire from that infernal star. Nothing.

On that particular morning, I entered my apartment on a mission. I walked with intense intent and purpose through the front room and toward my small office.

After a few moments, I could hear Toni's half-asleep voice yell out from the adjacent bedroom, "Todd? Todd is that you?" I didn't answer.

After another few moments, I heard her flop out of bed and walk toward my office. "Todd?" she says as she approaches.

Still no answer. I continue shoving my items into an oversized gym bag. "Damn, Todd! You could let me know when you're coming home so I don't have to think someone's trying to attack me!" she said through heated breath. I assured her that no one was trying to attack her, but it didn't temper Toni's intensity. "How am I supposed to know that? You could've been anybody! So, what? Are you

replenishing your wardrobe for another vacation away from home?”
she asked.

“Something like that,” I responded.

“We’ve got problems here, Todd. Eventually, you’re going to
have to come home.”

“Eventually.”

As I continued to pack, Toni moved closer to me. With her
attitude cooled a bit, she told me we should talk about our current
situation, but I rejected the idea, stating that we had nothing to talk
about. Toni asked for leniency, hoping, praying, that I would at least
agree to have some sort of dialogue. I was sure she was thinking
something, anything, was better than nothing, but yet and still, I
continued to dismiss her requests.

In her most feeble tone, she said, “These issues we have,
Todd, they’re going to end us if we don’t talk about them.”

“I don’t want to get into it! I already said I don’t want to talk.
Now, I just came over here to get a few things— . . .”

“Darryl kissed me last night. I thought you should know.”

This threw me for a loop. Naturally, I took a long pause to get my thoughts together. *Is she serious or is she just saying these things to get me talking?*

"We were working late over drinks again, and before I knew it, he leaned in, and it happened. I pushed him off and left the restaurant. I'm going to ask to be taken off of his team. It won't matter as far as my promotion goes, and the new project I'm going to go after actually lines up better with my goals. It's for the best in all cases."

I couldn't speak. All I could do was shake my head. She asked me if I still loved her, but I couldn't answer. She told me that even though the moment with Darryl happened, she hopes it didn't affect anything with us. She went on to maintain that she loved me with all her heart and couldn't bear to lose me. Honestly, even with all that had happened, I was affected by her admission, but ultimately I remained silent.

She squatted down next to me and gently placed her hands on my shoulders, her patented go-to move. She kept this tucked away in her arsenal for only the most crucial times. Her warm, soft hands stayed on my shoulders for a few seconds, and I begrudgingly reveled in her caress. Oh, how I'd missed this. She leaned in close behind my neck and whispered, "I'm sorry," through her sincerest emotion. She hugged me close, and I sank into her remorse for a moment, then broke free of her cradle.

I jumped to my feet, closed the closet, and hurriedly resumed my packing. I scurried around the room, tossing odd items into my duffel bag—books, pens, notebooks, vitamins . . .

"Will you at least tell me where you're going to be staying?" Toni asked firmly, to which I remained silent.

"TODD!" she yelled.

"WHAT? WHAT DO YOU WANT?" I yelled back.

"I want to know where you'll be staying."

"Not sure."

I zipped up my duffel bag.

"Will you please talk to me?" Toni asked.

I put on my coat and walked to the door.

"Wait, wait. Before you go, please talk to me!"

I continued my walk toward the door and reached for the knob.

"TODD! Tell me that we're going to be okay!"

I paused, my hand curling around the cold doorknob. I finally felt enough air fill my lungs to speak. When I pushed the air out, I heard myself say, "I can't."

I exited the apartment, duffel bag in hand. As I galloped down the stairwell, I could hear Toni weeping through the acoustics. She was in pain, and so was I. Selfishly, my pain was the only thing I cared about at that moment, and I once again employed the necessary armor to bar myself from being completely broken. In that moment, I compartmentalized Toni and all that came with her, and walked feverishly down the cold, windy street toward my immediate future.

11

Not surprisingly, I had my best rehearsal of the run on this day. Being finished with Toni, while painful, was a weight lifted off of my shoulders. I felt totally free and unburdened, yet there was definitely a deep wound inside of me that I couldn't reach to soothe. It was going to take time, but what always helped me in those times, what helped me get through the last time, was the work. The work saved me each and every time.

After rehearsal, we were all sitting on the wooden floor as Trent and Vincent stood before us. As opposed to many of the days in this sweat chamber, there was an energetic, upbeat vibe in the room. It was the culmination of a full month of rehearsals, and we were ready to hit the road. We were feeling good, rested, and excited as Trent read through the final rundown of how things would transpire in a few moments. ". . . once we have all the gear locked and loaded, we'll run through the checklist one more time, and we'll be off. Sal, please remind me to give you the spare key for the passenger van," he said.

"Yes, sir," Salvador responded.

Trent reminded us that there was an early call tomorrow, six a.m., much to our dismay. He went on to promptly warn us that tardiness would not be tolerated and reminded us of the contracted fines that were tied to being late for call times. Afterward, he turned our attention over to Vincent, and we applauded heartily as he stepped forward.

"Please. Please. Save your strength. Well, we've made it. We've worked extremely hard in here so you won't have to work as hard out there. What stands before you, my pets, is a privilege. A mission reserved only for those blessed enough to carry it out. And thanks to the highest, we are those blessed ones. To do what we do, to breathe life into a lifeless vessel, elevates us to deity status. We are the masters of the unconscious. Our actions inspire, our words teach, and our silence—my God, our silence! Our silence heals! Our silence converts! Our silence ripples and creates shifts! Being the keepers of these coveted treasures, we have an obligation to give back, to share our gift with the world. This obligation was created by the world itself out of the desperate need for enlightenment. Therefore, never underestimate your value as a player. You are fulfilling the required role subscribed by the gods of the universe, to provide balance to its four corners. Be proud of your penance. Use it each time you hit the stage to convey the souls of these characters. Keep it with you even after you dismount, because we are truly not worthy to possess such a bountiful endowment. Good luck out there, and have safe travels," he concluded.

We erupted in applause. We knew from the beginning that Vincent wouldn't be taking this trip with us, that he was just to prepare us for survival on the road and give us the tools we needed to be successful. Now that that work was done, our next steps would be on our own.

We all stood and individually thanked Vincent for his tutelage and words of wisdom. He took in the appreciation, and like a mother releasing her young cubs into the wild, he relished the final moments he had with his pupils.

"Take care of them," he said to Trent.

"I will," Trent responded.

We giddily said goodbye to the stuffy crucible-like confines of the rehearsal room and filed downstairs to the busy, windy New York streets. Just outside the building, a large silver Sprinter van packed with luggage sat near the curb, doors open. Just behind it, a large, weighed-down cargo van sat idle. The majority of us stood near the Sprinter van chatting amongst ourselves as Salvador performed a quick head count.

"All accounted for, sir," Salvador said.

"Thank you, Sergeant. Ladies and gentlemen, we are all here and accounted for on time. Give yourselves a round of applause,"

Trent said as we applauded affectionately. He dangled a set of keys above his head. "Who has the first shift?"

Johnathon emphatically raised his hand, and Trent handed him the keys.

"And his navigator?" Trent asked.

"That'll be me," I said.

Trent handed me a map and said, "The route is highlighted in red just in case we get split up and GPS goes AWOL. Reception is bad in these parts. Who's my navigator?" Joey reluctantly raised his hand. Trent handed him a map and said, "I'm sure I know where I'm going, but just in case . . ."

"Route's highlighted in red. Got it," Joey interjected.

"Okay, ladies and gentlemen, let's literally get this show on the road!" Trent shouted.

A few members of the cast let out a few "woo-hoos," then piled into the Sprinter van. Johnathon climbed into the driver's seat, and I rode shotgun. Trent and Joey hopped into the cargo van, with Trent at the wheel. After a few chokes and pulls, both vans were ignited, and began to pull off, with the cargo van leading the way.

***

BUFFALO, NY

Heavy snow fell as both vans pulled into the Red Roof Inn parking lot and parked. I was extremely grateful for this particular stop because my bladder was about to burst. The ladies' bathroom was broken at the last rest stop, and for some idiotic reason, I continued to drink water like a fish. I couldn't wait to relieve myself.

Trent and a well-rested Joey exited the cargo van and made their way over to the Sprinter van as the rest of us were dismounting.

Molly exited first. "Thank God," she said.

Trent walked over from the cargo van to greet us as we inspected our new surroundings and said, "Welcome to glorious Buffalo! You guys can sit tight until I go check us in. Sal, I'll be needing your assistance."

Salvador and Trent walked toward the hotel as a sulking Molly retreated back into the van and as the rest of us grabbed our luggage. As we marveled at the winter wonderland, Sally said, "It's beautiful."

"Can't get enough of this stuff in these parts," I said as Sally stuck her tongue out to catch some flakes.

"We barely see snow where I'm from," Sally stated.

"Believe me, you're lucky, sister. When I'm on tour with my band, it never fails that we get stuck on a major highway for hours due to some freakin' blizzard. Winters in the north bite me where it hurts," Johnathon said.

"It's not so bad. I can think of a hell of a lot worse," Joey said.

"Like what?" Christian asked.

"I don't know. The desert," Joey responded.

"Hey, hey. I was born amongst cacti," Sally retorted.

"It's too hot during the day, it's too cold at night. Whaddya gonna do? Then there's all those longhorn skulls lying all over the place . . . it's unsanitary. Unsanitary and unattractive," Joey jested.

"I'll tell ya what's unattractive, mister," Sally said through a crooked smile. We reacted with *ooh*s and *aah*s as Sally had clearly won that round with her spunk and sassiness.

Salvador appeared from the hotel's innards and waved us in. As everyone headed toward the hotel, I tapped on the van window to signal to Molly, and she obliged. When she dismounted, I tried to walk with her to the hotel, but she left me in the dust, once again, shutting me out. I absorbed rejection's slap, then realized I wasn't alone. Todd had intentionally lingered behind to wait for me. I caught up to him, and he asked, "Now or later?"

I watched the remaining cast members enter the hotel, the playful jargon continuing well into the hotel's innards. "Now," I responded as a nervous tingle shot through my spine. "But let me use the bathroom first!"

***

An old, beat-up laundromat sat about a mile away from the hotel. The rickety sign could barely be seen at night; however, the neon OPEN 24 HRS sign blazed away, clearly the most recent investment for the aged and faded establishment.

The passenger van was the only vehicle parked in the parking lot, and the bulky silver spinning machines could be seen through the large glass windows. Just a few of the machines were active. Not too far from the activity, Todd and I sat quietly across from each other at a table. The subtle metallic knocking and humming provided a hypnotic soundtrack for us as we positioned ourselves in the center of the mechanized labyrinth.

I, attempting to mask my curiosity about the svelte gentleman sitting across from me, read a hard-covered comic book while Todd wrote in a notebook. We caught glimpses of each other looking at each other, only to quickly look away and chuckle off the silent encounter. Eventually, Todd decided to break the tension. "Gettin' hot," he said.

I didn't say a word; however, I wondered if he could read my thermal body temperature, as it had been on fire ever since he and I had been alone. I prayed that wasn't the case. I just stayed very still, like an insect that knew it had been spotted.

"The dryers. They're getting hot. Seems like the last load dried faster than the others," he continued. He took a peek at the cover of my comic and laughed. "Wow. Never figured you for the colorful stuff."

"Oh, this? Don't be fooled, this is pretty deep material I'm dealing with here. Dark side of the moon, severed consciousness, birth in shadow, that kind of thing," I said.

"What are you, a witch?"

"Yes, I am. I plan to add you and the other little children to the cauldron before the year's out."

"That's gonna be some sour stew."

"Don't worry, the sugary-sweet adolescents will curb the tart tartness you expel, my deary." Satisfied with my comeback and feeling the warm, pleasurable sensation of confidence, I inspected his notebook of scribbles and said, "So, you're a writer too? Is there anything you can't do?"

"Juggle. I can't juggle to save my life."

"Don't worry. Not all clowns can juggle. You can drive the little car," I quipped.

"Drive it to run you over? Yes indeed, though I think I'll need a bigger car."

Ha ha! Asshole.

"I think you're right," I responded.

We both went back to our separate functions for a while, me reading, Todd furiously writing away. The sound and tempo of the frantic pen scratching the frail notebook paper revealed Todd's passion. He was writing as if he'd reached the climax of a whodunit and an earthquake couldn't pull his pen from the page. Whatever he was writing, it was intense, and the intensity intrigued me. "Anything good?" I asked.

"Well, there's no adolescent cannibalism, so . . ."

"Oh, well, there's my answer, then," I responded.

We took a pause to let some air in between our continuous verbal spar, and we both enjoyed a laugh. This wasn't the first time we'd had a round, but it was the first time we individually acknowledged this addictive and delicious blood sport for ourselves. We loved it, and I could tell that we both wanted more.

"Seriously. How's it coming along?" I asked.

Todd continued writing and commented, "It's coming."

"What is it?"

"It's . . . it's . . ."

"A song, a novel . . ."

"A play," Todd said through pressed lips.

"A play! That's great." I reveled in my accomplishment for a moment and watched Todd as he continued to feverishly write. I relaxed for a second, then I just couldn't help myself. "May I ask what it's about?"

Todd stopped writing. "Uh. Don't take this the wrong way . . ."

"You don't like to talk about it . . ."

"Not until it's finished," he said.

I surprised myself by not being crushed by his gentle rejection. I continued to watch him glide his pen over his personal canvas and commented, "Sure, no problem. I understand. Believe me, I've heard that before from other writers. I respect that." I calmly reopened my comic book and flipped through a few pages. I waited a few moments before I recharged my courage. "Do you have others?" I asked.

"Yeah, a few."

"You should let me read some of your work."

"I really don't . . ."

"Oh, come on! You're gonna reject me twice in one night?"

"No, it's not that. It's just . . . I really don't let anyone look at my work."

"Don't be embarrassed. I promise I won't be cruel."

"It's not about being embarrassed. My writing is very . . . I don't know . . . revealing. It's very personal. True to life. It may scare you," Todd said.

"Believe me, nothing you could put in front of me could scare me, Todd," I replied.

"You sure about that?"

"Positive."

Todd smirked, flipped a few pages in his notebook, handed it to me, and said, "First paragraph." I began to read Todd's composition, a scene in his play where the lead character is writing a love letter to his betrothed. The writing was beautiful and twisted, his words conveying split sentiments of adoration, eroticism, and madness. It revealed something about him, something dark, something passionate that I indeed found frightening. I really had no idea who I was sitting alone with in this secluded field of steel. No one would think this quiet, intelligent man would have these kinds of thoughts, but there they were, his gray matter spilled out onto the page before me. The idea of being alone with a stranger whose mind dove this deep into the recesses of human need and perversion was an extreme turn-on, so much so that I began to tingle. Something was building inside of me, something with the momentum of a freight train, and it had just pulled off from the station.

I finished reading the scene and handed the notebook back to Todd. I was flushed from all the excitement, and from Todd's subtle grin, he had clearly noticed. "You are one sick puppy!" I said.

"Told you."

"But it's also beautiful. You're really talented."

"Thanks. It's about you."

This . . . this is about me?

An electric rush shot through me like a live current. Heat. All I could feel was heat. "No way! Stop . . . stop kidding around," I managed to say through the inferno.

"I'm not. There's something about you. Haven't put my finger on it yet, but for some strange reason, you have my attention. Scared yet?"

"Yes. Very," I replied. I was aroused and swollen to the max. I was ready to explode. At that very moment, the buzzer on the dryer exploded with sound as another load had just finished. The sound lifted me out of my seat and made me gasp.

"Sit tight. I'll get this one," Todd said as he folded his notebook closed and walked to the dryer. I watched every fiber of him as he approached and unloaded the hot box.

This guy's trouble. Absolute T-R-O-U-B-L-E.

***

Todd and I drove up a long, dark road and eventually reached a large statue of a water buffalo adorned with a pair of angelic wings. The statue sat just outside a tavern that had a large sign draped over its awning that read THE ANCHORBAR: HOME OF THE ORIGINAL

BUFFALO WING. We located the silver Sprinter van in the lot, parked right next to it, and hopped out.

The first thing we saw when we got inside was a large tray of glossy-sauced wings and neon-green celery stalks being carried through the mayhem of the busy eatery. The server holding the ridiculous platter dodged several fatal mishaps before reaching her final destination: a long buffet-style table that housed the majority of the cast. We followed behind her as the cast enthusiastically greeted her when she approached.

The server put the large tray down in the center of the table, and the cast rabidly attacked the sizzling mound of enflamed poultry. For a few moments, the sounds of popping gristles and sweetly glazed torn flesh was all that was heard. Eventually, Christian lifted his head out of the pile for air and said, "Holy mother, these are good!"

"I like spicy food, but I don't know. This stuff sounds pretty lethal," Johnathon said.

"What sounds pretty lethal?" Todd said as we approached the table.

"Welcome! I assume laundry went okay?" Leroy asked.

Todd pulled two chairs up to the table for us, and we sat.

"If you call being stuck alone with this guy okay," I quipped.

"Hey, I told you, cottons only! I'm not touching that polyester shit! Gives me rashes," Todd responded.

"Oh, those rashes aren't from the polyester, buddy. But don't fret. You can get a special cream for that," I responded.

"Oh, can I borrow yours?"

"All of my creams and lotions are for beautifying purposes. Not for itchy rashes and crabs . . ."

"Hey, hey, hey! We're eating here!" Salvador yelled.

"You two must've had some time doing laundry," Christian said.

Molly raised an eyebrow and said skeptically, "I sure hope it was done correctly."

"Don't worry, the laundry's fine. If there's any problems, blame Nurse Ratched over there," Todd responded as he gestured toward me.

I playfully cut my eyes at him as he grabbed a menu. "So what's this lethal decision we're making?" he asked.

"I'm trying to decide if I'm going to get the 'hot as Satan's balls' wings," Johnathon stated.

"I don't think I could eat any balls that hot," I said.

"Oh, you're a big girl. I'm sure you could jaw juggle those if you put your mind to it," Todd said.

"I guess you would know. I mean, you being the expert of having flaming-hot balls in your mouth!" I snapped as the table laughed. Everyone noticed and was supremely enjoying our newfound chemistry.

"Do I need to separate you two?" Leroy asked.

"I'm just starving, that's all. I'll be fine once I get some food in me," I stated.

"Sounds like you need something else in you," Todd replied.

Jazzed by the jargon and determined to win yet another round, I come back with, "No thanks. Wouldn't want to catch a rash." Game. Set. Match.

"All right, all right! That's enough talk of hot nuts and flashy rashes at the dinner table. I'm trying to enjoy my tasty salad and its subtly spicy cool water dressing, so relax, will ya?" Salvador said.

Todd and I make sly eyes at each other. I knew I'd gotten the best of him not once, but twice, and he knew it as well. We were the greatest of foes at this wordplay, and we had the utmost respect for each other's skill set. It was a stimulating competition.

Todd finally broke from my magnetic draw and took a look at the menu. He asked Johnathon about the wings he was considering ordering. Then he got the attention of the server and asked about the intensity of the wings, and she told him she was not able to talk for three days after eating them. That seemed to appeal to Todd, as well as Johnathon. They both seemed to be thrill-seekers. Johnathon, seeing that he had a partner, became reenergized about attempting the feat before him.

"What about the show?" Leroy asked.

Todd sucked his teeth as if he'd just been reminded of something that was going to take his fun away: the safe, practical path versus the dangerous, adventurous one. "That's right. You're right," he said.

"Don't worry about the show. How many times will you get a chance to taste the Antichrist's colon? Do it!" I said. My encouragement seemed to be all that was needed to get Todd back in the game on this challenge of endurance as he warmed to the idea again.

"Do it! Do it! Do it!" we enthusiastically started to chant. Seeing that her customers were on the fence, the server threw another log onto the fire by commenting, "You know, no one's ever been able to finish more than eight of these things."

"What? A challenge?" Johnathon said as he made eye contact with Todd.

Even with the added incentive, Todd was still hesitant. Out of nowhere, Salvador said, "I'll tell you what. If each of you make it through six of those, I'll eat three."

Johnathon and Todd contemplated. We continued our chant and even the server contributed to the rowdy repeating chorus. Johnathon and Todd looked at each other, smiled, and gave confirming nods. "Two ten-piece orders, please!" Todd yelled, as we cheered.

Not long after, the server presented Todd and Johnathon with their wings, and we marveled at the task ahead of them. Todd and Johnathon wiped their eyes from the potent fumes, then slowly attempted to nibble away at the volcanic carnage. Each bite was met with heavy breathing, more tears, and large gulps of the closest beverage.

We kept count of both of their conquests on a small chalkboard the server left behind for our amusement. Johnathon submitted after swallowing seven lava-soaked morsels, and Todd surrendered after six.

Eventually, Salvador was presented with his serving, and made it through all three wings, but not without needing four pitchers of water, and several cooled towels to counterbalance the pools of sweat being secreted from every pore of his body.

All in all, that was a good night.

12

Excitement filled the backstage area of the Paul Robeson Theatre as we feverishly made our way through our load-in, in anticipation of our first show. Christian, Joey, Salvador, and Molly were assembling the stage pieces, Leroy was testing the microphones, Sally was situating all of the props on a nearby table, Todd and I were unloading wardrobe and its accompanying racks out of the van, and Trent was speaking with the theater's owner about what was about to transpire. Everyone was filled with a zest that hadn't been seen before. Finally, it was about to be showtime.

Todd wheeled two oversized clothing racks to a secluded area in the wings. Each rack had a massive garment bag on it. As Todd unzipped one of the bags, I entered the area holding another and asked for assistance. The consummate gentleman, Todd helped me hang the heavy monstrosity on one of the racks. The rack shifted and bent when the bag was lowered upon it. "It's like someone's in there!" I remarked.

I moved away from the loaded rack and began to extract and assemble an oversized steamer from a box-shaped bin sitting in the corner of the room. As I worked, I realized something felt a bit strange about our load-in session. While Todd and I worked around each other, it felt like he was intentionally keeping his distance from me, and had been abnormally quiet, even on the ride over to the theater. Something was up.

"So how did we sleep last night?" I asked. Todd shrugged.

"Warm? Cozy?" I continued. Todd remained silent and continued to arrange the clothes on the rack without uttering a word.

Now really feeling like something was amiss, I slowly approached him with an instigative twinge in my gait. "So . . . are we supposed to separate these by act or by character?" Todd shrugged again.

"Say something," I said. Todd continued to hang items on the rack, oblivious to my request.

"Say something," I repeated.

When he reached for another bag, I stopped him from picking it up.

"Say something."

Todd finally opened his mouth to reveal a severely swollen tongue. It was so fat and limp that it mimicked a canine's; it fell, listless, and dangled toward the ground. When I erupted with laughter, Todd snatched the wardrobe bag from me and said through a severely slurred filter, "We've got work to do."

"Holy shit! Brilliant! Just brilliant! It was the wings last night, wasn't it? I was only kidding when I encouraged you to have the hottest ones on the menu, the ones you had to sign a fucking insurance waiver for before eating them! Christ. I can't wait to see how this turns out!" I laughed.

"Shut up!"

"Ha! It gets better with every word! Is Johnathon the same way?"

Todd nodded sadly.

"You two are classic. First day of the show and you guys can barely speak because of chicken wings! Chicken wings! Ha! I'm convinced: you two are the real men of the tour. *Muy macho!*"

"Leave me alone, all right? I've learned my lesson."

"Your lesson hasn't even begun, buddy boy."

"Last time I try to impress you."

"You mean that act of lunacy was for me? Well, since you put it that way, I'd like to bear your children."

"Whatever."

"Seriously! That type of valiant action you displayed last night only helps a submissive cavewoman like myself confirm their suitable dominant mate!"

"Get outta here."

I approach Todd aggressively and say, "Just thinking about how you ate that sixth wing on my behalf completely turns me on! You're the one . . ."

"Get away from me, woman!"

I pull him close by his collar, press my body against his, sniff the air, and seductively say, "I can smell the pheromones. Can you smell the pheromones? I want to breed with you."

Todd was turned on. With our bodies still close together, I could feel him swell, and I was immediately impressed. It was just what I'd imagined.

Joey and Sally entered the room just as I shouted, "I NEED TO BREED WITH YOU!" My intensity was so convincing that the both of us weren't sure if I was kidding or not. Todd looked extremely perplexed., as if he was trying to figure out my angle and what to do about it once it was deciphered. We hovered in that gray area for a moment until we slowly realized we had guests. I carefully released my grip, brushed the wrinkles out of his shirt, then smiled pleasantly and said to Joey and Sally, "Todd can't talk."

"Johnathon too. Guess y'all know now what happens when you mess with fire, huh?" Sally said.

I cheerfully walked back over to the rack and resumed my assembly. Todd snapped out of his lustful trance, wiped the sweat from his brow, and got back to work. I once again reveled in my strength. I knew I'd gotten to him, and I knew I'd bested him again. A strong sense of power washed over me, and my confidence was soaring. I'd never felt like this before. My ability to affect the opposite sex had never been fully embraced, and my ability to sway a situation or another person with my sexuality had never been a primary part of my arsenal. I'd always been the brains of an outfit, not the sex. Most men in the past had seen the sex in me as a secondary function of my persona, with them being attracted to my personality and my creative mind first. However, I'd just realized that I had some semblance of power over this one. I could be the dominant with him, and being the one in control was appealing, sexy, and addictive. It made me want to take more risks, to venture into places that I wouldn't have in the past, all to cement my place as the one that was really in control of the interaction between me and this strong, beautiful, ultramasculine man. I could live assertively while with him. I could live like I hadn't lived before, and I loved the idea of that.

***

Oh my fucking God. I cannot believe I just did that. I am just not cut out for this.

The stage had just gone black. The rousing applause swelled the filled-to-capacity theater house as the lights re-illuminated and shined on the entire cast. As we took our final bows, the audience continued to applaud, hoot, and holler for their spent entertainers. We graciously applauded the audience, then jogged backstage with significant pep in our steps.

Once backstage, we headed straight for the large dressing room and began to decompress.

"Woo-hoo!" Sally exclaimed.

"One down, and one hundred to go!" Leroy yelled.

"Amazing. Truly amazing. I have never, in all the years I've been doing this, had a show quite like that one," Christian said.

"And have nobody walk out or boo at the end? Neither have I," Salvador commented.

"First, the piece of the stage wall falls off during the opening, Mercutio and Benvolio sound like their tongues have been stapled to the roofs of their mouths, and then the coup de grace: Romeo moves to 'sack the hateful mansion' and realizes he doesn't have the knife! Nursey forgets to tuck it into Romeo's jacket before his wardrobe change! Ha! Ha! So Joey tries to do himself in by attempting to choke himself with his bare hands! I almost lost it," Christian continued.

I, sullen, sorrowful, and in the pit, attempted to give my sincerest of apologies with, "I'm sorry, guys." Having just ridden the steepest emotional roller coaster I'd ever been on, I was doing my best to mask my colossal heartbreak.

I don't belong here. I was crazy to even think I could pull this off! Thought I was starting to come around, that things were getting better, but they're clearly not. I'm way out of my league. Need to end this. Need to get out of here somehow, some way.

"I almost couldn't hold it in either," Leroy said.

"Were you hoping to use it later on at dinner or something? Get a head start on the utensil-hoarding process before we got to the restaurant?" Todd shouted toward me with a less-swollen tongue, giving rise to the cast.

Ugh. Not now, Todd. Not now.

"I just forgot to grab it from the prop table. I'm so sorry," I responded.

"Next time, why don't you just leave a banana peel or something onstage so Romeo could at least he can trip or fall on something sharp. Don't make him have to do himself in with his bare hands!" Todd continued as the cast laughed louder. "You just left him out there with nothing. At least bring the man a rope or a chicken bone he can choke on!"

I contributed awkwardly to the cast's laughter, however, I clearly wasn't fooling anyone. "I'll just tape it to my arm, that's all. Problem solved."

"You should probably tape it to your forehead," Todd quipped.

That fucking asshole!

"I know something you can tape!" I snapped, filling me with an ounce of pride for my stoutness in this, one of my most feeble dispositions.

"Will you be supplying the tape? Because, you know . . . I wouldn't want you to forget it," Todd cleverly snapped back winning this verbal spar. His first victory at my expense.

I accepted defeat, laughed it off, and expelled some needed frustration with, "ARRGH! Go to hell! All of you!"

Amongst the hubbub, Trent arrived backstage looking at his watch. "Ladies and gentlemen, you've got five to get undressed. Another fifteen to get this load-out completed. You can chitchat afterward. Now let's move!" he said as he exited. We all looked stunned at Trent's stern outburst. We quietly resumed changing out of our costumes and began our load-out duties in silence.

Saved by authority, I felt some of the load being lifted off of my back. I exhaled a small sigh of relief once the focus shifted off of me, and onto the task at hand. However, my internal torment remained.

As the cast, now turned crew, worked toward the end of the load-out, my eye caught Joey and Christian carrying a large steel beam toward a pair of exit doors. Trent was standing just beyond the exit doors, stopwatch in hand. "Let's go, let's go, let's go!" he yelled with his eyes fixated on the stopwatch. The rest of the cast was hurriedly reloading costume bags, props, and smaller pieces of the set into the cargo van, which sat directly behind Trent. When Christian and Joey finally arrived at the van with the steel beam, they were greeted by Trent. "Is that the last one?" he asked. A struggling Joey responded in the affirmative, and Trent continued, "Let's get that thing in there so we can push off. Leroy, has that sound equipment been stowed?"

"It was the first thing in," Leroy stated.

"Good job, Corporal."

"Corporal?"

Trent, a man on a mission, checked his stopwatch again, then hollered, "We're behind schedule, people! It should only take us twenty minutes to do this, and we're at twenty-three minutes. Pick it up, pick it up!"

Our pace quickened. This process felt like we were involved in a regimented calisthenics class or a military boot camp.

When it became a bit too much for her, Sally took a breather, and Trent noticed immediately. "Our job here is not done, missy! Get it in gear!" he shouted.

Sally pleaded, "Could . . . could I just . . ."

"Get it in gear NOW!"

Frightened and embarrassed, Sally grabbed the nearest crate and hustled to the van as best she could. "You all can rest when the tour's complete. But until then, we're here to work!" Trent said as he continued to crack the whip. The quiet, operational, utilitarian that Trent once was had gone full-out Mussolini on us, bringing our new reality to light: we weren't in Kansas anymore. We weren't in New York either, with laws, large crowds, and civility to protect us. We were out on the open road, in seclusion, with a madman calling the shots.

***

"There's a spot Todd," Johnathon said to me as I pulled into the parking lot of a local strip mall, just a few minutes away from the Paul Robeson Theatre. Inside, the majority of the cast was assembled at a large table in the center of the food court, and were quietly eating their fast-food lunches as we approached with our

Chinese takeout. Trent sat alone at a nearby table, eating aluminum-packed food rations.

"I feel like I just got run over," Johnathon commented as we sat with the group.

"Tell me about it. I honestly didn't see this coming. Normally you can tell," Leroy said.

"I must say he fooled me too. Played it really cool at the beginning," Joey commented.

"Then he Jekyll/Hydes us with no warning. The company should do background checks on these people so they'll know if they're putting us on the road with some psycho," Sally stated.

"Maybe they knew they were putting us on the road with some psycho. To keep us in line," Joey suggested.

"I thought he would've flipped when Johnathon and I had tongue trouble after those wings. Go figure," I said.

"What did he say to you? Did he put his hands on you?" Christian asked Sally.

"No, he just barked a few loud orders at me, that's all. Enough to scare me," Sally confirmed.

"If it gets out of hand, I'll report him to the Union. We don't have to take any crap. You let me know if he goes there again. If it gets worse, I'll sanction his ass," Christian said.

"The Union won't do anything. The company knows what they're doing when they hire these managers. They only hire ballbusters. They figure if the manager runs a tight ship, the head office'll have less work to do to support us. This shouldn't be a surprise. It happens every year," Molly commented.

"Still. I haven't ever seen a transformation quite like that," Leroy said.

"Welcome back to reality. Hope you enjoyed your trip," Molly said as she stood with her tray and began to walk toward the trash receptacle.

"The trip wasn't long enough, honey. Wasn't long enough," Leroy said.

As I got up to throw my trash away, Molly threw her garbage into the open mouth of a nearby tall container, and I did the same. Our steps mirrored each other as we both walked toward the exit. I could see her patting her hip and coat pockets. She reached inside her coat, located a pack of cigarettes, then placed one between her lips. With dramatic flair, she whipped out her trusty lighter, and flicked it at the protruding cancer stick. After a few sparks, the lighter ignited, and she gratefully puffed on the cylindrical filter.

"Got another?" I asked.

She blew a saturated cloud of smoke into the air as she pulled out another square and handed it to me. I put the cig to my lips and she lit me.

"Thanks."

"No problem. I expect the favor to be returned," she said as she began to slowly stroll the parking lot. Her blissful walk continued until she reached the passenger Sprinter van. I watched her as she leaned backward onto the front bumper as if she were Joan Jett and continued to bask in her manufactured cool.

Mellowed to the max, I watched her hair begin to gently sway, almost as if the van she was leaning on were softly rocking back and forth. I stealthily moved in a bit closer, and I heard the sound of quiet-yet-violent whimpering and swearing. Molly eventually noticed the sound and followed it to its origin, as did I from a distance.

Sitting on the rear bumper of the van, a distraught Anne hung her head and tearfully whispered expletives to herself, "Stupid. Fucking stupid. Dumbass . . ."

Molly watched Anne continue to rock back and forth and maliciously attack herself with vile utterances, unmistakably thinking she was reveling in a private moment. Molly took a deep toke of her precious calming agent and extended it toward Anne.

"Hey," Molly said, startling Anne.

Tears streaming down her face, Anne looked up and noticed Molly and her gesture. Shamed, she immediately retracted. "Take it," Molly said as she stretched the cigarette a bit farther toward Anne.

Defeated and spent, Anne limply took the cigarette from Molly's hand, brought it to her lips, and inhaled deeply. Her tension and panic seemed to dissipate as she slowly exhaled the venomous vapor. Molly looked off into the distance and said, "Don't sweat it, kid. I once forgot to bring the dagger into the tomb. You tell me, how's Juliet gonna die if she doesn't have the damn dagger? What are you going to do? You figure your way out of there, and you forget about it. The scene'll forgive you after you forgive yourself."

She grabbed the cigarette back from Anne, took another long puff, and said, "One thing I learned out here is life is too short. It's too damn short for these types of distractions." Molly then gave the cigarette back to Anne, and entered the van.

Anne continued to smoke and calm herself down in her supposed solitude. I continued to observe the chaos melt from her person as she eventually wiped the tears from her eyes, extinguished the barely lit butt, and reentered the food court. I wasn't quite sure what I'd just witnessed, but what was certain was the supreme sense of guilt I felt sitting on my chest. It got so heavy that it became hard to breathe. I wound up tossing my barely smoked cigarette to the ground and going for a walk through the vast parking lot, alone.

13

The stale, worn double-bed room was packed with luggage. The packed-in space and tight quarters provided for sufficient insulation on that cold night. I was in one of the beds, writing in a journal. I heard the sound of light rain outside and Molly brushing her teeth, as a soft bathroom light and the lamp over my bed illuminated the room.

I scribbled, *I lost it today. My factions, my couth, my knife, everything. Gotta keep it together. This is a good thing. Gotta keep it together. Don't fuck it up!*

I could hear the water in the bathroom sink turn on and the sound of rinsing and spitting. The light in the bathroom was flicked off and Molly emerged, toothbrush in hand. She noticed my attention to my journal. "You sing too? Booked any musicals so far?" Molly asked.

"Excuse me?" I responded.

Molly placed her toothbrush into her bag, hopped onto her bed, and said, "I asked had you booked any musicals yet. I saw you writing, I figured you were like all the other triple threats that go on these types of tours, constantly writing new lyrics for their upcoming album so they can hit the ground running when they get back in town. The tour's just to pass the time between Spotify releases."

"I don't sing."

"Then what are you writing? A new play?"

"Just some thoughts."

"It's not like I'm going to ask you what it's about or anything."

"Seriously, it's just a few thoughts, that's all."

"Yeah, yeah, okay, whatever, just forget it. Just don't take too long to write that scene. I'd like to get some sleep without having light shining in my face," Molly said stiffly as she slid under the covers and turned away from me.

And she's back. Was fun while it lasted, I guess.

I let the silence sit awkwardly for a moment, then said, "Hey . . . I—. . ."

"Sleeping!" Molly interjected.

"I just wanted to say thanks for earlier today. It really helped."

"Don't mention it."

"I've never done that before. Forgotten a prop. Took me totally off guard. I hate that you saw me like that. I normally don't let my emotions get the best of me."

"Yes, you do."

"No. No, I don't."

"You just do it in private, that's all. I know your type," Molly said.

"My type? What's my type?"

"Go to sleep, Anne."

"No. I'd like to know what you think my type is. You barely know me. I appreciate the cigarette and everything, but don't think just because you saw me the way I was doesn't mean that you know my type or anything about me. Like I said, I'm not like that all the time," I snapped back.

"Okay, fine. You're not like that all the time. You're the most emotionally stable person I've met. You're a fuckin' rock, you're a steel trap, you're unbreakable. Now will you let me get some sleep?"

Before I could respond, Sally entered like a ball of energy. "Ladies, you will not believe what just happened! Joey and I just fed a deer!" she said.

"That's amazing!" I responded as Molly buried herself underneath the covers.

"We were walking near the little wooded area out back and we . . . well, Joey really saw it . . . Joey saw it grazing in the marsh. I was so excited, I almost scared it away. I'd never been so close to a deer before—I mean, I was raised on a farm with tons, I mean *tons*, of animals, but they were all farm animals. They don't count. Something in the wild, something in its natural habitat, that's where it's at, y'all."

"Ladies. I am trying to get some sleep," Molly moaned.

"This'll be really quick, Molly, I promise. So Joey, venison whisperer extraordinaire, took a bag of sunflower seeds out his pocket and started approaching it. I kinda really didn't know what he was doing, but I followed him anyway. It was fun!"

"Sally!" Molly yelled sternly as she threw the covers off of her.

"Okay, all right! Joey dropped a few seeds near it, and it ate them. Then he filled his hand with seeds again and stuck it out at the deer. The deer looked at him for a while, and then it slowly started to walk toward us. Oh my God! I almost fainted. It was so sweet, so innocent. I'll never forget that. Nature is so beautiful. There. I'm done."

"Thank you," Molly said as she receded back into her bedding.

Sally whispered to me, "What's her problem?"

I shrugged.

"Anne needs to get laid—that's my problem," Molly said from underneath the covers, sounding like she was buried under an avalanche.

What the fuck?

"Why? What happened?" Sally asked.

"I do not need to get laid!"

"Yes, you do, but never mind that. Did something happen?" Sally asked.

"Sally!" I exclaimed.

"Oh, come on, honey, don't deny it. It shows up in your walk. Your switch speaks volumes," Sally stated.

"I do not need to get laid!" I said.

"I need to get laid," Molly confessed.

"Oh boy, do I need to get laid!" Sally concurred.

"Well, I don't, so just leave me out of all that," I said.

"Come on, Anne. It's just us girls. Your secrets are safe here. Don't you want some good lovin' right about now?" Sally asked.

Yes. Hell yes, I do!

"No. No, I do not," I stated.

"Come on. You can tell us," Sally said.

Molly unsheathed herself from her bedcovers again. "You have a boyfriend, don't you?" Molly asked.

"Fiancé, yes."

"And how long has it been?"

"What do you mean how long has it been? How long has what been?"

"Well, if you don't know, then that's more reason for you to get laid!" Molly exclaimed as Sally laughed.

"Sally!" I yelled.

"It's been too long for me. That's why I'm a total horndog right now," Sally shared as she began to change into her pajamas.

"Finally, some honesty around here!" Molly said.

"It's the truth! I'll probably need y'all to leave the room at some point so I can play with my friend in my suitcase," Sally said.

"Eewww!" I said as I shivered.

"I'm beginning to like you. I don't know about Miss Goody Two-Shoes over here," Molly said.

"There you go again. Don't assume I'm a Goody Two-shoes," I responded.

"Could've fooled me," Molly said.

"She's no goodie-goodie. She's more like a rattlesnake. It's just under the surface, huh, Anne?" Sally said as she moved her way to a small sleeper sofa, pulled out the bed, and laid down.

I remained silent. "Huh, Anne?" Sally continued.

If they're asking me what I think they are, this'll be a pretty big reveal for me. I haven't even admitted this kind of stuff to some of my best friends! Have I even known these ladies long enough to start revealing deep dark secrets? No, not even close. But this could be my way in, a way to bond, a way to start a relationship, and if there's anyone who needs a friend on this tour it's me. I don't know, this might be a bit too much for them. Hell, it might be a bit too much for me.

I could feel the hue in my cheeks beginning to activate.

"That true?" Molly asked.

"Kind of."

"See there, told ya! I got a sixth sense about these types of things," Sally said.

"So just how bad have you been, missy?" Molly probed as she struck up a cigarette.

"I'm really uncomfortable talking about . . ."

"Come on, honey. I'm probably skunking you both on scandalous, freak shit. Auntie has had a life, ladies! I've got the written memoirs in my bag; take a look at them whenever," Molly commented.

"I'd like to put down an early reservation on that," Sally said.

"All I'm saying is that we're all adults here. We should be able to talk about adult situations," Molly stated.

"Yeah, it'll be fun. Swappin' stories, techniques," Sally said.

"So early into the tour?" I asked.

"That's the whole point. What better way to get to know one another? Whaddya say, Anne?" Sally asked.

I hesitated, then said, "Yeah, all right, but I'm not spilling it first."

"Fine. I'll go first. Ask me anything. Anything you want to know," Molly said.

"Why do you feel you have to get laid right now?" Sally asked.

"First off, I don't do the vibrating plastic thing; too cold, too informal for me. Maybe if they came with a set of arms that carried me over a threshold to a satin-sheeted bed, I'd be into it, but until then, I'm going to have to pass. My encounters have been and can only be with flesh. I just haven't found someone who's worthy enough in a long time," Molly said.

"Worthy of you?" I asked.

"I need someone who can take care of me, okay? And I'm not giving myself to anyone else until they can totally, unequivocally, without any hesitation, doubt, or pretense, take care of me, body, mind, soul, and of course financially," Molly replied.

"Sounds fair," Sally said.

"Sounds like you're a pretty tall order," I stated.

"Sounds like both of you are absolutely right," Molly said.

Acting as if she's unable to hold it in any longer, Sally contributed with, "Well, I think I'm all hot and bothered because . . ."

"Oh, I know why you're *en fuego*, sister," Molly interjected.

"Why do ya think?" Sally asked.

"That hard-talkin', rough-lookin' Joey has lit your fire," Molly said.

"And this one's a five-alarm! It's got to be extinguished or else I'm just gon' burn up!" Sally acknowledges as the ladies laugh. "I don't know what it is. He's just so not what I'm accustomed to, but at the same time, he is, you know? He listens, he's nice, he's funny, but he's just in a different package than what I'm usually attracted to. I know I'm different for him too, but he seems willing to learn. And dammit, I am so willing to teach!"

"I bet you are," Molly said.

"I don't know. It's early, but it could be more than just a little fling here, if you know what I mean."

"But if the opportunity presented itself . . ."

"I don't know if I would. Yeah, the smoke's rising, but I think I'll fan the flames awhile just in case there's more than meets the eye."

Two confessions down, one more to go. The ladies gave the conversation an organic breath as they gave me an opportunity to volunteer my contribution. When I didn't budge, Sally nudged with, "And you, madam?"

Fuck.

"And . . . and me?" I responded.

"Yup. Why are you so hot and bothered?"

"I am not . . ."

"Don't even try it. We shared. It's your turn. Now spill it!" Molly said.

"Yeah, spill it, dewdrop!" Sally said.

"Well . . . I don't know. I seem to have an aggressive appetite when it comes to sex."

"How aggressive?" Molly asked.

"Really aggressive," I answered. I could tell they believed me. "I'm kind of like a guy. I need it so much so often. I find myself thinking about things I really shouldn't be thinking about and feeling ashamed about myself. I love sex, but some of the things in this head of mine are just wrong. Indecent. If they were just fantasies, I guess it would be okay, but sometimes my need to experience these things completely overtakes me and I just can't seem to control myself."

My tone was filled with absolute truth and terrific terror. I surprised myself as I heard the words slipping from my lips. The girls paused in astonishment.

"That's no rattlesnake, honey. That's an anaconda," Sally said as she giggled a bit to lighten the mood. I could feel Molly continuing to observe my demented disposition. She kept her eyes on me as I shriveled back into myself, embarrassed that I'd shared such a personal revelation to people I barely knew. Couldn't help it. It snapped back like an old dusty accordion, one that had been played too much. The slow, weighed-down retraction was clearly visible and, according to Molly looking away out of what I interpreted as pity, somewhat painful to watch.

***

Johnathon lay on his double bed as he talked to his girlfriend on his cell phone. ". . . it was pretty good. Glad we got the first one under our belt . . . Well, I got in pretty late. We had to break down the set then I hopped on a call with the band that lasted four hours, so it's been a pretty long day. No, I didn't mean that, I just meant . . . No, no, no, I want to talk to you, that's why I called . . ."

I exited the bathroom, towel wrapped around my waist. The steam from the shower followed me like an apparition, and the brisk air prickled my skin as it whisked by.

". . . I wasn't complaining, I was just saying that it's been a long day and . . . No, you don't have to let me go, I'm okay . . . No, I really am, listen . . . Hello? Christy?" Johnathon lowered his phone as I continued to dry off.

"What time is van call again?" I asked.

"Six thirty a.m., my friend."

"Damn," I said as I picked up my phone. "Six o' clock good for you?"

"Whatever."

I set the alarm on my phone, slid on a clean pair of black boxer briefs, grabbed my pen and notebook, and climbed into bed. This was the time of day I relished; my golden time where it was just me and my writing. I could stay in this sphere forever if I could. I knew I couldn't, though, which made those moments extra precious for me.

"Say, you have a girl, dude?" Johnathon asked.

"Something like that."

"How long?"

"Too long."

"I hear you."

"How long for you?" I asked.

"A year."

"Things are good when it's new."

"Believe me, they're not that good. Things have started to get pretty stale, if you ask me."

"Then why do you stay?" I asked.

"I don't know. Love? How 'bout you?"

I shrugged and said, "I have no idea. The rent?"

Johnathon chuckled, then asked, "Is it worth it?"

"Not even close," I responded.

14

SYRACUSE, NY

Bustling activity could be heard outside of the theater as we were just beginning our morning load-in. This space was very different from the last one we were in.

The last theater was saturated with lavish artwork and a rich history. This new theater, a two-and-a-half-hour drive away in the morning darkness, had the same feel as an abandoned warehouse with stand-alone seats and a raised partition. While the glamour-less outfit had an underdog's charm, it lacked the necessary pomp befitting a live professional performance. In short, it was a dump.

The cramped dressing room was pitch black until Todd flicked the light on. He rolled an industrial clothes steamer and a rack of costumes behind him as he entered the sour-smelling room. I followed with two extra costume racks.

"This'll never get old," I said as I parked the racks next to his. "Why don't you hook up the steamer and I'll go get the shoes?"

"Why don't *you* hook up the steamer and *I'll* go get the shoes? I steamed yesterday," Todd responded.

"But you were so good at it!"

"No, no, no . . ."

"Yes, yes, yes, you were! You're like the King of Steam! King Steamer! Steam King!"

"I hate steaming. I think you should give it a try. You'd probably like it. You know, with your ability to wither and wilt those with whom you come in contact, I figure it would be a perfect fit," Todd said.

"Not everything."

"Not everything what?"

"Not everything I come in contact with wilts," I said as I exited with a sexy sashay. Todd, as if hypnotized by my sway and bounce, whispered, "Touché," almost to himself as he began to set up the steamer.

***

We completed another wonderful performance, which was met with a rousing standing ovation. Two performances down, and it was clear that we had gelled and were hitting on all cylinders once the curtain was lifted. We'd made the entire producing team back in New York proud, as the wonderful reviews had extended themselves all the way to the Big Apple. The praise was abundant and had been given en masse from the New York team to the top-notch company.

That day happened to be a double-dip—two performances in one day—so there wasn't much time to rest on our laurels. We systematically finished the load-out like a tight-knit detail unit, then the majority of us piled into the passenger van to await instructions.

As we waited, a scarlet-faced Sally approached the vehicle while on her cell phone. Her conversation ended just as she entered the van. She paused for a second, then said, "My boyfriend just broke up with me, y'all. Like, just now. "I don't even know why! I have no idea why!" As she began to weep, I quickly moved in close and embraced her.

Leroy also moved in closer and gave Sally a comforting rub on her back. "I'm sorry, sweetheart," he said.

"This was just so out of nowhere. If I just knew what I did wrong . . ."

"Don't blame yourself. Who knows what that guy's thinking?" I said.

"He's crazy. It's his loss," Joey chimed in.

"Damn right. It's his loss. Not yours," I said.

"Here, kid," Molly said as she handed her a tissue.

Sally took the tissue, wiped her tears, and blew her nose. "I'm sorry, guys. This is just all so sudden."

"Don't apologize, little lady. You're fine," Salvador commented.

"Everything was fine, then BAM! We're done. Just like that . . ." Sally said. Just then, Trent entered the van with lasers in his eyes. He attempted to interrupt Sally with, "Ladies and gentlemen, hear me but speak a word."

Sally, so caught up in her emotions didn't hear Trent's request and continued to gush.

Trent then yelled, "Hear me but speak a word!" Sally gasped in shock and stopped speaking. She continued to sob heavily into my shoulder. "This second performance is going to be challenging, so I need all of you to listen up. I want everybody to know what's going on." Sally's muffled crying could be heard under Trent's instructions. "Next we will be performing at Nottingham High. This place is known for the students trying to disturb performers during the show by throwing things at the stage. Therefore, I'll need all of you to stay back an extra ten feet from the footlights."

"Can we throw anything back?" Johnathon asked.

"No, you cannot. Now, listen, when we get there, I will have security provide us with a safe so we can lock our valuables up." As Trent continued to give instructions, Sally pulled away from my grip

and tried to motion for Molly to pass her another tissue.
Unfortunately, Molly was having trouble deciphering Sally's gestures, so she whispered to Sally, "What is it?"

After some back and forth under their breath, Sally was still not able to convey her message. Finally, she said out loud, "Do you have another tissue? I need another."

Trent became enraged. "HEY! Be quiet! I'm giving out important information here, and you need to listen! You've already made us late by showing up after our call, and now you're making it worse by making me repeat myself!" he said.

Before I even realized it, my maternal instinct kicked in, and I yelled, "You are such an asshole!"

"Excuse me?"

"Can't you see she's having a rough morning?"

"All of you are going to have a rough morning if you don't listen to what I have to say."

"And what's that supposed to mean?"

"Try me and you'll find out. You of all people need to listen. Wouldn't want you to leave any other precious things backstage during the performance or after the show. We just might not be able to forgive you for making us look bad this time around!"

"That's enough, Trent!" Christian interjected.

The tension between us, this group of newly bonded strangers, was at an all-time high. This was the second time Trent had lashed out in as many days, and it was the second time he had made Sally his target. Those outbursts were highly disturbing to us; however, we understood that there was a fine line between protecting our castmate and ostracizing the person that was in charge while out on the road. Sure, we could've called the Union, but what would that do at that point, so early in our journey? He hadn't done anything physically to Sally, and his verbal tirades, while personal and effecting, hadn't been so far over the line that they would've been deemed as abusive to someone reading or listening to a report of the activity. At best, Trent would've been talked to about his behavior, and given a warning. The real casualty of that outcome would've been the damage done to the relationship between him and the rest of us, and we would've gotten the worst of the deal, as he would've made life on the road a searing hell like no other for us, and made it look justifiable. We knew we had to tread lightly, but we also had to defend our comrade to the best of our ability, and we would, within reason.

There was a very tense moment of silence as Trent caught his breath, eased his intensity a bit, and said, "Each time I bring a group into this place, something happens, and I don't want that streak to continue, so allow me to tell you how not to end up injured, robbed, or sabotaged. Okay? Important enough for you?"

The tension eased a bit with Trent's new approach. We provided the necessary nonverbal cues to let Trent know we had his full attention, and he continued with us still on edge.

Eventually, a puffy-eyed Sally rejoined me in an embrace. When in place, I stroked Sally's arm in an attempt to comfort my injured sister.

∗∗∗

We arrived at Nottingham High and began the load-in in complete silence; we'd been that way the entire forty-five-minute drive over to the school.

I was in the dressing room, steaming a complicated wardrobe item. I squatted near the ground to improve my reach on the long, ruffled monstrosity. My steaming hand aggressively fired up and down like a juiced piston, heating the wrinkles out of the garment with blazing speed.

Not too long after, Todd entered with an empty clothing rack and said, "I love the school spirit here. In the bathroom, all of the urinals have a nice little message about the principal sucking or biting something. And wait till you see what they've sewn into the back of the stage curtain!"

Caught up in my own thoughts, I didn't acknowledge Todd's presence.

"Is this the last of it?" he asked as he walked to a table next to me and eyed a mountain of wrinkled clothing stacked upon it.

I quickly snatched the gown I was working on from the steamer hook, and jabbed it onto an empty clothing rack. I grabbed another piece of wardrobe from the heap and slung it onto the steamer hook.

"Guess not," Todd said. "Has Joey come in here yet? He has been looking for the strap that goes on his left boot. Says he'll definitely need it for his fight with Tybalt as things tend to get a little rough between those two."

Still no response from me.

"You okay?" he asked.

Nothing. Then . . .

"You were right, you know? He is an asshole. He had no right to say those things to you."

Christ. How does he know exactly what to say to me? It's like he's in tune with me. Like he can listen to my silence and hear what I'm saying.

My grip on the steamer hose tightened and I could feel myself beginning to turn red. The *glub-glub* from the steamer seemed to increase in volume as I began to speak.

"It's the truth," I said.

"What's the truth?"

"I knew it. I knew I wrecked everything."

"That's not . . ."

"You all hate me . . ."

"No, we . . ."

"To you guys, I'll always be the girl who constantly fucks up and embarrasses you . . ."

"Will you stop it . . . —"

"That's it. I can't do this anymore. I'm going to call Vincent right after the curtain and tell him that this was my last show— . . ."

"Stop it! You stop it right now, you hear me? You're killing yourself over what some idiot said? It's not true. That son of a bitch has no idea what we think. He doesn't speak for the rest of the cast, and he surely doesn't speak for me."

"What he said confirmed my worst fears," I responded.

"Your worst fears are a fallacy. No one here hates you. We love you! We're ecstatic that you're here! The way you stood up for Sally back there was great! We all appreciated that. Especially Sally."

He's so sweet.

"I just feel like I'm causing problems and letting all of you down."

"No . . ."

". . . like this tour would run a whole lot smoother if I wasn't here."

"That's furthest thing from the truth. I alone would lose my mind if you weren't here."

He's really doing his best to lift me up right now. Impressive. Impressive and ultra sweet.

"Come on . . ."

"I'm serious! You keep me on my toes with all your quick remarks and sarcasm. I'd die if this tour became mundane and bland. I need stimulation. You stimulate me," he said.

And you have no idea how you stimulate me, good sir. These days, you're the bright part of my day. The reason I've been halfway excited to get up and go to work each day.

I smirked and said, "Good to know I still got it."

"Oh, you got something, all right. You should at least stick around long enough for me to find the cure."

"Fuck you!"

"That's an approach, but I don't know if that'll solve your problem. It very well might, though!"

It very well might!

"You're the asshole, mister! You!" I said, somewhat breaking out of my funk.

"Seriously, though, you shouldn't be so hard on yourself, kitten. It's not what you think it is."

"I know I can do that from time to time, but generally, there's something behind me beating myself up."

"Something like what?"

"The truth," I said.

"It's your truth. Not ours. Get out of your own head and you'll see that's the case," he responded.

"Impossible. I've tried, and it's absolutely impossible. You wouldn't understand. If you only knew half of the shit I carry around with me."

"Like what?"

"You really want to know?" I asked.

"Yes. I'm interested," he replied.

I took a long, deep breath, faced Todd, and plunged in. "What the hell. Where do I start? How 'bout here; I'm a six-foot-two, twenty-six-year-old actress living in New York whose first acting job in two years is this tour. Two years without a gig. Can you imagine? Don't even know if I can still call myself an actress. I'll never be who I aspire to be. Bette Davis, Meryl Streep, Audrey Hepburn. . . I don't know where I fit. I'm trying to figure it out, but the answer's not coming to me. I'm trying to be patient, but time's a-ticking. Hell, I'm almost thirty! Along with that comes the unescapable pressure from family, friends, and myself to invoke some convention and 'do something' with my life. I know you feel it too, but mine is worse. You know why? Because I get it twenty-four hours a day from the people that mean the most to me. I'm guilty of it myself. Even now I'm thinking about how much easier my life would be if I weren't programmed to do this. These problems lead to other problems. I don't value myself as highly as I should, and most times I feel that I am not worthy or deserving of good things. I feel as if I'm a burden to those I'm closest to. I've hurt people, and I've never been able to forgive myself for that. sometimes I take things too far and I can't seem to stop myself even when I know it's happening. It's not enough that I see the pain I inflict on these people, but not having enough self-control to cease and desist makes me hate myself. It makes me a stain. Knowing all of this, my mother . . . She never misses an opportunity to compare me to my other siblings."

I started to get emotional. Tears were welling up in my eyes, but before they fell, Todd gently placed his hands on top of mine and began to deliver a slow, comforting rub to my extremities.

"I am a fragile being, Todd. That's dangerous, you know? Something that's fragile, you keep in one spot, you know—in a cupboard, in a display cabinet, in a padded room or something. You don't whip it around from room to room, taking it out each time someone visits and throwing it back and forth like it's a football. It could get broken," I said.

"I understand," he replied.

"Well, there you go. I'm a mess. Repulsed yet?" I asked as I wiped my nose.

"Not in the slightest," he said.

My eyes were red and streaming with tears, and my nose was running like a fountain. I was sloppy, unkempt, and Todd had the nerve to say, "You are beautiful, Anne. Inside and out."

"Stop it."

"I'm serious. This is one of the most beautiful sights I've laid my eyes on in a while."

My blush deepened so much that it was starting to get painful. A rush of warmth ran through my body so quickly that it felt like my entire body was blushing. My emotions were out of control.

I had to almost pinch myself when I felt Todd leaning toward me, as I couldn't tell if it was real or not. *Am I hallucinating? Is my depth perception off due to me being worked up right now? Nope. Todd is leaning in. Oh my God. He's about to kiss me.*

All of my senses were ignited at the first taste of him. It was like everything was magnified to the thousandth power. I started to cry harder, and tremble uncontrollably.

His lips are so soft. He tastes and feels so good. This is wrong. It's so wrong, and I'm sorry, but I need this right now. I need this so much.

A tidal wave of emotion poured over me, and I let myself go. I gushed like a deluge, and had a good, soul-cleansing release, something that had been a long time coming.

I wrapped my arms around Todd and held him close, squeezing the life out of him. When I finally loosened my embrace, I was finished. Unable to take any more, I released my ghost to the heavens, and fell limp in his hands.

Even though I was out, I could still hear and feel everything. I heard Todd panic, and I could feel him gently lay me to the ground, and check my breathing. He started touching my face and calling my name. "Anne. Anne." My God. It was like a reverse siren call, his voice luring me back to consciousness. It was incredibly hot to me in such a twisted way. Lying unconscious on that cold floor, in Todd's arms, him calling me back to him: it was enough to totally soak my panties through and through.

After a few moments, I began to moan and slowly open my eyes.

What the fuck is in Mr. Happy's lips? Electricity? Pure H? Some super-freak power given to him by aliens? Damn. Never have I had a reaction like that from one kiss. Unreal. What he must think of me.

Relieved, Todd exhaled and said, "Hey. You left me for a while. Are you okay?"

"Yeah, yeah, I'm okay. Wow, my head . . ."

"Let me get you some aspirin."

"No, no, I'll be fine. Just let me sit here for a minute."

"Whatever you need."

Todd lifted me onto a chair, and I slowly began to get my bearings.

"Wow. Thanks—for listening, I mean. I guess I needed that."

"Anytime. You sure you're okay?"

"Yeah. Yeah, I think I am."

From the wings, we could hear Trent giving the five-minute call. Showtime was approaching. Todd gave me a bottle of water, told me to stay seated, and began steaming furiously. I drowsily watched him through a haze, and resumed my internal debate on whether or not Todd is a man or a super being from another planet, a super being with superpowers. I remained undecided by the time I regained

my strength, and began getting dressed for the upcoming

performance.

15

That. Was. Awesome.

I was alone in the dressing room wrapping my hair in a scrunchie as I put the finishing touches on my redressing. Surprisingly, I'd just had one of my best shows; a virtual miracle considering the mental and physical condition I was in just two hours ago. Nonetheless, my performance went off without a hitch. Every beat, every moment was played to perfection, and my emotional life soared while onstage. The previously deemed "troubled children" at

Nottingham High were captivated by the Nurse's outpouring, and gave me the loudest of ovations during the curtain call.

I sat still for a moment to take in all that had happened to me that morning, and while my performance had put me on cloud nine, I realized that it was Todd's kiss that got me there. As a matter of fact, it was Todd's kiss that was still resonating with me and supplying short, tingly bursts of electricity to all of my extremities. It was like I had a new heartbeat, pulsating and charged with fire, ignited by the taste of Todd's lips.

Eventually, I shook myself back into consciousness and began my load-out duties. I wheeled the costume rack near the door, and placed each of the large shoe bins on one of the two square dollies left in the room. Suddenly, a beautiful bare-chested Todd entered the room. His half-unbuttoned costume pants hung very low, exposing his chiseled hip bones. I misplaced my breath upon the magnificent sight. "Do you have my pants?" Todd asked.

Still trying to locate my oxygen, I asked Todd to repeat himself, and he replied, "My pants. Do you have my pants?"

"Why would I have your pants?" I answered.

"Would be just like you to hide 'em from me."

"Don't flatter yourself, sweetheart. I do not want your pants."

"Then where the hell are they?" Todd asked as he continued his search.

It was an understatement to say I was incredibly turned on by Todd's body. It was perfection. I stared as he bent, pulled, and lifted heavy boxes as he looked for his lost article. His ripped muscles twitched flexed and tightened with every movement. His chiseled shoulders looked like mountains, and when they tensed, it looked as if the earth were shifting. Diamonds could be cut on his shredded midsection, and his massive back looked strong and sturdy enough to support two planets. *My God, this man is a god.*

I could feel the rouge starting to settle in my cheeks again, and my breathing started to accelerate. I tried to calm myself down by taking long, deep breaths from my diaphragm. Todd's back was to me, so he wasn't a witness to the chaos going on behind him. That shallow safety net proved to be deep enough for me as I boldly and uncontrollably began to pinch and rub one of my nipples without hesitation or a second thought.

With Todd's back still turned to me, he asked, "You promise you haven't seen them?"

I was over the top in terms of arousal. Not only were the visuals stimulating me, but danger and risk were acting as equal catalysts to this sexual rush. I responded to Todd with a faint, "Mmmm-hmmm."

"Promise?" Todd asked.

"I promise, Todd," I mumbled through my heated lips.

Todd turned in my direction, sending a sharp current through me, but he kept his eyes engaged in his search of the ground. The shock I felt only added more fuel to the fire as I boldly continued to pull and caress my taut protuberance. A bead of sweat ran down the center of Todd's chest, and I began to salivate. *What I wouldn't give to lick the sweat from his bare chest.*

I tried to condemn the thought, but I was too caught in my lust to do so. *I'd lick every crack and crevice on you, Todd. Let me taste every inch of you. I'm a dirty slut. Treat me like a dirty slut!*

All he had to do was look up and I would be exposed, but I could not stop myself. The uncertainty was too delicious and addictive. The red in my cheeks reddened even more, and I expelled a breath of rapturous air that consumed the room. Todd remained oblivious. "They've gotta be in here," he said.

Todd kneeled as he searched inside the bins I placed on the dollies. Still standing directly in front of him, his head positioned at the exact height of my crotch, I slowly, carefully slid my hand down my pants. I kept a close eye on Todd as he searched, looking for any split-second sign that he might glance upward and discover my appetite.

I was determined to cum right in front of him, right before his face, without him knowing. *Now you're gonna eat this sweet pussy. Now you're gonna be my bitch!* I rubbed harder, faster, all the while keeping my hand in control so as to not make any eye-jarring movements that would alert my subject. I could feel the wave building, his strong arms looking so tensed and toned as he shuffled through the cluttered bin. What I wouldn't do to be able to grip those chiseled shoulders, those godlike monuments affixed onto a deserving physical deity.

Oh my God, I'm close. Look at me. Watch me cum.

I bit my lip as I could feel the rumbling begin and I could taste my own salty sweat, along with the smooth, creamy taste of my lipstick. It was almost like splash of dessert, the sweat/salty taste in my mouth.

Just a few more strokes and I was going to share my explosion with him, albeit privately. My clit was so wet to the touch I could barely keep my finger on it. The slickness helped me circle and tease it at light speed, which was appropriate for this unspoken encounter. I had fantasized doing this with him for real, with his hands on my body, with him bringing me to the ultimate satisfaction, and this would be the closest I would ever get to that. I had to reach the top of the mountain and dive off into the abyss—I just had to.

Todd began to grab the items he placed outside of the bin and pack them back inside. The shine and pop of those arms moving, gripping, and contracting all at once, coupled with the thought of the magnetic kiss we shared a few hours ago, was enough to send me over the edge. *Oh fuck, oh fuck me, fuck me, Todd!*

I came. Hard. I was able to swallow a few moans before he placed the lid back on the top of the bin. I quickly ceased my fondling, folded my arms, and turned away from him, with every fiber of my body still pulsating.

Todd finally looked up at me and asked, "Where's our stuff?"

My back still turned to him, and barely able to speak, I motioned toward the back of the room with my head and whimpered, "Over there."

When Todd went to inspect the rear of the room, I was able to exhale the remaining remnants of my pleasure into the atmosphere; however, my face remained severely stressed and was beet red. I still couldn't face him. I tried to calm myself down by taking a few deep breaths, and when my motor functions solidly returned, I resumed my load-out duties. After a few moments, I felt the buoyant blush dissipate, and the tension seep from my face.

Eventually, Todd made his way over to the rack where his and my personal items were hung, took his coat off the rack, reached into the sleeve, and pulled out his pants. "I'm such an idiot!" he said.

I looked at Todd with new eyes, and reacted by laughing at his folly. "I forgot. I put them in there because of the . . . environment," he said as he took his wallet out of his pants. "Good idea, you just can't lose your fucking pants! Just let me get dressed and I'll be back to help you," he continued as he exited.

I, still a bit winded and amazed from my stunt, buried my face in my hands. *What the fuck have I done? Am I becoming a worse animal than I've been in the past? I have no idea, but I do know one thing: it felt good, damn good. I've never felt so free, so bold. I'm ashamed, yes, but I can't deny that I fucking loved it. I can see right now that Todd is bad for my health, that this shit can become addictive for me and this is just the tip of the iceberg. I don't know if I should be alone with him anymore.*

While my appetite has been ravenous in the past, my loss of control had never gone this far. I'd seen a glimpse of what I was capable of, and I was now legitimately frightened. I did my best to catch up to my breath and calm my nerves in this new, ultra-uncomfortable solitude.

***

My hotel room was dark, moody. Only the desk lamp

provided a dim glow near the back of the room. I liked it like that; it

helped me get my thoughts together.

I was sitting at the desk as I dialed a few digits on my cell

phone. Against my better judgment, I was compelled to call Toni on

that night. Fearing the worst, I let it ring for a while, and was relieved

when the call went to voice mail. "Just wanted to see, ah . . . I was

just calling to, ah . . . I don't know . . . you don't have to call me

back," I said. I hung up feeling an even stronger urge to talk to her

than before I dialed.

I wondered why I felt this way. I'd had this same urge to talk

to Toni soon after I'd suspected she'd done me wrong before, and I

could never place why. Maybe it was my body or the universe telling

me I should've reconsidered my suspicions? Maybe I was wrong? I

didn't know. What I did know that even though Toni put me through

the wringer and stressed me out to no end, I couldn't deny the

connection we had. It was so real that even when I thought the worst

of her, I still had a need to fuse with her, to tap into her. She nurtured my spirit in a way that I'd come to depend upon, and when

we were at odds, I definitely felt the void.

A knock at the door snapped my melancholy. I opened it, and

found a shower-fresh-looking Anne. Her hair was still wet. "Ready?"

she asked. I nodded, then exited with her, my cell phone left on the

bed.

***

Todd and I traveled in the passenger van through hilly terrain.

It was cold and windy, and snow flurries fell from time to time. Both

of us were silent. The only action in the van was the active ghosts of

our breath as we expelled the warm bursts of air into the chilly frost.

Both of us seemed severely distracted on our journey.

Eventually, we came up on our destination, a twenty-four-

hour laundromat just on the edge of town. Both of us leapt out of

the van as if we'd reached Disneyland, with the anticipation of arrival

outweighing the actual overpriced payoff. We grabbed the soiled wardrobe, entered the establishment, and began to make what was currently dirty, clean again.

The amount was substantially larger than we'd had in the past, most likely due to the extra skins worn during the double-dip. The added work seemed to be welcomed by us as we were able to clear our minds while doing something mundane. Silence, and not having to think tonight seemed to be well appreciated by the both of us.

We worked our way through the mountainous pile, and I folded the last few items in front of me. As I worked, Todd startled me a bit by dumping another load of hot skins and undergarments in front of me and broke our almost-three-hour silence with, "That's the last of it."

"Finally," I replied.

"That was a huge load."

"Seemed like it would never end."

"It's the same every night, Anne."

"I guess. Tonight it just seemed longer than usual, that's all."

We began to fold the clothes through a few moments of uneasy tension, and then Todd hit me with it. "You know . . . I know about you, you know. And I like it," he stated.

"What are you talking about?"

"This afternoon in the dressing room."

Oh shit. Oh fucking shit! I freeze. My body was locked. The only thing I could move was my mouth. "What about it?" I asked.

"Come on, Anne. It's a dressing room. There's mirrors all over the place."

Oh fucking shit! Shit, shit, shit!

I mumbled to myself, "Oh my God."

"Yeah. Pretty intense," Todd responded.

"I'm so embarrassed."

"Don't be. Like I said, I liked it. It turned me on. I wanted to look up at you so badly."

"Why didn't you?"

"I wanted to see how far you were going to take it."

"You kissed me earlier, and I just . . ."

"I know, I know. I shouldn't have done that. You were in a bad place, I was trying to comfort you, and it just got out of control. Emotions took over," he said.

"I can't control it," I said.

"I understand."

"Do you?"

"I feel the same way," he confessed.

"You do?"

"Ever since we met."

"I don't think you understand . . ."

"I just didn't want to throw it out there right away."

"Well, it's out there now."

"Sure is."

Silence filled the room. This wasn't the calming, soothing silence we both enjoyed earlier. This was the silence that people dread. The type of silence that woke the neighbors.

"This is weird," I mentioned.

"What's weird about it?" he asked.

"I don't know. You . . . me. We barely know each other. You have a girlfriend, I'm engaged, we're talking about this while we're doing the laundry . . . It's just weird," I said.

"I guess. Even with all of that, it doesn't change the fact that I want you," he responded as my face turned scarlet once again.

In disbelief, I acted like I didn't hear what he'd just confessed. I asked Todd to clarify, and without a beat, he replied, "You heard me. I want you. There's no denying it. And you want me too."

"Uh . . . Todd . . . let's change the subject."

"You can't hide your attraction from me. I can smell it on you like a perfume. The way you look at me, the way you blush, the way your voice trembles when you speak to me. This flame burns deep down. Admit it," he said.

"Admit what?"

"That you want me as much as I want you."

I paused. The scorching garment I had been attempting to fold was now clutched tightly in my knotted fists. Finally, I relented and said, "More."

Both Todd and I took a moment to digest the new reality spawned by my bold admission. Only the fuming pile of wardrobe separated us.

With nothing left to say, we finished our work in the laundromat and drove back to the hotel in complete silence—the noisy kind.

***

Later that night, in my hotel room, I soaked in the bathtub as the water continued to slowly trickle into the murky pool. The humid room was filled with fog and a subtle scent of jasmine. I laid back in complete relaxation as my mind began to wander. The interaction with Todd had been on my mind forever, or at least it seemed so. Was I dreaming? A man of this caliber wanted me. I'd never dreamed or aspired to dream of having a man like Todd be a suitor of mine. I simply hadn't believed that I could draw that kind of attention from a man like that, that I could appeal to someone who had their pick of the litter.

Did Todd know about my flaws? At that point, he couldn't. It was too early. What would he think when he discovered them? Would he still be drawn to me? Brody knew I had flaws, but I knew he had them too, and we were perfect for each other in our imperfections. Neither one of us felt "too perfect" for the other. We celebrated our shortcomings and found peace with each other in the valleys. We felt as if we were on the same level, neither one higher than the other, neither one trying to outdo or live up to the other person's shadow.

Todd, however, was someone to look up to. He was at the top of the mountain. He was bright, successful, talented, and an Adonis. He was a king. He was an ideal. I knew I wasn't his equal, and yet, just the thought of him desiring me pleasured me more than Brody ever had or could. I'd literally stepped into the fantasy realm when dealing with Todd: a living dream that injected me with life, hope, and excitement. I clearly could not brush that off as a passing phase or an apparition. I felt it just as he did. It was real, it was alive, and I was living an unexpected fantasy, such a delicious catastrophe.

Still, remorse and doubt remained. Thus, I fell back on my trusted companion, the sturdy horse that was always with me, and always uncontrollably calmed my ills. With Todd remaining at the forefront of my mind, slowly but surely I began to caress and softly squeeze my chest. My other hand eventually moved below the waterline and began to fondle my femininity. The swirl and bubbles from the running water only added to the effect as I delicately beat my drum until I heard a symphony in my mind. The rousing chorus crescendoed to a climax that made me grip the side of the bathtub and hold on for dear life, lest I be sucked down the drain with the rest of the trickling drink.

When the waves subsided, I let go of my anchor and sank into complete relaxation. After a few moments, I completely emerged from my trance, realized what I'd done, and began to silently weep.

16

KUTZTOWN, PA

Morning came too soon for all of us. Even though the day was set up as a day of travel, it felt even more weighted than our normal day, filled with at least one rousing performance. Those performances, at a minimum, allowed for a release for each of us, a release from the real-life pressures and stressors we individually carried. Without the opportunity to do what we love, we were lost; our life forces were severely dimmed. Thus, after three and a half hours of travel, we spontaneously decided to visit the Schaeffer

Auditorium, our next performance location, to get a feel for the space.

After getting clearance from Trent and the theater staff, we entered the rickety building one by one and tested the acoustics and views from the orchestra and balcony, and the lighting package. It was a solid space, suitable for a hallowed performance.

With all of us assembled onstage, Salvador began to orchestrate an impromptu fight call, calling for us to rehearse our combat scenes for blocking and safety purposes. First up, Molly and Christian began walking through the fight scene between Lord Capulet and his daughter, brought on by her resistance to marry Paris.

Salvador looked on with an unforgiving eye as the two actors grappled in a heated battle. Eventually, Christian tossed Molly to the floor as rehearsed, but she landed awkwardly.

"Hold it, hold it, hold it! Why are you falling like that? How did I teach you to fall?" Salvador asked Molly.

"I know, but it's kinda hard to . . ."

"I don't care if it's hard! You've gotta do it!"

"I'm trying!"

"You want to get hurt? Fall like I taught you!"

"I'M TRYING!" she yelled.

"DON'T TRY! DO IT!" he yelled back.

"You're an asshole! I can't work with this brute!" she said as she began to storm off the stage.

Salvador snatched her by the arm and said, "Hey! I'm only looking out for you, sweetheart. You want an injured tailbone again?"

"No, I don't want a fucking injury, you fucking moron! I also don't want some two-bit drill sergeant talking to me like I'm some kind of peon that's forced to take it. You WILL NOT treat me as such!"

"I'm in charge of your safety up here on this stage. You WILL take my orders or— . . ."

"Or what? Or what Sal? You're gonna drop me from the cast? You're gonna lock me in the dressing room so I miss my curtain? Hmm? Really, what are you going to do? That's right, nothing. You can't do anything to me because you have no power on this stage. None!"

"I'll tell you what I do have. I have the authority to . . ."

"You don't have any fucking authority . . ."

". . . have you written up."

"You wouldn't dare!" Molly responded.

"Try me sweetheart. Now do the damn scene again and fall like I fucking taught you!"

Molly and Salvador continued to argue. The rest of the cast tried to simmer them down, but to no avail. Todd and I pantomimed our assistance as our attention continued to gravitate to each other.

***

The next morning, on the other hand, couldn't come quick enough, as the last twenty-four hours had been torturous. All of us had been snippy, devouring each other at every opportunity. It hadn't been safe to have three of us in the same room ever since the sun went down.

Now, however, things were back to normal as we were in our sanctuary of refuge, the theater. We'd scattered ourselves in the various creases and crevices of the backstage area as we individually performed our final warm-up rituals before taking the stage.

The audience, just beyond the jet-black curtain, provided a buzzed murmur to the atmosphere. As I stared at the crowd through one of the folds in the huge drape, I suddenly felt something brush by me, and an object slide into my hand.

I looked into my hand and found a small, exquisitely folded note. I whipped my head around to identify the stealth postal person, but he/she had dissolved into one of the deep black shadows behind the proscenium. I looked back through the curtain at the audience, then back to the note. Trent's five-minute call came about three minutes ago, so I needed to stay in place. However, my curiosity consumed me, and I just had to inspect my private package.

I rushed into the bathroom, moved into one of the stalls, and took a few breaths as I stared at what was written on the top of the freshly folded piece of paper, the words *Wanna Dance?* I examined the weight of the decision that stood before me, as I now knew who the note was from. Did I really want to know what was contained within this capsule of communication? Why couldn't whatever was inside be spoken to me? Was what was written within so lofty that it needed the weight of the pen to carry its message to its intended recipient?

Bravely, I opened the page, and when I did, I was immediately enraptured, so much so that I heard the scribe's voice in my subconscious.

I'm preparing myself. Tux's prepped, shoes polished, cuff links primed. Can't afford to not be ready for the inevitable. We're negotiating with a merciless combustible agent capable of erasing our archives. Needless to say, we should tread lightly and live in our breasts. Even with that dusty limitation, my application will be submitted to my loins as I look to die from the vocation. And I'm ready to die! I've thought about it since our conjoined steps began. The war inside of me has been unstable and lopsided. Our mutuality has only upped the behemoth's charge, slowly but surely wiping out the preexistent stain. A choreographed dance this havoc has become. An unpleasant mix of tension, eagerness, shame, and hunger. Movement is the unorthodox cure for the queasiness. So I ask, may I have this dance?

Signed,

Interested and Intrigued

I slowly folded the letter closed. I leaned against the side of the stall, as the airy prose made me weak. *Who is Mr. Happy really? Cyrano, with an exceptionally large bulge instead of a schnoz? What am I getting myself into? Am I really getting myself into something I can't handle, and if so, why am I so excited about it?*

While I had no real answers for my questions, I couldn't deny that I was absolutely giddy and tingling all over. Just as a small smile began to curl on my lips, Sally quickly entered the bathroom and called for me. When I responded, Sally told me the curtain was up and we were next.

I yelled that I was on my way, flushed the toilet, rushed out of the stall, then hustled toward the door.

"You're not going to wash your hands?" Sally asked as I grabbed her arm and pulled her out the door.

"There's no time. Let's go!" I said.

"Ewww! Let go! You guys are gonna have to wash this shirt twice!"

***

The show and subsequent load-out went off without a hitch. Anne and I performed with added zeal when we were onstage together, with and without an audience. Even the other cast members noticed our extra playfulness while in the wings, during the load-out, and in the van as we made our way toward a gas station to fill up. We began to get labeled as "the married couple" due to our public affectionate bickering and sweet yet biting comments about each other. When I acted out of line, Anne always heard, "Get your 'husband' under control, please," and vice versa. Both Anne and I seemed to enjoy being attached to the hip in pretend matrimony and never let a public moment pass without stating our claims to each other in so many edgy words or playfully devious actions. Leroy continued to threaten to separate us, but we wouldn't have it. This crazy yet comfortable union couldn't be broken.

Both vans arrived at the gas station and pulled up to adjacent gas pumps. Trent quickly exited the cargo van, stood in front of the passenger van, held up both hands, fingers outstretched, and said, "Ten. Be back in ten."

As Trent began to manipulate the buttons at the gas pump, we all slowly exited the passenger van and lumbered toward the station. Sally remained inside, stoic.

"Hope they have those peanut butter cups they had at the last station. They've been calling me," Johnathon said.

Joey looked at the decor and set up of the small convenience store attached to the gas station and commented, "Looks like the selection in this place is pretty . . . limited."

"Don't crush my dreams, man. Don't crush my dreams," Johnathon replied.

As I walked toward the station half-asleep, I felt something slip into my hand. When I turned my head to see the culprit, I saw the back of Anne's beautiful hair swaying back and forth as she passed by and continued walking at a quickened pace. I smiled at the familiar covert operation, then diverted my route to a secluded area on the outskirts of the lot. I unfolded the note, began to read, and heard Anne's voice through the page.

I thought of responding to your note in conversation, but I'm wondering if writing would be more appropriate. A parry to your thrust, if you will. I hope you understand most of this, for I mean for my words to land, not crash and burn into you, but perhaps they will shake you a bit.

A dance, eh? I've got a spot free on my dance card for you. We could continue the moves, the styles, the music for the next few months, the whole tour! And why not? Being with you is a thrill. And being away from you . . . I have to confess, I think of you more than I should. The imagination is a powerful tool.

But we are feeding a fire. The more we are together alone, the closer we come to exploding (for now, I think we are imploding in ourselves, a bittersweet release). I know you know already, but I did want you to kiss me the other day. In fact, I've wanted it more than once. Honestly, though, now I wish you hadn't. Can we stand on this precipice? Can we tango on a knife's edge?

One last point. My body is a spark, and sometimes when you look at me, I become enflamed. Blood rushes forcefully to all parts of me . . . heat, heat, heat. My knees are weak or not there at all. With a caress or a kiss, I am set ablaze, trapped in a deep blue flame, the color of stars after you close your eyes.

Signed,

Amazed

I was astonished by what I'd read. *We have another writer in our midst. Who knew?* I dwelled in my astonishment until my thoughts were interrupted by Christian yelling, "Heads up!" as he tossed the van's keys toward me. Luckily, my reflexes were as quick as a cat, and I was able to snatch the keys out of the air before they crashed into my face. "You're up next, right?" Christian asked.

"Right," I said as I folded the note into my pocket. I then walked back to the van, entered, and sat in the driver's seat. It was just Sally and I. We sat silently as we waited for the cast to return, both with differing impatience.

17

PENNSYLVANIA HIGHWAY

The scenic surroundings zipped by as our souped-up passenger van pushed through the area at warp speed. We were a bit behind schedule, and Trent, responsible for setting the pace in the cargo van, had effectively put the pedal to the metal in order to make up time. What would have been a day for appreciating the panoramic views of scarcity brought on by a harsh Pennsylvania winter had now turned into a schedule-induced grinder, with the driver and navigator of each van bearing the brunt of the habitude.

Fine luck of the draw for me, getting the driving responsibilities after the gas run, but everyone either had or would come up on the short end of the stick during this tour; at least that's how I rationalized it for myself. Things weren't so bad, though, as Johnathon was my navigator. We'd struck up a solid friendship while out in the thick of things, and there was no one else I would rather be stuck with for the next three driving hours, minus the obvious substitute.

I looked in the rearview and saw Anne, situated near the rear of the van, reading a book, looking as peaceful as ever. This was when she was most beautiful to me: when she was alone with her own brain. There was kind of a twisted beauty in her face when she was like this, a kind of warped elegance molded and shaped by stress and past experiences. Seeing her like that made me want to know more about her, find out what was behind the magnificent tension I could so clearly see in her. When she was with me, that tension melted, and to watch it slip away from her gave me a shot of adrenaline. Knowing I affected her that way made me feel like I could conquer the world. I'd always been a fan of magic, and with her, I could be a magician. I could make shit disappear.

As we crossed another state line, a wicked idea developed. I carefully reached for my phone while keeping my eyes on the road . . .

***

My cell phone vibrated in my pocket. Perfect timing. Always happens when I'm near the end of a chapter. Devil's in the distractions. I immediately knew it was a text due to the vibration style. I took out my phone, swiped it to activation, and read the message:

u r hot.

I tried to decipher the origin of the message, but I didn't recognize the phone number. I quickly typed my response. *Thanks. Who is this?* With my initial annoyance quickly subsided, I blushed as I eagerly awaited a response. Eventually, my phone sprung to life again with a healthy vibration, and I rapidly checked my message inbox.

I am who I am.

I sank back into my seat. Disappointed, I closed my phone, put it back into my pocket, and resumed my reading. After a few moments, I felt the phone vibrate again, but I ignored it. It vibrated again. Annoyed for a second time, I took the phone out of my pocket and swiped it on.

Don't give up so easily.

I scrolled to the next message.

Hint: We're riding in the same van.

I began to observe my surroundings. Todd was driving, Johnathon was busy navigating while riding shotgun, Christian and Salvador were asleep, Leroy and Joey were playing cards, and Molly was riding in the cargo van with Trent. I was baffled. I texted back, *Oh really? If so, then what am I wearing?*

I'll tell you what you're not wearing . . . panties.

Offended, yet aroused, I texted back, *WHO IS THIS?* as I feverishly searched the van for a culprit. My phone rattled yet again.

I'm right, aren't I?

WHO? I wrote back, almost cracking my screen with the impact of my thumbs.

Check the driver's seat.

I looked toward the driver's seat, and all I could see was the back of Todd's steady head. I peeked into the rear mirror and observed Todd's alert eyes as they scanned the highway. Just when I was convinced that Todd's focus on the highway was razor-sharp, Todd looked slyly at me in the mirror.

I gasped, then composed another message: *How are you doing this?*

I sent the message, then watched Todd react to the vibration in his lap. He picked up the phone and held it waist high. I watched his eyes rapidly glance from his phone to the road as he typed his response with one hand.

So you want to play you clever, dangerous devil? Well, I'd love to play.

When Todd finished composing, our eyes briefly met in the mirror. Soon after, my phone vibrated with the message, *Am I right?*

I waited a few moments, re-blushed, then typed, *No. I am not wearing n e panties.*

Knew it. So fuking hot!

Don't get us n2 a accident.

It'll be your fault. Distracting me. Thought about u last nite.

So did I.

Did u touch yrslf?

Yes.

Cum?

Yes.

Hard?

Very. I shook for 20 minutes afterward.

Me too. Wanted to call u during.

I wanted more than just a phone call.

Tell me what you wanted.

u to touch me.

Where?

My back, my shoulders . . ."

tits, ass . . ."

Wanted you to grab those. Hard. And pull m/hair.

The van began to drift past the yellow line. Johnathon noticed and said, "Dude, watch it," Todd jumped to attention, swerved the van back into the lane, and apologized.

I sent him another message: *Want to touch me?*

Yes.

I want you to touch me now. RIGHT NOW.

Our eyes met in the mirror for an extended period of time. I was visibly worked up, and I'm quite sure Todd could see the fire in my eyes. Finally, I broke the voltaic gaze and wrote another message: *Come taste me. Please.*

Then I quickly fired off another one, causing him to blush: *Pull the van over right now and eat me.* I could see little beads of sweat beginning to develop on Todd's forehead. I sent another message right after that: *Let me taste you, Todd.* Another: *Feed it to me Todd, I NEED IT NOW!* Another: *Pull the van over and come give it to me. I want it! I WANT U!*

Todd sharply pulled onto the shoulder of the highway and stopped the van. He quickly jerked his seat belt off and sat still as he breathed heavily.

"What's wrong?" Johnathon asked.

"What's the problem, guys?" Joey asked from the center of the van.

Just then, Trent's voice chimed in over a walkie-talkie that had been attached to the driver's-side visor, "What happened back there? Is everything okay?"

Todd picked up the walkie and responded, "Ah, yeah, everything is okay. I just needed to pull over for a minute, that's all. We're getting back on right now."

"We'll be at the hotel in a few hours, so try to catch up. Don't want to have to wait around for you guys to check in. We're already late enough as it is," Trent responded.

"Ah, shut it!" Johnathon yelled into the walkie, then clicked it off. He then turned to Todd and said, "You all right? I can take over for you if you want."

"Nah. Only a few hours left. I think I can stick it out," Todd responded.

He pulled the van back onto the highway and met me again in the rearview mirror.

I win.

With both of us out of breath and still trying to catch up, we continued to gaze at each other, our eyes totally glazed over, as we charged toward our destination.

18

LODI, NJ

Leroy and I entered a crowded aquarium-laden restaurant. We walked past the elegant decor, and through the airy aroma of sautéed seafood, toward the large rectangular table positioned near the rear of the restaurant. The rest of the cast, seated at the table, greeted us.

As I sat down in the empty seat across from Todd, Leroy said with van keys in hand, "Don't worry, it fit. Barely. I thought I'd have to squeeze it into one of the handicaps, but I got it to fit in a regular spot. We're back near the dumpsters, but we're in there."

"Sometimes that's the best place to be," Johnathon said.

"Near the dumpsters?" Christian asked.

"Some good things have come out of dumpsters," Johnathon said.

"Like what?" Salvador asked.

"I found one of my best guitar amps ever in the trash. Still use it today," Johnathon said.

"What else?" Salvador asked.

Johnathon takes a long pause then says, "I actually found a perfectly good cheeseburger in the trash once."

"That's just gross," Molly said.

"It was completely untouched," Johnathon retorted.

"It was trash!" Molly said.

"Not to me. It was just like a fresh one. Believe me, if it looked tampered with or if someone had taken a bite out of it I wouldn't have touched it. I mean, I'm not some merciless scavenger or something," Johnathon stated.

"I'll say," Molly commented.

"I don't know. Once it's in that can, I can't touch it," Todd stated.

"Yeah. Say hello to hepatitis for me," Christian jested.

"Why were you digging through the trash anyway?" Leroy asked.

"Life as a musician is not all that it's cracked up to be," Johnathon answered.

"Neither is life as an actor," Anne commented.

Leroy lifted his glass of water and said, "I'll drink to that." All of us lift our glasses as Leroy begins his toast: "To the actor's life. One full of heartache, promise, rejection, and sustained hunger. And thank God we're not musicians!"

"Hear, hear!" Johnathon applauded.

We collectively saluted, then clinked our glasses. We individually sipped, then delved into energized banter. Conversation topics seemed to divide the table into sections, with each contributor being grossly engaged in their separate lyrical choruses.

***

It was late. Dinner had concluded, and we were the only remaining patrons in the restaurant. The bar was closed, and the servers and staff were working feverishly to close and clean their stations. Molly, Joey, Todd, and I continued to be engaged in the enthralling conversation that began just after Leroy's toast: a smorgasbord of topics that continued to grow as time passed.

"How'd you do? With the zombie in my room, I mean," Molly asked Joey.

"I don't know. I'm kind of worried about her," Joey responded.

"Sally'll snap out if it eventually," Molly responded.

"It's been almost a week," Joey said.

"I think she's coming around. I saw her looking very intensely at what I had for lunch today. Give it a day or two," I added as my eyes rolled past Todd's. Todd wore a look of lust on his face. I did a double take and became enraptured by his gaze for a few seconds. I blushed, then broke the eye lock.

"It's a shame. Letting someone have that much control over your life. I didn't even know she had a boyfriend," Molly said.

"Neither did I," Joey replied.

"I mean, I know she's hurting, but come on. Life goes on, you know? Ah, the shortcomings of youth."

"I don't think that has anything to do with it. The girl was in love."

I repeated my quick glance at the swelling lion sitting across from me. Todd's focus had not changed. I boldly held my gaze even longer this time, the heat pulsating every pore on my body. Eventually, I smiled to myself, then looked away.

"Young love. It's different. Young love is dangerous. It's wild, it's impulsive, it's primal. It's war. The casualties are severe in that type of love," Molly continued.

"What's the alternative? Old, decrepit love? Who wants that?" Joey asked.

"Seasoned love is the alternative. Both parties have fought through the potency of that young contraband when it explodes and leaves bodies in its wake. They lived through it and survived. Now they're ready to try it again, but now they're wiser, battle tested. They know how to not just run in there with their head down. The whole thing is still unpredictable, but at least they're armed this time around."

"I don't know. I think I'd rather sign up for the juiced version. I don't want some run-down, careful version of love. Is that even love? You're not supposed to walk on eggshells and tiptoe around your feelings. I wanna be abrasive! I wanna throw it against the wall!"

Our eyes met again.

"It's dangerous," Molly said.

"It's supposed to be! It's not some instructional video on traffic safety. It's X-rated!"

I, still engaged in the most intense optical fuck I'd ever had, shifted in my seat. I crossed my legs and tightly pressed them together.

". . . it's offensive. I don't want some censored version. Give me the authentic thing with all the tangy spices and fruity flavors I can handle!" Joey continued.

With the heat in the room at its maximum, I re-crossed my legs, locked them together, and began to slightly rub them against each other.

"That is the exact kind of thing that kills hundreds of adolescent girls every year, the thing that makes young women physically harm themselves by going on hunger strikes, amongst other things. I don't wish that kind of love on anyone," Molly said.

"Don't you see? That kind of love is the only kind worth having. You wouldn't do all of that with your watered-down version. Not palpable enough. The experience of young, wild, untamable love is what earns the pain afterward. Some people would starve themselves or would even be willing to die just to have that kind of experience, if only for a little while."

"It's different for us ladies. Our emotions are just subject to too much. Back me up on this, Anne."

Me, being as valiant as I ever have, was still locked in with Todd. My hand slowly stroked my tense neck as I tried to subdue the lump in my throat.

"Anne?" Molly said, jarring me out of my trance.

"Yes? Yes," I replied with my face beet red.

"Back me up. Women dive into relationships, heart, mind, body, and soul. We expose ourselves completely and leave ourselves open to the scathing side of love. Yes?" Molly said.

"Yeah, I agree with that. We are emotional beings. We can't help that," I agreed.

"But don't you prefer it that way? Throwing yourself all in instead of half-assing it?" Joey asked.

"Depends," I said.

"On what?" asked Joey.

"The relationship. Sometimes it's not worth being totally there. You'll only expose it all if you're with the right one. And in that case, it's not like you have a choice anyway. You won't be able to control it," I replied as my eyes met with Todd's again.

The fire in Todd's eyes had increased. I began to tremble. I mumbled to God under my breath, then said to the group, "Could you guys excuse me for a second, please?"

I forced my jelly-filled knees into action as I got up from the table and headed toward the restroom. I could feel Todd's eyes on me as I departed.

Into the bathroom I went, whizzing past the door and heading straight for the sink. I was extremely flushed and breathing heavily.

"Jesus Christ!"

I ran cold water in the sink and smacked a few handfuls onto my face. I looked into the mirror at my reflection and slowly began to regain my breath. When it was all caught up to me, I let out a gut-inspired sigh and dropped my head. I remained hunched over for a few moments, listening to the sound of my breathing.

"What are we going to do about this tension?" Todd's voice rang through like a beacon, startling me. I turned around to see him standing in front of the closed bathroom door. His brooding masculine sexuality was atomic. He undid all the work I had done to calm myself, with one look. I quickly looked away. "I can't even look at you. I can't speak to you. I cannot touch you," I said.

"Why not?"

"You know why."

"Do you want me?"

Don't do it, Lamberty. Don't you dare confess it out loud!

I hung my head again. On the verge of tears, I quietly replied, "Yes."

Todd slowly began to approach me. I made an attempt to defend myself with another whisper, but nothing came out.

Don't.

Todd continued his approach until he had pressed himself against me, chest to chest, pelvis to pelvis. The smothering induced more tears from me.

We can't, Todd. We just can't.

Todd softly caressed my hair. He seemed enamored with my cheekbones and neck as he stroked my limp locks. He began to tease my neck with his lips and breath. A severe chill ran up my spine. "Todd . . ." I whimpered.

He began to gently kiss my neck. The soft plunking sounds of his pecks added a sensual percussion to the sustained melodic buzz of the florescent lights in the room.

I exhaled. The turmoil inside me could be seen on my face. ". . . Todd, we can't do this."

Todd journeyed up to my cheek. He rubbed his flesh against mine, and my breathing intensified. My verbal attempts at pleas began to transform into pleading moans.

Todd . . . please . . . stop . . .

He kissed me on the lips. Slow, meaningful pecks turned into long passionate kisses. As the passion increased, so did the waterworks. My face was literally saturated with tears when Todd lifted me onto the counter and began to slip my dress from my shoulders. "The door, Todd. The door," I said, my voice filled with anticipation and regret.

Todd made it to my breasts and began to suck and fondle my nipples. He flicked them with his tongue and squeezed my breasts. I lifted his shirt off of him and began to unbuckle his pants. He hiked my dress up just enough for him to get a good grip on my panties and yanked them off. I felt the cold marble counter underneath me for the first time, and it was that sharp sensation that woke me up from the fantasy for a brief moment.

Is this really happening? Am I really going to have sex with this man, right here, right now? Ugh, I can't stop myself, he's making me feel like I've never felt before. I always knew he would.

He pressed his body against mine, and entered. I deeply inhaled and fully embraced the pain and ecstasy I experienced the moment he broke my threshold. I could feel Todd taking special care to see that he was not hurting me. He was gentle and strong simultaneously.

He filled me up so completely I could feel him in my throat, and I felt like I could barely exhale. I held the air in my lungs for a few beats and, when I couldn't take it anymore, expelled it slowly, methodically, a severely satisfying release.

Once I'd fully emptied my lungs the first time, I found it was easier to breathe, and I adjusted to being at capacity. Upon that adjustment, I fully surrendered to the sensations that crackled throughout my entire body. It felt like I was being pleasurably stung by thousands and thousands of jellyfish all over my body, and I responded in kind. My body trembled and shook, and I began to incoherently speak. I started to open up, and unleash pieces of what had been inside of me for so long, the once-dormant lustful beast that, to that point, only Todd could release.

When he saw my lust being slowly unleashed, he increased his tempo and ferocity. He hung my legs over his arms, gripped my hips hard with both hands, lifted me up, and swung me back and forth on him. It felt like I was hanging from two stone mountains, and his dick was a pleasurable anchor, holding me in place, making me not want to get off the ride as I bounced back and forth on him.

He tensed every time he repositioned me, and the continuous quick swell of his muscles made me even hotter. When he finally set me back on the counter, I could feel the puddle left behind from the intensity, and I was shocked. I'd never pooled before. That unexpected surprise added it to the experience even more, as I felt totally saturated by him, by us, and the mess we had made. I began to revel in it. I began to love it.

The acoustics in the empty, unlocked bathroom added to it as well. They transformed the location into a steamy sex den, amplifying each moan, grunt, and combative thrust tenfold, as both of us continued to throw caution to the wind.

We continued for another fifteen solid minutes, and we had not one visitor.

19

I sat alone in my hotel room, staring at the wall. My face was the definition of "welcomed turmoil" as I smiled through my twisted and worried disposition.

My cell phone rang. I looked at the caller ID and saw that it was Brody.

Of course. Couldn't have happened any other way.

I silenced the ringer and continued my internal conversation with the wall. After a few seconds, I heard my phone chime again, indicating a new voice mail. I reluctantly picked up the phone and listened to the message.

"It's me. Just wanted to give you a call, see how you were doing out there. Hope things are okay. Everything's fine here, just missing you. Give me a call when you can. Just want to hear your voice. Okay. Bye."

Universe, you are one harsh motherfucker.

I closed my phone, shut my eyes, and leaned my head against the wall. After a few moments, my phone chimed again, this time signifying a received text message. I reopened my phone.

R u ok? - T

I wrote, *What did we do tonight?*

I waited a few moments for a response. Finally, my phone chimed again.

Lived and died.

I closed the phone and reaffixed my attention back to the solid and sturdy room divider.

20

Todd and I were laying out the wardrobe for the day's show in a very tightly cramped dressing room. A few traditional makeup mirrors with large-bulbed lights heated the tiny space into almost sauna-like conditions, and the room reeked of newly dried paint. A cracked window allowed for a much-needed release from the toxic fumes and stuffy fever of the sweltering hotbox.

Both Todd and I were silent while we worked. The only sound in the room was the constant *plub-plub* coming from the steamer as it warmed up.

Even though we were not speaking, we were communicating heavily with each other via glancing looks, uncomfortable tension, and nervous/uneasy body language. The small, crowded room only added to the tautness of the situation as both of our bodies were forced to rub and slide against each other in order for us to navigate the area.

"Excuse me," Todd said as he brushed against my hip.

"No. I'm sorry. Let me get out of your way," I replied as I shifted my weight to the opposite side, a maneuver that added even more grind to the situation.

Steam began to stealthily fill the room as the physical tension between our restraint-filled bodies heated up with every bend, twist, and twitch. The more we moved, the more entangled we became, forcing us to engage in a hypersexual game of multiclothed Twister. Our contortions and sensual stretches mocked an outlandish Kama Sutra diagram. Both of us were visibly affected by the highly stimulating setting, and it didn't take long for the once-incidental shifting and grinding to subtly start becoming intentional.

As the steamer pumped at full force, I attempted to reach past Todd for a wardrobe item. Todd stopped my advance, and we stood face-to-face. The steamer shot strong puffs of steam at our sweltering bodies, increasing the tension and heat between the two of us with each expulsion of vapor. Consumed by the swell, we erupted with passion.

We utilized the small space well by tightly pressing our bodies together and physically restricting our movements. The restraint only fueled the inferno inside of me even more as I violently ripped Todd's shirt open and attacked his bare neck and chest. I viciously worked my way down to his pants, tore them open, and furiously forced him into my mouth, whole.

Todd knocked down most of the prearranged wardrobe items and kicked over a few clothing racks as he reacted to my passion. I noticed my strong effect on him as he quipped and shuddered at every flick and slap of my tongue. He tasted like dirty cologne, and I loved it. It was a hearty, masculine taste, one that fully satisfied my appetite. When I licked the head, I could also taste his sweet-and-sour combination of precum, and it only excited me more. I was anticipating his climax like nothing before.

Aggressively, I pinned him to one of the shelves in a small corner of the room and devoured him whole. Gripped his muscular thighs to hold him in place as I sucked his shaft and tickled his balls until he began to tremble. Feeling him shake and break down gave me a type of confidence I hadn't experienced before. I reveled in my dominance and continued to recklessly and sloppily pleasure him until he was unable to resist succumbing to me. He came in my mouth, and I almost climaxed as I felt the thick, creamy fluid snake down my throat and into my stomach. I had conquered him, and I was on cloud nine because of it. My unbreakable satisfaction was challenged, however, by a few thoughts of post-lust regret, as if I'd just woken up from an uncontrollable trance.

I strode confidently toward the door as I left him drained, sitting alone on the shelf, his pants around his ankles. As I exited the room, I mentioned, "Better get yourself together. We're late."

Moments later, I arrived onstage as the rest of the cast was in the middle of our customary preshow fight call. Todd arrived soon after, ripped shirt and all. Salvador was in the middle of his opening remarks, commenting on the fight technique in the previous show, and when he saw Todd and me running onto the stage in a frenzy, he commented, "Glad you could join us. Fight call was at nine thirty."

"Sorry. Had a lot of things to steam," I responded.

As Salvador resumed his commentary, Leroy noticed Todd's shredded shirt. "You've . . . you've got a little tear there," Leroy whispered.

"Thought I felt a draft," Todd responded.

***

We performed flawlessly in front of a jubilant, accepting crowd. Todd and I continued to make eyes at each other throughout the performance, and in the wings. I felt a certain thump in my stomach each time I looked at him, like something new was birthed in me every time—something electric, something wonderful.

After the show, I was back in the cramped dressing room, reminiscing on what took place in that space earlier, when a feeling of melancholy swept over me. I felt dirty; I felt less than. It was almost like what happened earlier was part of a terrible dream, and now I was awake, taking inventory of my soiled thoughts and actions.

I'm a horrible person.

That once-proud feeling I felt when I broke that musky piece of manly stone down to a pulp had now dissolved into feelings of self-loathing.

However, even with this newfound gloom, a twinge of excitement and satisfaction remained that I couldn't get rid of. I punished myself for this small piece of me that survived the tidal wave of guilt, but I couldn't deny it. As much as I hated myself for what I'd allowed to happen with Todd so far, I hated myself even more for liking it, undeniably.

As I began to change out of my costume and into my street clothes, I reached into my bag to take out my socks and came across another folded, untitled note. I felt the thump in my stomach, and even though I didn't want to, I smiled to myself.

I teased myself by not opening the note right away. Savoring the anticipation, I waited until everyone had piled into the van for transport, then hopped into the large storage space in the very rear, along with all of the luggage. I laid on my back, in a semi-euphoric state, my legs stretched toward the rear window as I watched the treetops, disabled highway lights, and cell phone towers whiz by.

Eventually, I unearthed the folded note, unfurled it, and set it on my chest. I breathed in those last few moments of intentional anticipation, then happily picked it up and began to read the intoxicating prose. Once again, I could hear each syllable in Todd's voice, clear as day, as I scanned each word, each letter.

One touch. That's all I need, all I need to step into a volcanic wonderland. You are the Ash Queen, walking through the area, sprinkling cayenne on everything. The tips of your fingers singe my skin and send all of my sensors in motion. Some people call them butterflies, but butterflies don't flutter that fast. We'll call them hummingbirds.

And I'm not just talking about the physical touch, oh no! It is also cerebral. I have become a willing partner with the id as it battles the ego. Your subtle tickle has allowed you to live in two separate worlds, the conscious and subconscious; an extraterrestrial in the latter, but welcomed with open arms. Stay as long as you like. The fruits are sweeter and the air is cleaner since you've arrived. I want to smell your scent. Douse myself in your pheromones and eliminate my most acute sense. If all I smell is you, hopefully my eyes, hands, mouth, and ears aren't incapacitated at the same time, because my answer every time will be the same: amazing.

The discreet caresses under the table, in the backseat, outside the hotel, make me long to explore your temple. I'd admire the complexity of its exterior, tactilely examine its structure, bends, creases, sweeps, and arches, but never fully enter. Oh, how I desire to touch your fleshy lobe, rubbing it between my fingers and generating the aforementioned heat. As we joust with each other in this tickle game, I simply would just like to sample your cuddle. Spoon myself tightly around your skin, like a glove. I'd surely need to wear one, or risk bursting from the flame. You don't know the power you possess in one of your plush palms. Enough power to crumble my empire. To make dust out of what I have created for myself. Regardless of the danger, I am still drawn to the heat. One touch does it. One touch, and I'm ready to be consumed by the fire. Ready to die.

I laid my new confidence booster back on my chest and reintroduced myself to the heavens. I glanced over and caught Todd subtly peeking back at me through the seats. I felt the thump again, then smiled at him.

Thank you, Mr. Happy. Thank you again.

21

CEDAR FALLS, IA

We hadn't had a day off in two weeks, and it was starting to take its toll. We were being overworked due to the positive reviews we'd been getting since our first performance.

Once the word got out, requests for us to come perform at more venues flooded the production office. Never one to turn down any form of currency—pay them in pennies and aluminum cans if you like—they selfishly booked us for almost a dozen new shows on top of our already-packed schedule. Because of the uptick in performances, tensions and quick tempers were abundant and Trent's iron fist had been hardened even more in order to keep us constant and on schedule.

In dire need of a release, we spontaneously pulled into a local theme park as we came upon it while driving on the highway. Trent protested but was quickly and forcibly overthrown. He knew we needed the break, and hell, I was certain he needed one himself, so he conceded.

The small outfit was equipped with go-karts, batting cages, a full-scale arcade, miniature golf, wall-climbing, and a few mini, uncomplicated roller coasters. Our excitement was through the roof. As we de-vanned and made our way toward admissions, Todd and I lingered toward the back of the group.

As we walked, he put his hand flush on the small of my naked back. His touch ignited my senses, and I suddenly was on fire. I felt his hand flinch a bit, and I could only imagine that he could feel the strong current of heat emitting through me and his fingertips got singed.

He looked at me and smiled, as if he was delighted to know that he caused an impact on me. Our silent, secretive connection revealed itself even further in my hardening nipples, which were beginning to protrude through the fabric of my loose-hanging, backless shirt.

After purchasing tickets, we all collectively conquered the Tilt-A-Whirl, Zipper, and Spinning Tubs, all while having a tremendous time. Laughs and screams from the gut were constant as we were whipped and thrown in all directions from the rickety steel. Outside of being on the stage, this was the best time we'd had together as a group to date, and we all realized it as the sun set on an exquisite day, quelling the former built-up strife and angst.

***

A few hours later, near the entrance of the park, a roller-coaster operator was stepping down from his post as Todd and I, sweaty and out of breath, ran up to him screaming, "One more! One more!"

The coaster operator apologized and told us the park was closed.

"Oh, come on! We ran all the way from the batting cages!" I said.

"We're only here for one night. We can't leave without experiencing the Twistanator!" Todd chimed in.

"I know you've got one more in you. Please?" I pleaded.

The burly coaster operator rubbed his gruff beard for a moment, then said, "All right. One more." Todd and I yelled triumphantly as we hopped over the barricade to the ride, then strapped ourselves into the loosely hanging front seat.

"Now, this'll be a quickie, so hold on tight," the coaster operator said as he pulled the rusty lever, activating the aged, hulking beast. The track was worn and slow, and the seat jostled from side to side, almost as if there was a screw or two missing. Nonetheless, I couldn't feel a bump or bounce, as I was fully captivated by Todd, and he looked like he was fully captivated by me. We exchanged lustful looks as the train slowly curved around the preliminary track and began to clink its way up the initial drop.

It didn't take long before we were kissing passionately and engaging in heavy petting. Midway up the incline, we looked at each other, each longing for something more. We silently confirmed our thoughts through our eyes, then took our first step toward the unthinkable.

Todd unzipped his pants and slid them down past his waist as I hiked my skirt up and slid myself out of the bar harness around my lap. I straddled and hovered over Todd as I attempted to line up our flesh.

"Don't worry. I've got you," Todd spoke through the breeze. He bear-hugged my waist with one hand, opened my shirt with the other, and began to suck my chest. When the slow-churning train finally made it to its pinnacle, it slowed almost to a stop and teetered on the mountaintop. Slowly, surely, the brake released and the mechanized monstrosity submitted itself to earthly physics.

Our union was simultaneous with the train's furious decent. As the raging leviathan twisted and turned around sharp corners and narrow passageways, Todd receded deeper into me, and I felt each adrenaline-induced grind with g-force strength. The wind whipped my hair to and fro, and acted as a third and fourth hand on my body, as it smacked and pushed me around. The sugary smell and taste of funnel cake was in the air; it made me high and acted as a counterbalance to what Todd was doing to me. Childhood memories mixed with adult desires, and all of it enhanced the experience in my twisted mind.

As I grinded on him tightly, I could feel myself dripping all over his cock and down my thighs. I was turned on that we were christening this contraption for ourselves, and anyone else who rode in that compartment would mingle with our DNA.

As we rounded a sharp bend, I grabbed his collar and used it as leverage as I pulled him into me even harder, causing me some pain coupled with intense pleasure. I stayed there and wiggled on him in short, sharp movements. He was right where I wanted him, right in my spot, and I could feel the tide rising. I never wanted to get off.

"You got me?" I asked.

"I've got you," Todd responded.

"Yeah?"

"I've got you."

"You got me?"

"I've got you. Oh, I've got you!"

We continued, completely engrossed in our percolated senses. Halfway through the ride, we each experienced gargantuan orgasms, the biggest I'd ever experienced.

22

PEORIA, IL

Late night, at a dusty laundromat, a bundle of clothes swirled around in sudsy water. Todd and I, alone, were watching the garments slosh and slush against one another through the clear window of the washing machine. My head rested on Todd's shoulder, and Todd's hand was on my skirted thigh. We mindlessly observed the clothes as if we were watching an episode of television.

While taking in the dialogue of the active clothes, I began to get a bit introspective. I wondered who I really was now, in that new space, with that new man, and wondered if I liked my life better that way. I was wild, wilder than I'd ever been, and I was taking more and more bold risks every day. My confidence was growing by leaps and bounds, and I was finally becoming comfortable in my own tall, lanky skin. However, I clearly noted to myself that I was cheating on my fiancé, and those specific actions were contributing to those newfound feelings of zest and liberation. Did that make me a bad person? Did my reveling in and enjoying being a "harlot," as I'd termed myself, make me a person not fit for society's norms, or was I simply putting my needs first and becoming empowered by doing so? Eventually, I gave up on my internal monologue and turned my attention to the catalyst of my newfound form.

"What are your dreams?" I asked Todd. "What do you want out of life?"

"Not sure if I know. I mean, I want to be happy."

"And what'll make you happy?"

"Being able to showcase my work on a grand scale, the grandest of scales. Inspiring others and living forever."

"That's cool."

"What about you? What'll make you happy?" Todd asked.

"I don't know. Being able to act full-time without having to worry about what the next gig's going to be or how I'm going to pay my rent. Traveling the world, visiting my homeland, and researching my roots," Todd then asked me about my origins, and I responded, "My father is Panamanian."

"Would have never known."

"I only found out a few years ago. After twenty-four years of believing the man I grew up knowing as my dad was naturally my biological father, my mother decided to tell me the truth—on the day of my sister's wedding, no less! There I am, all dolled up in my horrible teal bridesmaid dress, ready to join the line of five other unattractive, sweaty bridesmaids, when mom pulls me aside and says she has to tell me something important. I guess the stress and sentimental emotions she was feeling from the reality of her first daughter being moments away from walking the aisle must have gotten to her, because right then and there she decided to come clean. She told me that I was conceived out of an adulterous relationship that came about while she was in the peace corps. She said she became involved with a man she just couldn't resist, a man she fell in love with. Needless to say, the relationship was over when her term ended, and she only realized she was pregnant after she got back home. That's the moment, she told me, that she realized that she'd done a terrible thing and that she'd never be able to forgive herself. Ever. I see it every time she looks at me."

"I'm sure it has nothing to do with you."

"I don't see regret. I know she's not sorry that I'm here. It's guilt. It's the hundred tons of guilt I see in her eyes that breaks my heart. My dad has long since forgiven her, but I'm sure he sees the same thing I do," I say.

"Have you?"

"Have I what?"

"Have you forgiven her? Todd asked.

"It's funny. When she told me, I wasn't mad. Actually, I kinda understood."

Todd took in the piece of my soul that I shared with him, and for a second or two, I wasn't sure how he felt about it. Then he took my chin and lifted my head from his shoulder so we were facing each other. He looked deep into my eyes.

Ugh. Those fucking eyes.

I still got weak. As the look lingered, I felt the thump in my stomach and braced myself.

Todd brought my face to his, and we kissed, softly, slowly. We took our time enjoying each other's lips, each other's taste; his was like Corona, and I'm sure mine was the same. Eventually, the passion increased, and we embraced, holding and gripping onto each other for dear life. We both were each other's safety net, and were determined not to let go while standing on our precipices.

Todd lifted me onto the running washing machine. The spin cycle was activated, causing the body of the cold, hard steel to vibrate and kick rapidly. Immediately, my arousal shot through the roof as I almost had an orgasm at the moment of impact with the machine. Unable to wait any longer, I reached down Todd's sweats and palmed his massive bulge, already on medium.

With the kissing and heavy petting continuing, I gripped and stroked him to a full, thick erection, pulled my panties to the side, and shoved him into me with one motion. He was deep inside, so much so, he touched my back wall. I held him there, deep, and said, "Don't you fucking move," as I began to grind him, hard. I loved being in control, and the combination of the cold, hard steel of the machines and Todd's smooth, chiseled body all added up to peak arousal for me. The knock-knock-knocking from the machines gave me a tempo I could match, so I became one with them. I became a machine, and mimicked their power, their precision, until my desired outcome was fulfilled.

The vibrations from the spin cycle along with Todd's girth filling me up made me extremely wet. I dripped all over the machine, and when I finally came, I gushed, a first for me. It went all over—the machine, the floor, and Todd. Todd then wiped some of it from off his body, rubbed it on his mouth, and, as if on cue, I sat up and passionately kissed him like I was dying of thirst, sucking the tangy elixir from his lips.

Aggressively, I pushed him off of me, then took off my panties, shoved them in his mouth, and said, "Clean 'em, bitch." Sure to my calculations, Todd was turned on to the maximum. He turned me around and bent me over the machine as it clacked and clinked toward completion. With the panties still in his mouth, he entered, and began to pound me, hard. The clapping sound of our bodies and our rhythmic banging into the machine echoed throughout the empty laundromat.

I was instigating all of this increased spunk by being very verbal, spouting dirty obscenities, and challenging Todd's manhood with each thrust. Pretty soon, the sex became loud and boisterous. We moved all over the laundromat, soiling the top of a line of dryers and a folding table with our filthy intercourse.

When we moved to the floor, Todd flipped me over onto my stomach and said, "I want that ass."

I was turned on to the max, hearing him tell me what he wanted from me. It made me want to give all of myself to him. With that said, I was still hesitant as I'd never done that before. I'd always been curious, but neither I nor Brody, nor my other boyfriends, had ever engaged in that act. I was petrified that was going to be painful.

Todd snatched me by the hair and said, "I want that ass. You hear me?"

I, extremely turned on by his aggressiveness and staunch masculinity, fought through my fear, arched my back, and gave myself to him willingly. Todd lubed himself with a generous mixture of his spit and my secretions, inserted slowly, and I immediately felt the pain. Strange enough, my eyebrows and forehead felt as if they were on fire. I think Todd could sense that I was tense, so he worked past the threshold very gently and told me to relax. He whispered filthy things into my ear as he continued to pulsate and grind. His words and constant, smooth motion eventually turned my pain into pleasure, and I relaxed. Once able to move freely, Todd went to work. He smacked me on my ass, and continued to pull my hair.

"Is this ass mine?"

"Yes! Yes, it's all yours, Todd!"

I was his slave, helpless to defend myself against his trance, and he was my brooding master, dominant in service to me. I'd always wished Brody would have been that assertive. I always wanted Brody to assume control like that and take what he wanted, yet he'd shy away from those scenarios. He always said he had too much respect for me to dishonor me like I wished. However, I needed that from him specifically, and I'd always desired the feeling of being ravished, or being used to an extent, and Todd was fulfilling this deep carnal need of mine to the maximum.

We were absolutely rampaging beasts in that session, especially me. I was wilder and more free with Todd than I'd ever been with anyone else. I embraced that fact and loved it. We continued our nasty, verbally charged intercourse to climax, and we concluded with my sweaty body lying on top of his in front of a large transparent window, in plain view of a busy trucker's highway.

23

CHICAGO, IL

All of us looked like we'd had a long night. While mine was glorious, I was still majorly fatigued and not ready for what was ahead of us on that particular day. All of us were drowsy and irritable as we sat in our seats, waiting to depart to the venue for the day, when the sliding door abruptly opened.

Trent and Salvador appeared in the opening. "Ladies and gentlemen, hear me but speak a word. First, I want to thank you for being here on time and ready to go. Your professionalism and punctuality has not gone unnoticed and will be duly noted," Trent said as some of us discreetly rolled our eyes. "Secondly, I have an important announcement about next week's performances. They have been canceled. The producers were not able to book enough shows for us, so they're laying us off for a week. We'll come back to pick up where we left off afterward, but after we're finished here in Chicago, we'll all be going home for a week. Are there any questions?"

No, no, no! I'm not ready. I can't go home now. Not now!

We were all stunned. Trent slid the van door shut, and he and Salvador walked toward the cargo van. As if saturated in molasses, we started our journey towards the venue with the collective mood and spirit of the group filled with extreme tremors.

***

Naturally, we went on to give one of our worst performances of the tour. Dropped lines, choppy combat blocking, and late entries and exits marred the display. While the majority of the audience wasn't fazed, Trent and the theater owner were not amused. Toward the end of the show, it seemed as if we all were thinking about the aftermath, causing us to make even more follies. All in all, we knew we were in for it.

Finally, the curtain fell and the lights collapsed. To curb some of Trent's rage, we began to tackle the load-out like never before. We snapped to it like a tight military unit.

"Adios microphones!" Leroy said as we de-mic'd each other.

"You've been saying goodbye to everything. We've still got a few more shows to do in the city, and the layoff is only for a week. We'll be back in no time," Salvador responded.

"My last layoff got extended for an entire month," Molly added.

"Goodbye ol' mic tape!" Leroy said.

"I gotta figure out how I'm gonna pay my rent," Johnathon commented.

"One word: 'unemployment,'" Molly replied.

"I don't know bout y'all, but I'm kinda lookin' forward to being off the road for a little bit. Get a chance to clear my head," Sally said.

"Yeah, well, while you're clearing your head, I'll be begging my old boss to let me bartend again for a week. Argh! I hate that place," Christian said.

"There might be room for another 'tender at the place where I used to serve. I'll make a call for you," Leroy commented. I could hear Christian thanking Leroy for the referral as Todd and I broke away from the group and approached the costume racks. We began preparing them to be taken back to the dressing room.

"You okay with this?" Todd asked.

"Yeah. Fine," I replied, then abruptly rolled my rack toward the dressing room, leaving Todd by himself.

The truth was, I wasn't really sure how I felt about it. My mind had been so enraptured with Todd these past few months that it had been difficult to think about anything else. Just the thought of being away from him was unbearable, and that made me extremely uneasy for more than one reason. On top of that, the very real threat of seeing Brody again terrified me.

I wasn't ready to see him yet. I just wasn't ready.

***

Seeking one last hurrah before the layoff, we all decided to visit the world-famous Shedd Aquarium situated on Chicago's glorious Museum Campus. We darted into the prestigious structure like kids on an unsupervised field trip, purchased tickets, and fanned out to take in the structure's eight thousand–plus aquatic inhabitants.

Todd and I strolled around the front of the huge oceanarium tank near the aquarium's entrance. We watched a deep-sea diver feed the colorful fish and provide knowledgeable commentary from inside the tank. I commented about the beauty of what was inside the massive tank, and Todd agreed.

"I've always loved the ocean and aquatic life," I said.

"Me too. It relaxes me," Todd responded.

"Did you know I was a mermaid?"

"Excuse me?"

"I'm a mermaid."

"I can see that. The long hair, the fishy aroma . . ."

"Fuck you!"

"I'm just kidding."

"I'm just not complete yet. I didn't want to be the kind who could only live in the sea. I wanted to be able to function on land and water, so I asked the Octopus King for both capabilities," I said.

"A special, bionic mermaid. The best of both worlds."

"Wouldn't that be great? When all this craziness became too much for you on land, you'd have another world you could escape to. Another world that forced you to live a completely different life than you did in your previous one. I just think that would be awesome," I said.

"You know, you can't have it both ways. It's either one or the other," he replied.

"Yeah. Haven't quite accepted that just yet, but it's slowly sinking in. I'm still a mermaid, though. Just one that's confined to land for the time being, that's all. I'm still holding out hope for my gills to develop."

We shared a laugh, and I could feel our current bliss tightening, almost to the point of being claustrophobic. I could tell it was mutual.

"I'm gonna miss this," Todd said.

"Miss what?"

"This."

"Me too."

"Think about how it's going to be during the layoff?" he asked.

"Trying not to think about it that much," I responded.

"But . . ."

"But I literally have not slept since Trent made the announcement the other day."

"Me either."

"I just wasn't ready for this to come so soon. Everything is so conflicted and confusing. I really don't know where I am right now, and I'm just not ready to have to figure it out," I confessed.

"We have complicated things quite a bit, haven't we?"

I faced Todd, looked him in the eyes, and said, "I can't sleep, Todd. I cannot sleep thinking about what we've done. What we've done to each other, what we've done to our significant others. I'm engaged, for Christ's sake! And yet, I can't deny that a sizable part of me is so happy to have met you and genuinely glad and, hell, grateful to have had these experiences with you. I love being with you. I'm such a bad person."

"No, you're not. We didn't plan this. It's not like we said, 'I'm going to find someone while I'm out on the road.' This just happened. There's a chemistry or something between us that I can't explain. That, and the fact that we simply like each other, added fuel to the fire, and we can't control it. We are out of control. But I have to tell you, I like it. I love it. For the first time in my life, I love not knowing what's coming next. It's a thrill. And when each unknown reveals itself, we keep getting closer and closer. Being out of control with you has opened my eyes to what true passion and zest for life are all about. I'd like to continue to not care about the consequences with you. This is the most excited I've ever been in my life, and I don't want it to end."

Flattered yet torn, I turned my attention back to the fantastically enormous tank, wishing and longing to join my marine brethren.

***

NEW YORK, NY

We engaged in an all-inclusive conversation as we drove over the slicked grates of the George Washington Bridge. Todd and I sat next to each other in the rear of the van.

Unbeknownst to anyone else, we held hands as we contributed to the significant talk-back. When we were with each other, time lasted for an eternity; however, a poignant time stamp was made when crossing over the last few feet of the bridge. Time was fleeting, and we soon would be injected with a stiff sense of reality once back on Manhattan's hallowed concrete grounds. When we finally arrived, a portion of the air in our lungs was purged.

The van pulled just in front of the initial rehearsal building in Midtown, and double-parked. We unloaded the van of its contents. It was chilly outside, so we were working fast, no time for idle chitchat. Once the van was free from luggage, trash, and the sort, we assembled ourselves on the sidewalk and waited for Trent's dismissal.

Quiet at first, but then we heard his voice cascading from across the street as he unloaded the cargo van: "Ladies and gentlemen, we will see you back here bright and early in one week."

Accepting Trent's words as a satisfactory dismissal, Leroy proclaimed, "Well, that, tha, tha, that, tha, tha, that's all, folks!"

"Stop it! We'll be back," Johnathon said.

"I sure hope so. You guys take care and have a wonderful break," Leroy responded.

"No matter how long it is!" Molly chimed in.

"Stop it!" Johnathon said as he and Leroy began to walk toward the busy avenue.

As Salvador and Molly started walking away, she said to the group, "You kids take care."

"Yeah, we'll see ya," Salvador added as he throws his hand up toward the street, trying to hail a cab.

"Anybody need a ride? Got a friend coming that's giving me a ride," Christian said. When the rest of us declined, he continued, "All righty, then. Seven days." We said goodbye to Christian as he positioned himself near the corner of the avenue and scanned the oncoming traffic for his friendly transport.

"I'm heading downtown, y'all, so I guess I better mosey. Y'all be good now," Sally said as she gave everyone a hug. When she embraced Joey, he whispered in her ear, "I'll call you."

"You better," she replied. She kissed him, then walked toward the subway. Joey lingered a bit, enjoying her walk away, then turned toward Todd and me and said, "All right, guys." He shook Todd's hand, gave me a hug, then strolled into a nearby bar.

Silenced by our solitude, Todd and I stood in front of each other for a while and enjoyed our final moments of momentum. The familiar New York street ambiance filled the space between us, sounding a few levels louder and a few paces busier than I remembered. The sounds reminded us of home, and of how we once were, before we'd left that sanctified sanctuary of steam and twisted steel. We could feel the dream, the fantasy, slipping away, as if we were on the verge of waking up, but fighting like hell to continue our fantastical slumber.

"You know, we could rent a hotel room for the week. Stay up under each other for seven days, rent movies, order in, go skinny-dipping in the hotel pool. It'll be great," Todd suggested.

That's so tempting. Just me and Mr. Happy, slathered in sex and each other. Heaven on fucking Earth! What's stopping you, Lamberty? Why not take him up on his offer? You know why. It's this place, it's this city. All of it reminds you of him. You two had your first date just a few blocks from here, around the corner and down the street is where he bought you the ice cream that you spilled on your favorite dress, and you're one train stop away from the park where he proposed to you. No matter how much you want to, you can't share this place with Mr. Happy. This place is off-limits.

I gave him a long, meaningful kiss, then hugged him and said, "You will be missed." I released him, turned away to grab my bags, and walked away without looking back.

24

(Blackout)

25

I lugged a large suitcase behind me as I walked down the dampened city sidewalk. I'd packed too much this time. I have no idea why I thought I would need more shit this time around, but apparently, I did.

Spring had sprung, and the colossal icebergs of snow packed up by the former season had begun to melt, leaving behind large puddles in abundance. In an attempt to keep my luggage from dipping into a bottomless pool, I zigged and zagged up the walkway almost as if I was trying to dodge a trained sniper.

I turned the corner and saw a welcome sight: the majority of my castmates standing near the open-doored passenger van. Salvador spotted me first and yelled, "There he is!" I bowed my head and waved.

When I reached the group, Sally gave me an enormous hug and said, "Hey there, honey!"

"Hey! How was everybody's break?" I said to the group, to which everyone responded in the affirmative.

"I told ya we'd be back in a week," a bright-eyed Johnathon said.

"Fortunately, you were right this time," Leroy commented.

"If we weren't back in a week, there would be hell to pay. I had the Union ready to go on speed dial just in case," Christian said.

"It's nice to know someone's looking out for us," Leroy commented.

"It is my pleasure! I love getting on the Union's ass. Brings me great joy," Christian replied.

"Could you tell those bastards to swap us out a new stage manager?" Sally asked as Trent rounded the corner.

"Speak of the devil," Molly said.

"Maybe the break has cooled him out a bit," Joey suggested.

"We can only hope," Johnathon commented just as Trent arrived at the van.

"Good morning, ladies and gentlemen," Trent said very stonily.

Leroy sighed and said, "Nope. Not a chance," under his breath.

"Glad to see we're all accounted for and punctual," Trent continued.

"Where's Nursey?" Sally asked.

"That's a good question. Anybody heard from her?" Leroy asked.

"Nope," I answered.

Trent checked his watch then said, "She's got about another minute before I have to write her a demerit."

Christian smirked then said, "Technically, you don't have to . . ."

"I have to! What's fair is fair. If she's late, she gets a demerit, and that's that!" Trent sternly replied.

The good vibes we once possessed had been instantly power-vacuumed away by Trent's authoritative tone and message. We stood quietly as we waited while Trent remained fixed on the ticking hands of his watch.

A few moments later, Anne came dashing around the corner like a superhero, cape and all. The rest of the cast erupted in cheers and applause, while I stood quietly. It was good to see her. She looked even more beautiful than before. Trent slowly drew his attention away from his watch.

Out of breath and frantic, Anne said, "Holy shit! Did I make it?"

"By the skin of your teeth!" Salvador replied.

Anne swallowed a few times, then said, "The fucking trains are all out of whack. I had to go all the way into Queens to get on the— . . ."

"Okay people, we're already behind as it is! Let's load up and move out now! Mr. Drivus, you're with me," Trent commanded.

"Guess I'll see you guys later," Joey said as he and Trent walked toward the cargo van.

"I'd hoped he'd change over the break," Anne commented.

"Nope. Still an asshole. How are ya, honey?" Sally asked as she moved to hug Anne.

"I'm okay, just that fucking train . . ."

"Don't worry about it. You got here, we're glad you're here, and that's all that matters," Leroy said.

The group concurred and began to pile into the van. Anne wheeled her suitcase to the back of the van to load it into the cargo space. As she did, I felt the coldest breeze as she walked past me without saying a word. It wasn't until she was completely past me and masked by the back of the van that I could speak.

"Need help?" I asked.

"No, I got it. Thanks," she replied.

What the fuck? Not even a hello, how have you been? *Nothing?*

Dejected and furious, I jumped into the front portion of the van. Anne finished loading her luggage, then sat down in the absolute rear of the van. Soon after, the van took off. A familiar feeling began to resonate through all of us as the strong smell of cheap petroleum burned our esophagi, and the jerked force from the slow-shifting accelerator kicked in.

"I love you guys. I'm so glad to be back," Sally proclaimed.

"The break was that horrible, huh?" Johnathon asked.

"I was dying without you guys. The first day felt so weird, you know, 'cause I wasn't riding in the van all day. I actually had time to sit in a quiet space and think by myself. Freaked me out, man," Sally continued.

"I hate being by myself. My mind goes places I don't need it to go," Salvador admitted.

"It's not a bad thing to fantasize about other men, Sal," Anne said through a giggle. Salvador gave her a look, and she quickly inhaled her jest.

"No, I understand what you're saying. It's like you're forced to face yourself. All of yourself: the good, the bad, the ugly, all at once. Since I'm a chickenshit, I did my best to stay active and to be around people," Sally said.

"You say that like it's a bad thing," Christian commented.

"It wasn't, until the day I ran into my ex at some stupid party. It was pretty intense," Sally replied as Anne gasped.

"What happened?" Molly asked.

"Well, when I first saw him I was kinda shocked, ya know? I mean, I hadn't seen him in so long, and then BAM, unexpectedly he's right there. We made pleasantries then went off into our separate corners. I was uncomfortable from the fact that we were both in the same room, so I gathered my things and was about to leave. Well, he stopped me at the door and told me he wanted to talk."

"Tell me you smacked the shit out of him!" Molly said.

"You damn well believe I wanted to, sister! Shucks, I've never wanted to lay a hand on another human being before, but at that moment, I wanted to strangle the life out of him with my bare hands. Ooh! Strangely enough, I didn't lay a finger on him. I saved my wrath for something that would last a hell of a lot longer than an ol'-fashioned beatin'. We stepped outside on the balcony, and I let him have it! I told him exactly what I thought about him and how I never wanted to see him again, ever! I told him what he did to me will never happen again 'cause I won't ever fall that deeply in love with another man. I won't allow myself to go that far and open myself up to that kind of hurt anymore. Boy, did I let him have it! My finger was waggin', my hair was thrashin'! I didn't even let him get a word in! When I'd finished laying into him, I actually thanked him for opening my eyes, and I told him he'd truly changed me and my outlook on life and love."

"Damn, how'd he take it?" Leroy asked.

"Well, I was getting to that. I started to walk away without even looking at him. But then I heard something as I reached the door. I turned around and saw that he was bawling."

"He was crying?" Salvador asked.

"Like a baby. I guess I was so worked up when I was spoutin' off, I wasn't paying attention to how my words were affecting him. Hell, at that point, I didn't care. But when I saw that I'd genuinely touched something in him . . . I don't know. It was almost like standing in front of some special mirror or something. He looked how I felt. I ended up sticking around to hear what he had to say. By the end of it all, we were civil with each other. I saw him a couple more times over the break, and . . ."

"And what?" Christian asked.

"I don't know. I don't know where we are. I guess we'll have to play it by ear," Sally said.

Everyone in the van was disappointed and shocked. We stayed silent for a moment, then Anne bridged the gap with, "Well, good for you, Sally."

"Yeah. Thanks," Sally replied.

***

ELIZABETHTOWN, KY

A new, uneasy vibe snaked through the cast as we prepared for our first performance after the layoff. We had only been away from one another for a week, but it seemed as if it had been several months. Anne and I loaded in and set up the wardrobe in complete silence. The atmosphere between us was filled with extreme tension and anxiousness.

Joey and Sally loaded in as a tandem, and Joey picked up right where he'd left off when the layoff began. Sally, however, seemed to be in a slightly different space.

The closest I got to Anne was during the performance, and when offstage, I watched her scenes from the wings. After the show, Anne separated herself from me, sitting in the passenger seat of the van and burying her head in a book. I then made my home in the extreme rear of the van, and wrote furiously in my notebook.

***

The majority of the cast was hungry after the show, so we drove to a festive rib shack on the outskirts of town. The smell alone could give one diabetes, and its smoky stickiness could be detected from miles away. Upon entering, we were greeted with a rousing "Howdy!" from the hostesses and hustling servers. "Great to see y'all this evening! How many is it of yuh?" a spry hostess asked.

Leroy answered, "We've got six."

"Possibly seven," I said.

Instead of walking, the hostess almost skipped as she guided us to our seats, a jaunt she seemed to enjoy each and every time she took it. Once we were seated, we collectively thanked her for her infectious attitude, and she skipped off into the chaos. As Joey scooted his chair up to the table, next to Sally, he said to her, "This place has got the best ribs in the country, hands down. We stopped here on our last tour, and I just about died with all the ribs I shoved down. I swear I gained about ten pounds from that sitting."

"Guess I better keep an eye on ya!" Sally responded.

"You can keep more than an eye on me, sweetheart," Joey replied slyly. Sally subtly retracted from Joey's pursuit. The reaction was small, but we could tell that Joey noticed and felt it.

An even more chipper waitress than the hostess approached the table, pen and pad ready to go. "Howdy, y'all!" she said. The cast greeted her rousingly, and she responded with, "Why thank you! Welcome to the Ranch, Kentucky's finest outback shack. Is this y'all's first time?"

"Some of us have been here before and some haven't," Joey responded.

"Nice accent you have there. Where are y'all from?"

"The New York area," Leroy replied.

"Gosh, New York. I've always wanted to visit that place. It's so big. All the lights, the glitz, the glamour . . ."

"It's a dump, honey. Trust me, stay where you are. You'll be much happier," Molly interjected.

"Don't listen to her. New York's a great place. It's not for everybody, but there's not another place like it in the world. You should visit," Salvador said.

"Yeah, we'll make room for ya!" Sally chimed in.

"Y'all are so sweet. I just might do that. Now since some of y'all have been here before, you know that we serve family-style here. If you order ribs, one big ol' platter of ribs'll come out that'll feed five to six people. How many y'all got, lemme see, one, two, three . . ."

"We have six now, but we'll probably have seven," I said.

"Oh, okay. Then one, maybe two orders of your favorite items should do it."

As the waitress continued to gush over the serving sizes and specials of the day, Molly discreetly tapped me and said, "I don't think Anne's going to make it."

"I thought you said she was coming," I responded.

"I said she might be coming. When she got out of the shower, she said she wasn't feeling well and she might sit this one out."

"Hope she feels better."

"She seemed like she was doing better when we left. Got a phone call from that fiancé of hers; kinda perked her up a bit."

I sat still for a moment as I deciphered Molly's words, then took my phone out of my pocket and began to text Anne under the table.

We need to talk. 11. Swing sets.

I sent the message, then uninterestedly rejoined the table conversation.

26

I got there early; I don't know why. It was probably because I was nervous and I needed the extra time to calm myself down.

I circled around for a few minutes, then made my way to the old, rusty swing set behind the hotel and took a seat. The wind was still, and it was insanely quiet. Even the crickets had ceased their symphony. I waited patiently, huddled over, elbows on my knees. I was totally at a loss. Did I say or do something or not do something that had gotten her upset? If so, I had absolutely no clue what it could have been, but I wasn't above apologizing for something I was oblivious to. If it kept the peace, I was all for it. Just let me know where I needed to sign.

I kept checking my phone for the time.

She's late. Is she even going to show?

For a brief second I contemplated walking to her room and confronting her, but I thought better of it. Didn't want to seem like a madman, even though I could feel some level of descent on the inside. I wouldn't let it drive me crazy. I refused to let her make me insane.

At 11:17, I heard a noise, then turned to see Anne walking toward me in the distance.

Once again, she was absolutely beautiful. Flawless. I was instantly turned on as I watched her walk through the thick humidity. Outfitted in an off-the-shoulder, oversized T-shirt, cut-off blue jean shorts and lime-green flip-flops, she was the definition of "casual sultry."

Okay. Breathe and relax. Get to the bottom of it.

When she arrived, she spoke, "Hey."

"Hey," I responded. She sat on the swing next to me, and her sweet, subtle fragrance reminded my nostrils of breakfast—pancakes and syrup. I could see little dewy beads of moisture beginning to bubble up and slide down her neck and exposed shoulders. She looked like such a delicacy.

"Feeling better? Heard you were a little under the weather," I said.

"I'm feeling better."

"You look good."

"Thanks," she replied dryly.

"I meant that you don't look like you're sick."

"Oh . . . yeah . . . well, like I said, I'm feeling— . . ."

"Not that you're looking ugly or something . . ."—"

"No, I didn't take it that way . . ."—"

"I was just saying you didn't look like you felt bad, that's all," I said.

"I understand," she responded.

We shared a strong moment of quiet awkwardness, with the preposterous silence filling the universe. Unable to take the tension, I asked, "So what's going on?"

"What do you mean?"

"Oh, come on. You know and I both know that things have been different between us."

"I know."

"Ever since the layoff, we've been . . ."

"I know," she said.

"What's the problem?" I asked.

"This is becoming too complicated."

"What is?"

"This whole thing between you and me."

"Thing?"

"What do you want me to call it? I don't know what it is. I feel like I'm not myself when I'm around you. Like I'm in a dream or something, like this isn't real. How do you define something that isn't real?" she said.

"This is something real. As real as it gets. The definition? Love," I responded.

***

LOVE? HE LOVES ME?

"Don't . . . don't say that," I said.

"What else is it, Anne? What else can screw your head up like this?" he said.

I have no idea, but . . .

"This is not love."

"My head's screwed up too. I don't know if I'm coming or going, if I'm up or down. That's what love does . . ."

Very true, but . . .

"It's not love . . ."

"It fucks with your brain! Do you know how miserable I've been since the layoff?"

"Yes, I do. Trust me," I said.

"Well, not being able to talk to you, to touch you, to smell you is killing me. That's love, sweetheart, and I love you," he said.

"No, you don't."

"Yes, I do! You're all I think about, you're the person I want to be with . . ."—"

"I can't be with you!" I said exasperatedly as I stood up.

"Why not?"

"Because I love somebody else! I am engaged! Soon to be married! We both knew this when we started, but did that stop us? No. We can't control how we feel for each other, but what we did was wrong, Todd. It was wrong."

"So what? Are you telling me that we should deny our feelings?"

"That's exactly what we should do. For the good of everyone involved."

Good girl. Stay strong.

It's almost as if I could see the gravity of my words landing on the center of his chest, and he gasped from the impact. I quietly gasped also, most likely due to me being surprised at how confident those words sounded when they hit the air. Inside, I knew I was attempting to draw a line in quicksand; however, I was certainly not confident in that line remaining intact, no matter my resolve. I could even feel my faux foundation starting to crumble, but instead of sinking and exposing what was underneath, I quickly decided that my best defense was a strong offense, so I remained committed to propping myself up on my bruised yet unbroken mask.

I backed away as if I were tethered to him, creating space yet still revealing a real, live connection. Todd stood up, closed the space between us, and said, "I can't. I can't deny my feelings for you."

"Too many people will get hurt!" I rebutted.

"And what am I supposed to do? Spare everyone else so I can have all the pain and misery for myself?"

"You won't be alone in your pain," I admitted.

He suddenly grabbed me, held me close, and said, "Tell me you love me."

"I can't."

"Tell me."

"I can't, now let go!" I yelled, and he released me. We sat in silence for a moment, the both of us slightly shocked at his actions. I'd never seen him like that before, even at our most passionate, and I hated the fact that all of this was turning me on. It really pissed me off to know that no matter how hard I tried to deny my feelings, he would still have a hold on me. No matter if this was really love or not, I had to get away from this guy. He was my drug, and it was too dangerous for me to be around him.

"We have to stop, Todd. We just have to. I couldn't live with myself if we kept doing what we were doing. I've already asked Trent to give my wardrobe duties to Christian . . ."

"Hold it, wait a minute . . ."

"And I've asked to only ride in the cargo van while we're traveling . . ."

"Wait a second here . . ."

I could feel myself starting to tear up, but before I completely lost it, I quickly said, "I ask that you respect my requests as this is the only way I'll be able to finish out the last few weeks of the tour."

"Anne . . ."

"Goodbye, Todd," I said as I walked off, desperately trying to not let him see me cry. As soon as I turned around, however, there was a deluge.

"Anne! Anne!" I could hear him yelling my name as I got farther and farther from him, disappearing into the night. It wasn't long before his calls for me ceased and all I could hear was the sharp, rusty, sashay of the swings. The piercing screeches became louder than ever as both seats swung back and forth, empty.

27

It was early morning. The sun had barely broken the horizon, and the nighttime vermin were still at play, at least for a few more moments. Most of us were standing in front of the van, engaging in lighthearted dialogue as we awaited entry, our breath producing a smoky fog over the collective. I led the discussion, telling a rousing tale that had the cast's entire attention.

Todd, the last one to join the assembly, approached us and asked, "What's going on?"

"Sal lost the freaking keys," Molly responded.

"I did not lose the keys. I just can't remember where I put them," Salvador replied.

Molly transitioned into her no-nonsense demeanor and said, "He lost them."

"Trent went back to the office to see if he can get back into Sal's room. Wants to search it himself," Christian said.

"Typical," Todd said.

Eager to get back to my opus, I drew the attention back to myself.

"So, guys, guys, listen. When my friend came into the room and saw that my fiancé and I were naked, he stripped off all his clothes, picked up his phone, and started yelling, 'Threesome, threesome!'"

The cast laughed; however, I noticed Todd wasn't amused one bit. In fact, he looked disgusted—not at the fact that I was giddy about a threesome involving Brody and me, but at the fact that I was mentioning Brody at all, on that tour, in that sacred space.

The audacity. Fuck him and his silent tantrum. I am in control of this, not him.

"Can you believe that?" I asked the group.

"I'da done the same thing," Johnathon said.

"Ooh! We would've welcomed you in a heartbeat! A threesome with a hot rock star? Hell yeah!" I responded.

"Yeah right. You guys would make me hold the phone," Johnathon said.

"I'd let you hold anything you wanted, tiger," I responded.

The cast *ooh*ed as they instigated a growing fire. Johnathon was at a loss for words and was visibly taken back by my frankness. I knew in my heart Johnathon would never take me seriously. We barely had a meaningful conversation while on this tour. He seemed pretty cool, though. Why not have a little harmless fun?

Johnathon and I stood quietly for a few beats, examining the hunger in each other's eyes. I moved toward him, still eye-locked, and stood ever so close to him, so close to where we weren't chest to chest, but that I could feel him beginning to become erect. Slowly, very slowly, I leaned into him, toward his mouth, and Johnathon lifted his head and extended his neck.

Suddenly, I burst out laughing, just before our lips locked. "Ha! Ha! I had you! Ha! Ha!" I cackled.

"You sexy bitch!" Johnathon replied.

To the rest of the cast's delight, Johnathon began to chase me around the van. When he finally caught me, he threw me over his shoulder and began to spank my ass. I kicked my feet and laughed hysterically. Eventually, he put me down and commended me on my performance. "You had me all right!" he said.

I playfully bent over and protruded my ass toward him. "Again, Johnathon! Again! I like it rough!" I said.

"You little . . . " Johnathon grunted as he aggressively approached me again, but I jokingly halted his pursuit.

"No, no, no! I'm just kidding!" I said.

Johnathon settled for giving me a smothering kiss on the cheek and another smack on the bottom, to which I gave a small yelp and giggle. Everyone laughed. Well, not everyone.

Everybody thinks this is so fucking funny. I don't get it.

I was the only person in attendance who wasn't applauding this performance, my stomach gnarled by the display. How dare she taunt and tease me in front of my face! This was the ultimate level of disrespect, and admittedly, I felt shamed. I was now an outcast, and she'd chosen others to replace my position of "fool" in Anne's royal queendom. Quite frankly, I wasn't even sure if I wanted my spot back after experiencing what she'd just put me through.

The twisting continued later in the morning during load-in as I wheeled in the racked costumes with my new wardrobe partner, Christian. As I was on my way to the dressing room with my rack, I saw Anne chatting it up with Sal, Joey, and Leroy. I observed the multiple affectionate arm touches she gave to Sal, the inviting laughter she contributed to Joey's wisecracks, and the playful docility she demonstrated to Leroy's commands. It burned me to my core. I continued to watch as she eventually executed a group hug with her new cohorts. As I approached the dressing room, I heard her say, "I love you guys," and received a sharp pain in my side, the knot tightening to its capstone.

＊＊＊

JENNERSTOWN, PA

The piercing smell of Tabasco filled the bustling Hooters restaurant in the heart of this tiny mountain town. It was lunchtime, and the locals were filling their bellies with the finest hot, greasy chicken parts this establishment had ever produced. The snapping of the saturated appendages could be heard throughout the local hobnob, adding a necessary percussion to the great room's soundtrack.

One of the large-busted servers placed a large platter of hot wings on our table. All of the male eyes followed the perky server as she bopped and bounced away, toward the kitchen. Even Todd's eyes followed her, to my surprise. I admit I felt a slight pang of envy, but it barely registered.

"You sure you guys picked this place for the wings?" Sally asked.

"Who said that?" Leroy asked as he teared into a meaty drumette.

Molly hesitated a moment just to see if anyone was going to cop to this caper. When all was quiet, she began to blow the whistle. "Johnathon, Joey, Sal . . ."

"The real shocker here is that we believed them," I said.

"What are you talking about? This place has some of the best wings on the planet! Go 'head. Try one," Joey said.

"I've had their wings before, and trust me, they're not the greatest," Molly replied.

"That's because you're not considering what all goes into these wings," Johnathon responded.

"I'm sure presentation counts for a lot here," Sally said.

Johnathon thought about it a bit, then answered, "Yes, presentation does count for a lot at this establishment . . ."

"Uh-huh! . . ." Sally interjected.

". . . but that has nothing to do with it. It's all about the taste of the meat," Johnathon said.

"I'm sure you would like to taste some of the 'meat' in this fine establishment, but what we're talking about is poultry, jackass," I commented.

The table laughed as Johnathon bit all the flesh from a thick wingette and held it in his mouth like a Neanderthal in response to my jab. I laughed, then playfully pushed his face away from me as he continued to chomp. He ended the process with a hearty belch, firmly planting his masculinity flag, and leaving no doubt as to why this restaurant was chosen for dine-in.

Ha! This guy's a riot!

When the song on the electronic juke ended, a new one began to spin. I recognized it immediately and went into my own world. "Oh my God! This takes me back," I said. It was a song I discovered while in college, "Crazy Bitch" by Buckcherry.

The cast watched as I slowly became entranced by the music. In turn, my movements and chair dancing became increasingly seductive.

"Are you okay?" Salvador asked.

My hair flipped loosely over my face, creating a sexy mess. I bit my lip and said, "I have had A LOT of sex to this song."

"Ooookkkaaaayyyy," Molly responded.

"You guys don't understand. Every time I hear this song . . . it's just . . . oh my God . . ." I said.

"You're blushing, sweetie," Sally commented.

I got up from my seat and began to slowly dance with myself. While my specific attention to the music and my own body was hypnotizing me, I happened to snap out of the trance for a split second to read the mood of the table. I had all of the guys' attention, including Todd. This shot a warm current of electricity through my spine.

"Whoo! Do it, honey!" Sally encouraged.

Sally's whooping drew the attention of some of the customers in the area, and I was ignited even more by the random audience. All eyes were on me, and I was on fire—it showed in my face and hip gyrations.

As the crowd got more into it, I walked behind Johnathon's chair and began to perform a short striptease with him as the focus. I slipped off my shirt, wrapped it around his neck, and taunted him with my bra-clad bosom. I then used Salvador as my strip pole, seductively flicking my tongue out at him like a venomous viper trying to sniff its way toward its next meal. I eventually made my way around to all of the males in the cast and gave them an awe-inspiring tease—all of the males except Todd. I timed it so the song ran out before I could get to him; didn't want to make it so obvious, but I had no intentions of reigniting that flame again.

When the song concluded, the patrons erupted with applause. I took a bow, half-dressed, rejoined the table, and began to clothe myself. The bouncy server reapproached the table and asked, "Want a job, honey?"

All the cast members laughed and commended me on my performance—all the cast members except Todd.

Fuck him. I'm living my life, having fun. Fuck him.

***

I was hot, sweaty, and in desperate need of a shower. I'd started running again, something I missed during the first half of the tour. Running cleared my mind and kept me balanced. When I felt myself becoming a bit unhinged, it was normally a run that snapped me back into place, and I felt like I needed to take a long one after the shenanigans at the Hooters that day. I didn't know why I was acting out like that. A part of me said I was trying to protect myself by being wild; the other part said I was trying to cover up and deflect what was really going on inside of me. One thing I was certain of was that even with me experimenting a bit, I'd been more focused during this portion of the tour than I was before. I felt like I had a handle on things, like I was steering the ship instead of just being a passenger. And that was how I intended to keep it.

When I entered our hotel room, I headed straight for the shower and turned it on. Then I exited the bathroom, walked near my bed, and began to strip naked. If the girls walked in, I didn't care. I needed relief from this suffocating stickiness. I threw my soiled clothes on the floor and began to head back to the bathroom.

Before I could reach the bathroom's threshold, a note was shoved under the room door. The paper looked familiar—yellow legal pad. I got closer to it and saw that it had my name on it. I stood in my nakedness for a while, just staring at the folded piece of paper on the floor. After a while I could feel goose bumps starting to form on my body as it reacted to the cool air falling on my sweat-saturated skin.

I approached cautiously and picked up the note, unfolded it, and began to read. As I read, the steam from the shower began to slither underneath the bathroom door and fog up my surroundings.

I've tried it for two days. It sucks not being able to inhale. It's a frustrating suffocation. It's like I'm staring at the large oxygen tank and my lips cannot reach the mouthpiece. The air that I desperately desire to fill my lungs is unattainable. The more I drown aboveground, the more I long to take a breath.

I have no idea why I feel like I need air! I've gone without it for twenty-eight years. Twenty-eight years without this breezy vapor, and now I crave it; I don't want to be without it. Not only do I want to breathe it, I want it to surround me at all times, never leaving my side. Blowing me hard, blowing me gently, a constant force I could spend time with and play with. I'd converse with it all day as it made its way through the trees and around the sharp corners of castles.

I envy surfaces when I see others breathing freely and I cannot. Why should they get to and I cannot? Because if I were to take one breath, not one, but two people would suddenly have new life? Because others would suffocate if I inhaled? Why must I be the sacrifice? Is this pain or pleasure? Is this euphoria I

feel from being afloat in the wind or is it because my brain is oxygen deprived?

My homeostasis depends on my intake and release of this necessary propellant.

My mind was stuck on it all day today, proving to be a distraction as I

played to the house. The air was amazing in there, but I just couldn't take it in. I

tried to ignore it, but it stayed on my mind as my windpipe continued to shrivel.

The resuscitator takes pleasure in not giving me what I need. The

machine loves the fact that I want what it's able to give, so it takes pride in leaving

me without. All it has to do is turn the switch and release me from this

frustration and agony. However, it seems as if the switch has been broken off

and placed in the pocket of someone who breathes at will, yawning until their eyes

water. Meanwhile, I'm turning blue.

I folded the note closed and sat down on the bed,

exasperated. With Todd's voice still ringing in my ears, I heard a soft

rumble of thunder outside my window.

28

Loud cackles and rousing conversation emitted from room 319 at the Jennerstown Red Roof Inn. I knocked on the door and heard Christian yell from the inside, "It's open!" I pushed the door open, stepped out of the rain to enter the room, and was greeted enthusiastically by Sally, "Yay, Anne! You made it!"

Joey, Christian, Salvador, Sally, and Johnathon were participating in an abridged poker night. They'd pushed the twin beds as far apart as they could and set up a crude table, one with one leg shorter than the rest, in the center of the room for the action. The jovial cast members were seated comfortably around the uneven stand, their laps shielded from the room's illumination. A torn pack of imported beer sat on a nearby shelf, and bottles were scattered all over the dwelling.

"I couldn't miss it. We only have time for a few more poker nights, and I'm trying to recoup my losses," I said.

"Good luck. With the pigtailed card shark sitting over there . . ." Salvador said as he motioned toward Sally as she ran her fingers through her mountain of unstacked chips and Christian shuffled for a new game.

"I swear I don't know what I'm doing," Sally responded as the rest of the poker players let out a disbelieving groan. "I'm serious! This is like my first time playing!" Still not buying it, the players gave her a look, and she said, "Okay, maybe second."

"We're lucky to leave here with our shirts," Salvador continued.

"I'm just taking advantage of what's being given to me," Sally responded.

"Sounds like that's a common practice for you," Joey remarked.

If Sally felt the sting of Joey's intentional words and sarcastic tone, no one would know, as she masked it. She then calmly and coolly turned her attention back to the game.

"You in on this one?" Christian asked me as he continued to shuffle.

"Yeah," I responded.

"Okay. You know the game. Texas Hold 'Em. Deuces wild. Got it?" Christian said.

"Got it."

The door of the room swung open and a confident "Deal me in" was heard. All of us looked over and saw Todd standing in the doorway with falling rain and flashes of lightning following behind him. He was strong and virile in his stance, his masculinity radiating off of him. I was turned on immediately, extending my hatred for biology.

"Sure! The more the merrier. Have a seat," Christian said.

Todd sat next to me. The close proximity of the players forced our legs to touch, Todd's outer thigh pressed against mine. Heat.

As Christian began to deal, Sally asked, "Say, has Trent ever told y'all about his 'experience' with the opposite sex?"

"Don't even try it. We're not falling for it this time, sweetie," Salvador said.

"Seriously! He told me one time when I rode with him in the cargo van. Said it changed him forever," Sally responded.

"Ooh! I wanna hear this," Molly said.

"We're in the middle of something here!" Christian objected.

Molly and Johnathon both cooled Christian's jets and told him the game could wait. "It's your money," Christian said as he dropped the cards on the table and sighed deeply.

We all leaned in to hear Sally's account. With the drenching cloud burst, crackled thunder, and bright flashes of lightning happening outside, it was almost like she was telling a ghost story.

"So, I'm quietly riding shotgun, reading a book and whatnot, when all of a sudden he bursts out, 'Ever been in love?' I said, 'Hell yeah, I been in mud. Ever try to wrangle a hog back to its stable in a downpour? Can't help but get muddy.' Boy, did I feel like an idiot when he repeated himself louder. I also felt like I didn't want to have this kind of conversation with him, if you know what I mean. But I obliged and said yes. He said, 'It hurt, didn't it?' I said, 'Yeah, but how do you know it's love if it don't hurt sometimes?' . . ."

The sticky moisture began to build up where Todd's leg and mine were in contact. I pulled my leg away and felt the perspiration separate like a water-based glue. A cool breeze blew through and soothed the formerly engaged area.

Todd then put his hand on my leg underneath the table. I was startled and uncomfortable, but for some reason, I didn't pull away immediately. I let it sit there for a few moments and enjoyed the hate in its burn. Eventually, I pushed his hand off of me.

". . . he agreed with me and went on to tell me about his first and only love of his life, a lovely young lady appropriately named Sally."

"No way!" Salvador said.

"Yes way! Her name was Sally, and he adored her. He wrote her a letter every morning telling her exactly what he appreciated about her. Some letters would be one-liners: 'Your smell ignites me,' or 'The curve of your back is divine.' At the end of the year, Miss Sally had three hundred sixty-five reasons why she had his fancy. He said she was tickled pink by his letters of appreciation . . ."

I could feel Todd's hand creeping back into position on my leg. Again, I hesitated, and in that moment of indecision, his hand began to slowly move up my thigh.

Oh Christ.

". . . so much so that she started leaving him complimentary letters. Hers weren't as frequent as his, but she'd pen about half of his total output when things were said and done. She was in love with him as much as he was with her, and a book of evidence written by their own hands provided the proof."

"Sounds like she loved him half as much, according to the letters," Molly commented.

I didn't stop Todd's advance. I rebelliously wanted to see how far he was going to go literally and figuratively. I was being bold in my bluff, and selfish in my dominance. Admittedly, deep inside, I wanted him to touch me, badly. I'd wanted it since I saw him after the break, after I'd mentally put the brakes on our relationship. But this wasn't about that. My letting Todd's hand wander was about me seeing how badly Todd wanted to touch me. So I didn't stop him. I let his hand slide all the way to my pleasure point.

When his fingertips grazed it, I shivered noticeably and immediately rethought my boldness.

Oh Christ, no, no, no! Don't get started, Lamberty. Shut it down, NOW.

I could hear myself loud and clear; however, I let his hand play there for a few seconds and enjoyed the fantastic sensations crackling through me, almost like a Fourth of July sparkler. I pushed his hand away when I could feel myself getting too hot.

"He knew this. He knew it from the very beginning, but he was content with simply loving her. Even if she loved him just a tiny little bit, and she loved him more than that, but if it was only a fraction of love, he'd continue to overflow his affection, his admiration, his love on her. 'I only know one way to love,' he says to me . . ."

Todd revisited the well again. This time, I put up some resistance in the beginning, but I eventually gave in, holding and pressing his hand into the desired spot.

Fuck my life for missing him for weeks. Fuck me for loving how he touches me. Fuck me for needing this.

The danger and excitement of this stealthy act seemed to add to both of our intensities. To my knowledge, no one had a clue as to the happenings underneath the table but Todd and I, and we both were reveling in this public act of controlled, contained decadence.

". . . and in the same breath, he says, 'I also only know one way to hate.' He had some disdain in his voice when he said that. I wanted to, but I didn't say nothin'. I just let him go on. He went on to say that eventually, the notes from her got further and further apart from one another, then stopped coming all together. 'It dried up,' he said. 'I loved her more than anyone ever will, more than anything, but she didn't love me anymore,' he told me. When he asked her why, she said she couldn't breathe. He'd smothered her . . ." Sally continued.

I bit my lip and fingers as I twitched and shifted in my seat. I looked at Todd's face, and his demeanor was as cool as ice as his hand flipped, teased, and caressed me. He smiled at me devilishly. I couldn't smile back. All I could do was close my eyes.

"'How can you love somebody too much?'" he asked me. I told him there's a give and take. It can't be lopsided. 'Again,' he said, 'that's the only way I know.' He looked so confused. It was like this just happened."

"Did he say when?" Johnathon asked.

Uncontrollably, I expelled a nasally-charged grunt, then immediately bowed my head in an attempt to hide the tension and pleasure that had been smeared on my face. The rest of the cast barely noticed it.

"This was like fifteen years ago!" Sally answered.

"Fifteen years? And he still hasn't gotten over this?" Molly asked.

"Obviously not. At least we know how the Evil Empire was created," Sally said.

"You've gotta be some kind of fucking monster to poke fun at somebody who gave their heart to someone who didn't want it. A fucking monster!" Joey snapped back.

"I wasn't trying to make fun of him. I actually feel sorry for him, for how he turned out."

I let another grunt slip out, and my breathing intensified.

Do the others have any idea what he's doing to me? That I'm about to burst? I HATE this, but I can't resist. I need it, but don't want it. I can't let this happen. I just can't.

Molly noticed my severely flushed complexion and asked me if I was okay. I subtly tried to push Todd's hand from me, but he resisted and I couldn't overpower him. "I'm fine . . . got a little head rush, that's all," I said to Molly.

"Don't feel sorry for him. I'm sure he lives a wonderful life," Joey responded to Sally.

"According to who?" Sally said.

"According to him!"

"He still hasn't gotten past this. Fifteen years later, and he's still affected. This changed him, and not for the better."

"Well, what the hell do you expect? That kind of thing changes a person! Some people aren't casual with their feelings. Some people mean what they say. Some people throw themselves out there only to learn that what they thought was real was only a farce. That shit hurts. You wouldn't be the same if that happened to you too!" Joey stated.

The resisting tension in my arm slowly loosened as I gave in to my carnal urges and pushed Todd's hand deeper into my tender cavity. I felt alive again. My brain had been reconnected to my body, and all the nerves, synapses, and neurons were firing so fast I rejoined the metaphysical. I was glad to be back, to have this feeling again, but I knew I couldn't stay. I had to come back to reality. I just had to.

"I know it hurts, but life does eventually go on. It has to. Or else you'll still be pining over things that happened ten, twenty, thirty years ago," Sally said to Joey.

"I guess all of us are not as callous as you," he responded.

"What the hell is that supposed to mean?"

Oh my God, he's, he's gonna make me . . .

I squirmed and slammed my hand on the table, jostling the chips a bit. "Oh shit. Stop, stop . . ." I softly pleaded.

"You know what the hell I mean . . ." Joey said to Sally.

"Stop it . . ." I said louder.

"No, I don't. Why don't you tell me, Joey? What exactly do you mean when you say I'm callous?"

"Stop it . . ." I said even louder.

"Just think about it. I'm sure you'll figure it out . . ."

"No, I want you to tell me. Right here, right now, face-to-face!"

"I would, but I honestly can't stand to look at you!" Joey says as he stood up from the table and began to walk out of the room.

"STOP IT!" I shrieked as I leapt from my chair.

Everyone froze. After a moment of tense silence, Leroy burst into the room holding a half-empty bottle of Jack Daniel's and singing, "One! Singular sensation, every little step she takes! . . ."

Eventually he noticed the vibe in the room, realized something was wrong, and stopped singing. He took some time to survey everyone's faces, opened the door wide to invite in the shooting precipitation, and said, "You don't like that one? How 'bout this: I'm singing in the rain, just singing in the rain! What a glorious feeling . . ."

Embarrassed and feeling like all eyes were on me, even as they were clearly on Leroy, I pushed past him and bolted out of the room into the thickening tempest. As I ran off into the night, I could hear all of the cast calling for me. I heard Todd's voice over all of them, and eventually, his voice was the only one I heard as I continued to run through the pounding rain.

29

The Red Roof Inn was rocking. As on every Thursday night, a local band graced the small raised stage in the bar and lounge area, allowing patrons to shake off and expel the troubles of the work week before the weekend arrived. It was a much-needed release, and the hardworking locals in town came out in droves to get what they needed. Alcohol and music: it was their religion.

As the band pumped to a fast and hard punk rhythm, Joey, Christian, and I stepped up to the bar and placed an order for drinks. When the cute, friendly bartender picked up a few glasses and began to swirl the bitter elixir into their voids, Joey asked Christian, "So who won?"

"Sally cleaned us out. I'd hoped your little display would've distracted her or something, but nope. She was even more dialed in after you walked out. The whole thing took about thirty minutes. By the way, I thought you were going to keep things civil with her," Christian responded.

"Yeah, well, I guess it didn't work out that way. You know I can't stand hypocrites."

"I just don't want this to turn into some kind of war zone in the last two weeks."

I've got enough to worry about with Salvador and Molly. With how psycho they are, I should be filling out a union report on them every day. There haven't been any serious incidents so far, so as far as I'm concerned, we're ahead of the game. But after hearing you two back there, I must say, I'm pretty worried."

"Ah, no need to worry. Everything's all right."

"Is it?"

"Everything's fine. Come on. Believe me, you won't have to write me up for anything. It's done," Joey said.

The bartender emerged and brought us a round of nine shots. Christian paid for the shots, then we gathered up the small treasures and walked them over to a table occupied by Leroy, Molly, and Johnathon. I held on to my shot and immediately put it to my lips when the other glasses were placed on the table.

"Whoa, whoa, whoa! Can we get a toast in before you inhale that, Tex?" Christian asked.

When Joey placed a shot in front of Leroy, Leroy stopped him, swirled his three-fourths-empty bottle of Jack Daniel's in Joey's face, and said, "Thank you, but I've got my own."

Once everyone had a shot, we collectively raised them; however, there were three shots left on the table. Leroy noticed and said, "Wait a minute, where's Salvador, Anne, Sally?"

"Don't know if Sally's coming down," Molly responded. She put her fingers to her lips as if she were smoking a joint, and continued, "Anne and Sal. They'll be back soon."

"And they didn't invite us? I'm appalled," Leroy said through a chuckle.

I couldn't wait any longer. I downed my shot and forcibly slammed the glass on the table. "Wow. Okay," Christian said as he raised his glass. "To our health."

"To the tour!" Leroy said.

The rest of the cast gave a collective "To the tour!" chant, then clinked glasses and downed their shots. All but Molly reacted to the robust, one-hundred-proof intoxicant. "You guys are lightweights," she commented.

I headed back to the bar, and this time, I asked for a bottle.

***

The night continued to move at a fast pace, its dial being pushed ahead by the hard and fast tempo of the onstage band. Salvador, Johnathon, Molly, Christian, and Leroy were all dancing up a storm as the band pumped out a strong cover to "Whole Lotta Love" by Led Zeppelin. Anne had finally joined us, but she was high as a kite and completely out of control. I'd never seen her like this, and I didn't like it. Quite frankly, I was disgusted. It was like she was a totally different person. That being said, something inside wouldn't allow me to just let her go buck and not keep a protective eye on her, so I stayed close, and monitored the goings-on around her just in case.

I watched her approach an older seedy-looking man at the bar, with an unlit cancer stick dangling from her lips. "Got a light?" she asked him.

"For a beautiful lady like you?" the seedy man responded with his gravelly voice.

He was drunk out of his mind and looked like he reeked of alcohol and cigarette smoke. I secretly bet myself that the hottest fireball imaginable would ignite if a match was struck during one of his heavy exhales. I continued to observe as he took out his worn lighter and lit her up.

Anne thanked him, then turned toward the dance floor and applauded the wild moves from her castmates.

"Woo-hoo!" she screamed.

"What are you drinking?" the seedy man yelled at her through the music.

"Whatever you're buying, sugar," Anne replied. While the man ordered, she took another peek back at her castmates cutting a rug and yelled, "Whoo! You guys rock! Yeah!"

"Here you go, sweetheart," he said as he handed her a whiskey on the rocks.

"Thank you again, sweetheart," she said with a wink.

As I hovered near the bar, Joey joined me and also began to peek in on Anne and her new friend. We exchanged knowing looks, but didn't speak a word.

"So what's your name?" the seedy man asked.

"Anne."

"New in town, Miss Anne?"

"Just passing through, baby, just passing through."

"Well, that could be a good thing or a bad thing for the both of us, depending on how we play it." The man showed his scummy gums as he displayed the smile of a classic slickster. He also began to rub his hand over Anne's hip and ass while she took down her drink

in one gulp. A strong strand of fire streaked through my chest cavity.

"You're cute. Come on. You've gotta meet my friends," Anne

said.

Anne grabbed his arm and pulled him toward the dance floor.

I moved with them and left Joey at the bar. The rest of the cast was

now directly in front of the stage and were having an absolute ball.

Anne introduced her new friend to the cast, and they all began to

rock out with one another.

The older man was having trouble keeping up with everything

except his groping techniques, horrendously feeling Anne up every

chance he got, and every time he did, I felt my heart swell and my

breathing speed up. Anne didn't seem to mind this guy's hands-on

approach as she continued to dance close on him, her alcohol,

tobacco, and herb-tainted breath further intoxicating her partner.

None of the cast members on the dance floor were paying much

attention to her and her perverted partner as they were in their own

worlds, getting into the music and the electricity flowing throughout

the robust crowd. However, for reasons I couldn't seem to explain or talk myself out of, I diligently continued to keep watch over the situation from afar.

The extended cover of the song seemed to last forever, with the tempo dipping from fast to slow, and back to fast again. All of the people on the dance floor were sweating furiously. At one point, Anne took off her shirt and began twirling it around in the air. The fact that Anne was down to a swimsuit-type bra was an even further catalyst for the old man, as he touched and squeezed her breasts with more fervor. Anne didn't stop him. I moved in closer.

The song came to a rough, pounding end, with the man and Anne dry-humping each other until the song finally concluded with the crowd yelling their appreciation to the band. As Anne screamed wildly and jumped for joy, she caught the lead guitarist's eye as evidenced by him pointing toward her and giving her a round of applause. Immediately, she reached for the hooks on her bra, unclipped them, threw her bra at him, and blew him a kiss. He delightfully picked it up, showed the crowd, and they went wild. The guitarist then stepped to a microphone, pointed Anne out, and said, "Everyone give it up for the wildest bitch out here tonight!"

A spotlight was placed on Anne. Bare-chested and out of her

mind, she continued to leap and scream as the crowd went insane

with hoots and hollers. Even in the white-hot spotlight, the older

man could not bring himself to take his hands off of her. He cupped

her naked breasts from behind with his palms as she simply shot her

arms straight up into the air and screamed like a banshee.

That was the last straw. I began to push my way through the

crowd to get to her. As I did so, I could see that finally, finally, the

rest of the cast members were starting to get concerned for Anne's

welfare. They tried to convince her to put her shirt on, but before

they could get through to her, I made my way to her, snatched her by

the arm, and dragged her outside. I could hear the band and crowd

booing my actions, but to hell with them. I continued my trek,

unbothered by the response of the crowd, and even cursed out a few

of the patrons and some of my castmates on my way out. Their

venom didn't last long. The band quickly struck up another cover off

of their playlist, and the crowd began rocking once again, completely

oblivious to what just happened. Just before we exited the lounge area, I glanced back at the crowd and saw the rest of the cast watching us, shocked.

***

Once out into the night, Todd flung me to the damp ground. The heavy rain continued to fall, saturating the entire area, and soaking both of us instantly. He paced back and forth near me. The sound of his feet squishing into the muddy soil complemented the muffled sound of the band, which could still be heard inside the lounge.

"What the fuck are you doing? What the fuck is wrong with you?" he shouted.

"What the fuck is wrong with me? What the fuck is wrong with you, throwing me down like that? You can't fucking do that to me!" I screamed as I struggled to put my shirt back on.

"I don't know who you are anymore. You're out here smokin', drinkin'. Lettin' some old pervert feel you up. What the fuck's going on with you?"

"Don't worry about it! Why are you worried about it? What? Do you think you're my father or something?"

"I bet if I were your father, you wouldn't be as fucked up as you are now."

"Oh, you'd be great as my dad. A father who constantly wants to fuck his daughter. No, I couldn't possibly develop any problems from that kind of relationship."

"What is it? You don't care about yourself or something?"

Johnathon walked into the area and asked, "Is everything all right out here?"

"Go back inside, man. Everything is fine. GO!" Todd responded. Johnathon looked at me for a moment, then complied.

"Is that what this is? Some kind of punishment for yourself?" Todd asked.

"Fuck you!"

"I'm asking you. Are you punishing yourself for what happened earlier? For what we did?"

I aggressively approached him, punched him repeatedly, and said, "It's not just about what happened earlier! Everything we've done has been wrong. WRONG, WRONG, WRONG! I didn't want to do any of it! I didn't! You made me! You made me, goddamn you!"

Todd did his best to block my drunken onslaught, but he was unsuccessful, as he was unable to gain his balance on the soupy terrain. He took a few solid shots to the face before he was able to respond with, "You wanted it too! You didn't stop me. When you tried to resist, you couldn't because you wanted it just as bad as I did. Even more, remember?"

I quickly ran out of gas. Exhausted, I fell to my knees in the slop. The splash from the mud leapt up and splattered onto my shirt and face. Soaked to the bone, broken, and soiled, I looked up at him and said, "I can't stand you. I am literally sick to my stomach thinking about the things I did with you. I never want you to touch me again."

"You don't mean that."

"The hell I don't! NEVER TOUCH ME AGAIN! I hope you go to hell for what you've done to me."

"You don't mean that," he said as he approached me.

"The hell I don't! NOW GET THE HELL AWAY FROM ME! LEAVE ME ALONE!"

Todd stopped his approach, then said, "You know how I feel about you . . ."

"Doesn't matter. I love my fiancé—MY FIANCÉ, TODD! Us, you, me . . . we're done, so STAY THE FUCK OUTTA MY LIFE!"

I get myself to my feet, then began to run away.

Gotta get there.

Gotta keep going.

Please, God, let me get there.

I rounded a secluded corner, but before I could get too far, I slowed my sprint to a jog, then stopped. I put my hands over my face as I was sobbing uncontrollably. As I wailed, I heard Todd approaching. The quick-tempo splashes from his feet landing in shallow puddles of water sounded like ocean waves breaking on the shore. When he saw me, looking like a wet, distraught mess, he walked to me slowly and gave me the most tender hug I'd ever experienced. At first, I tried to pull away, but eventually I melted into his strong, safe arms.

"I'm sorry," he said.

Something about his apology opened me up. Maybe it was the way he said it or how it felt being whispered into my ear, but I could feel the vise grip around my brain unlock, and the barriers I'd intentionally erected recede a bit. I pulled away, and we locked gazes. His eyes burned through the rain like lasers, and when he stared into my eyes, I could feel him inspecting my innermost wants and desires. This only made my self-imposed barricades lower even further, unwantedly revealing even more of myself to him. It was like I was under a spell. I didn't want to, but something was pulling me toward him—something strong, something undeniable.

He leaned in and kissed me. His smooth, wet lips sent shock waves and chaos through my system as an internal battle was sparked. I didn't want this, but I did. I couldn't control myself. I rode the wave of his momentum, and returned the favor, kissing him gingerly at first, then more passionately. I continued to internally struggle against his advances, but I never verbalized my displeasure, even though my mind screamed in protest. By the time he spun me around and pressed my body and face against the cold, wet surface, I could feel myself beginning to show signs of raw, primal enjoyment amidst deep regret. I knew what was coming, and I loved it, yet I hated myself for feeling this way. It was almost an out-of-body experience, but the deep pleasure I felt in all of the physicality kept me tethered to my temple. I wished I could get away, however deep down I wanted to feel every bit of this, so I let myself fly, but just above the ground.

I felt my skirt being lifted and my panties being torn from my waist, and with a push, my insides enveloped him, sending splintering sensations from my eyelashes to my toenails. I held on for dear life as he pounded me hard, very hard, as hard as the rain. Even though I was drunk, I felt everything. My senses were so acute that each drop of precipitation felt like a sledgehammer on my skin. I felt like I was being pulverized all over.

We were also loud, very loud—as loud as the thumping music from inside the hotel that was vibrating the outer walls and the smashing thunder overhead. It was as if all of our inhibitions had been stripped away, and we were two animals in the bush, thrashing, and screaming our God-given urges into submission as the rain continued to slap the ground with untempered rage.

Soaked in heaven's tears, we continued until we experienced a simultaneous explosion. I had multiple. Much to my dismay, I thoroughly enjoyed it. I took a few moments to revel in the aftershock, the heavenly tremors taking me beyond the mystical clouds and fields of the loftiest portion of my imagination.

When I finally woke from my flight, I snapped. I pushed myself away from the wall and began to attack Todd in a fit of rage. I screamed my throat raw, and struck him over and over again until Todd pushed me off of him. We stared at each other, spent, and out of breath. He looked confused and surprised at what just happened, then sat down on the ground and hung his head. While I understood, I had no sympathy for him, or me. I watched as he sat in the shit; the rapidly growing pool of sludge seemed to encompass his entire body, inside and out. He covered his face and continued to soak. Broken, bruised, and satisfied, I walked off into the night.

All I could see was darkness, blackness all around. I was aware of almost everything else; I could feel the rain pelting on my face, I could hear cars passing, and I could taste and smell vomit, but I just couldn't see.

In the distance, I could hear someone saying something, but it wasn't clear. I moved my eyes around to try to see where the sound was coming from, but all I was met with was a void. Fortunately, the voice was getting closer, and I was starting to make it out . . ."Hello? Hello? Oh my God, Anne! Are you okay?"

The voice was right on top of me, and I could tell it was Molly. I could feel her hands. She rubbed my head and shook me at the shoulders.

"Christ, Anne, wake up! Open your fucking eyes!"

I struggled to lift my lids, but it wasn't working.

"Jesus. Help! Help! Come on, Anne, for fuck's sake!"

I continued to move my eyes around with the hopes of signaling to Molly that I could hear her and that I was making an attempt to be responsive. Hearing her panic was causing me to panic internally, and I didn't want to put either of us under any more stress. I fought with my eyes until they hurt. I begged and pleaded with them to open and strained my optic nerves until they almost burst from all of the rapid movement I was attempting to create.

Eventually, I could feel my lids slowly peel open slightly, but I still couldn't see anything. A minuscule sense of relief pinged me when I heard Molly say, "Anne! There you are! Can you hear me?"

I placed my last ounce of strength into my eyes and felt them drop into place from being rolled toward the back of my head. Finally, I could see colors and shapes, although blurry. I could make out the shape of Molly's face and her thick, wet hair as it dangled on my forehead.

"Hey, hey. Are you okay?" she said as my vision finally came into focus.

I couldn't really talk, but I mumbled something, looked down at myself, and realized that I was a complete mess. I was sprawled out in the parking lot, half-naked and covered in mud and vomit. Molly sat me up, then slapped my face a few times before I fully regained consciousness. When I did, I peered at Molly with a look of pure desperation. I needed her help. More than that, I needed a friend, any friend. Molly carefully stood me up, walked me to our room, and we entered.

***

Molly sat me down, and ran me a warm bath, being extra careful not to get the water too hot. She also added some of her Champneys bubble bath to the water, filling the room with the fragrant smell of Citrus Blush. The steam from the water seemed to stimulate the effervescence of the fragrance, providing the effect of a subtle smelling salt upon my entry to the bathroom.

I sat in the tub and almost immediately began quivering and crying when she started washing my back with a large sponge. She cleaned all the mud from my face and body, and also ran a thick, lathery shampoo through my hair with her fingers. All while grooming me, she gently hummed a soft tune. The song proved to be the antidote for my quivering, as I calmed down during the second stanza.

"Close your eyes," Molly whispered to me before she cupped her hands, dipped them into the tub, and poured the water over my head, washing out the shampoo. The rushing water running through all the strands of my hair and the warm pressure being placed on the crown of my head provided me with a release like no other. It was almost as if the vise that had my brain and emotions in its steel grip for the past four months had just been loosened, and I was allowed to expand. I was able to allow other possibilities, other scenarios, in, and I was able to process those scenarios with the full capacity of my intellect. I could clearly see who I was in that moment and all the circumstances, choices, and decisions that got me to that very moment; from as far back as I could remember, to sitting in this murky-watered bathtub.

Once confronted with the totality of my life's blueprint to date, I decided right then and there to make a choice, a choice that would change how my life would be governed and lived from there on out. Once my decision was made, and once I assured myself that this was the correct choice, all of my turmoil, strife, and misgivings were washed away, just like the shampoo in my hair. Finally, I was clean, free from the soot. That baptism changed me, and I was eternally grateful.

Molly stepped me out of the bathtub, then took extra care in drying me off. She patted and softly whisked the towel over every inch of my skin; every fold, pocket, and crevice was comforted with the warm, plush towel.

After I was dried and dressed, Molly walked me to my bed, lifted the covers, and I slid in. Molly slid in behind me, spooned me, and began to hum the same calming agent she used in the bathroom. She also softly stroked my hair while humming her melody.

Amazingly, Sally, who'd been sleeping in the other double bed, awakened for the first time and witnessed us. With a look of contentment, she rolled back over and fell back to sleep. It was almost as if Sally and I drifted deeper into our slumbers on account of Molly's sweet lullaby. Eventually, Molly sang herself to sleep as well.

30

Sunshine cracked the horizon. The birds cheerfully greeted the long-lost golden dollop with healthy, loud chirps of optimism and appreciation. As the dawn broke, and the dew settled, remnants of the previous night's activity became visible to the onlooker. Torn branches, loose papers, shingles thrown askew, and puddles, endless puddles, littered the earth, a testament to the unmovable force.

Inside the hotel, Sally and I were packing up our things. Both of us were groggy and sore from the night before. We moved extremely slowly and carefully, lifting and pulling items toward our suitcases with the utmost care and gentleness.

Like a quick burst of light, Molly entered from outside holding two cups of coffee. "For both of you," she said as she placed the cups on top of the television. Both Sally and I wearily thanked her for the gesture, then Sally closed her suitcase, grabbed her coffee, and wheeled her bag toward the door. Molly held the door for her as she exited the room. "You've got like five minutes before the emperor comes a-callin'," Molly said to me.

"I won't be much longer," I responded. Molly began to exit, but before she did, I said, "Hey Molly, wait a sec." Hearing the sincerity in my voice, Molly reentered the room and closed the door behind her. I took a moment to gather myself, then said, "Last night . . ."

"Don't mention it, kid," Molly interjected.

"No, really, Molly . . ."

"I know. Don't worry about it."

"That's the worst I've ever been."

Molly handed me the cup of joe from the top of the television set. "Drink it." I took the cup and sipped the steaming concoction.

"You mustn't lose yourself, Anne, no matter how crazy things get. Things can get pretty confusing out here. You can start seeing and believing things that aren't real, and it'll hurt like hell when you get back to reality, believe me. These kinds of tours are the ultimate magic trick: a magic trick for the blind. They create mirages for those who can't see where they're going. That's why you must always keep your head. You get too far away from yourself out here, and you won't return the same. All you got is what you've got, and you can't lose that."

"Don't know what I've got. Don't know if I've ever known," I replied.

Molly gave me a sympathetic hug as I shed a tear. Through our embrace, we fully and completely understood each other's pain. Molly stayed in her supportive state for a few seconds, then quickly inhaled her warming rays and snapped back to her icy demeanor.

"Now get a move on or you'll make us late," she said, then left the room, closing the door behind her. I cleaned myself up, finished packing my bags, and exited the room as well.

***

WILMINGTON, DE

The performance at Concord High was one of our best on the tour. The audience was extremely energetic and engaged as we belted out our scenes. Trent was especially pleased at how timely the operation was and that the load-in and -out were extremely efficient.

While our performances were on a higher level, Todd and I continued to be tormented by what occurred the previous night. We worked individually during load-in and load-out, and when we did happen to glance at each other, our eye locks were cold and stale. It was clear that we both were wounded from what transpired, and we avoided each other at all costs, intentionally walking in opposite directions when we saw the other approaching, and sitting as far as we could from each other at lunch and while traveling in the van. I'm certain we were both extremely relieved when we were finally finished with our duties and got to be away from the group, free to have personal time to ourselves. I know I was.

When I got some alone time in my hotel room, I called Brody. I felt so far away from everything, so far away from myself, that I longed to hear his voice and feel that type of familiarity again. I longed to be home.

We stayed on the phone for over two hours, the longest we'd ever had a phone conversation. The topics ranged from new happenings to the seven pounds our cat had gained since I'd left. There were also several significant instances when we both said nothing; we just listened to each other breathe, and enjoyed picking up whatever audible occurrences that took place in our separate universes. I never mentioned what happened the night before or the events that led up to the explosion. I figured confessions could come later, if ever. Right now, I just wanted the comfort of his voice, the comfort of him. When all was said, and we'd run out of dead air, I ended the call with, "Can't wait to see you. I miss you so much. I love you."

∗

I arrived back in my hotel room after a brisk nighttime workout, a much-needed stress reliever. Hadn't had the time or the facilities for a good pump of the iron, so when the opportunity presented itself, I took full advantage. It was like a gift from God.

Exhausted, I took my keys and cell phone out of my pocket, put them on an end table, then took off my sweaty shirt and walked to the bathroom. When I turned on the shower, my phone began to vibrate against the hardwood, then I exited the bathroom for closer inspection.

I picked up the phone, checked the caller ID, then hesitated. The buzzing continued in my hand as I contemplated answering. It seemed like an eternity elapsed before I tapped the screen to accept the call; however, I didn't immediately put the phone to my ear. I stood frozen for a moment, suspended in equilibrium. After a few seconds, I lifted the phone to my ear and said, "Hey, Toni."

31

KUTZTOWN, PA

I'd been wanting to go for a swim for some time now.

Outside of running, it was one of my favorite things to do away from

the stage. It cleared my mind, and allowed for the very rare instance

of me being fully focused on myself. It was me and me alone that

kept me afloat, and if I faltered, I'd succumb to the undertow.

I really missed the benefits of that release and internal focus

those past few months as I hadn't been in a position to totally

immerse myself in a large body of nature's life source since we'd started out on the road. Thus, when I found out that the rare Red Roof Inn we were visiting that night had an Olympic-sized pool within its confines, my pores leapt with excitement.

When I entered the warm, chlorine-essenced aquatic center, the smell alone put me at ease. A smile came to my face as I walked toward the long liquid cube, as I'd been dying to drown my stress in the bleached drink. I teased myself a bit by gliding a foot across the skin of the thick drip, setting off a massive wrinkle that swirled to the edge. Satisfied, I gratefully began to disrobe, then heard someone say, "Still frigid?"

I turned around to see Todd sitting nearby in a churning Jacuzzi. Tension began to rapidly overpower the tranquility I'd felt upon entering my place of peace. I closed the robe back over my swimsuit and said, "It's warm now."

"Good," he responded.

I looked back to the water and tried to find my center again as we shared a moment of severely uncomfortable silence. I knew I should have probably left as I knew he didn't want to talk about it— hell, neither did I. If I did leave then, though, it would emphasize that

something was wrong, and he'd most likely want to talk about it later.
I mean, I'm sure he knew something was wrong, and probably didn't
feel good about what had happened, so I didn't want to call attention
to it; it had happened, and we should just leave it at that. I was
embarrassed, yes, frustrated, and a little afraid, but I was just ready
for all of this to end. I was spent. I didn't have the energy for
anything else but getting in this water and floating my stresses away.

"How are you?" Todd asked.

"Good. Been better."

"Same here. It's been . . . different."

"Yeah. Different. I've hated it," I admitted.

"Me too, but I've accepted it," Todd replied.

"Me too."

"Kinda glad it'll all be over tomorrow."

"Yeah. All over," I said, the calm shrouding back over me. I
sat and let my feet sink into the drink.

"Know what you're doing after this?" I asked.

"I have nothing lined up. You?"

"I've got a couple of plays I've wanted to get up for a while. Figure I'll get started making some headway."

I took a moment to look at Todd's beautiful eyes, the first time I'd really taken a hard look at him since the incident. Ah, those eyes. They could start or stop wars. I lingered for a little, then smiled and said sincerely, "I'm sure they'll be wonderful."

Todd smiled back and responded, "Thank you. I'll keep you in mind for any roles you'd be good for."

"Thanks." Content with our exchange and newfound understanding, I turned back toward the water to enjoy the soothing feeling of the gentle waves I was creating with my legs. As I was doing this, I physically felt a lost part of me come back, and I instantly felt the best that I had in days. I could've played in this space forever.

"Sun's going down," He said.

Todd and I watched the glorious sunset from the large wall-sized window. As the colossal inferno made its way below the horizon, the conflicting audio of the still tranquility of the pool and the raging infernal rapids of the Jacuzzi seemed to blend perfectly as

the liquid symphony filled the room.

32

We had a certain spunk about us as we geared up for our last performance of the tour. We carried out the final morning load-in with the zest and zeal of Santa's elves. As Todd carried one of the wardrobe bags into the theater, he passed by me and joked, "Let's make sure the lights stay on for the entire show this time, Nurse Ratched. None of that faulty wiring you've been doing since you got your new position."

That crack stopped me in my tracks. It was just like old times, minus the high-voltage undercurrent.

"You know, I still seem to be missing a pair of white stockings that go with my nurse's outfit. Don't tell me that you've fallen off the hose-sniffing wagon again!" I quipped.

"Ah, no. Those hose are probably in the same place where you keep the knife. God knows you've never checked there," he said.

"You little shit. You little shit!"

"Nice to know you still care, Nurse Ratched. Now remember, each plug goes into a socket . . ."

"Oh, go bite one!"

I walked away with a huge smile on my face and an energized jolt to my soul. My feelings of bliss were carried into my performance. Brilliant riffs and risk-taking efforts were happening not only with me, but with the entire cast. The only thing that remained constant was the dialogue, as stage positions, reactions, and even costumes had new life and inspirations.

While Johnathon, Todd, Joey, and I were performing our sole scene together for the last time, per the scene, I scolded the three Montagues for being crass and rude. The entire time, Todd had his back to me, which was a different interpretation than all of our previous performances. When it was time for him to deliver his line, he faced me and revealed a freaky fish-eye contact lens he'd purposely put into his right eye. I didn't see it right away, but when I did, I nearly tripped over my line. A consummate professional, I gracefully turned my near flub into a part of my performance, further entertaining the audience.

Todd and Johnathon fulfilled their obligations to the scene, then exited, leaving Joey and me on the stage. I could feel Todd watching me from the wings as Joey and I finished the scene. When I got a break from my dialogue, I caught a glimpse of Todd's grin as it glowed at me from backstage, shot him a *you got me* look, then picked up my onstage dialogue right on cue with the audience totally unaware of the silent conversation. I was on fire. I could do no wrong that day, and everyone in the house knew it, so much so that I had an incredible breakthrough in my performance that everyone felt.

The caring and protective nature of the Nurse toward Juliet had new meaning to me. The text, the circumstances of Juliet being so hopelessly and tragically in love, and the Nurse's role to try to save Juliet from love's darkest ills, spoke to me like never before. I poured myself into the concern and worry for my treasured fawn as a parent

would, taking Molly under my wing and hoping and praying that she

accepted my tutelage. The connection felt real.

Just a few days ago, this real connection with this same

person was reversed, and it was clearly fueling today's creation. Molly,

and all who were witnessing the performance, felt my intent in their

hearts and were moved. It was the first time something like this had

happened to me in my career: a palpable, organic connection that was

transmitted through the entire audience and back to me. In that

moment, as my last performance as the Nurse, I fell back in love with

my craft, and myself.

After the final line of the play was delivered by Salvador and

the curtain fell, we all engaged in a rousing curtain call. The crowd

gave us an energetic standing ovation, and we responded with

unprecedented high fives and singing. We took our final bows, then

trotted off the stage.

The entire cast let out a collective "Whoo!" once shrouded

from the audience, then gave ourselves a round of applause. We

shook one another's hands, gave one another hugs, and congratulated one another, then arranged ourselves in our standard positions and began to de-mic one another. Johnathon held up a small roll of mic tape and announced to the rest of us, "I think I'm going to keep this as a memento."

"No! Burn it! Burn it!" Molly proclaimed.

"We'll sacrifice it tonight at the wrap party," Leroy suggested.

"Throw that fucking freaky eye on the fire while you're at it," I said.

"I have no idea what you're talking about," Todd responded.

"I can't believe all of you were in on that! Sally? Et tu, Brute?" I asked.

"I was sworn to secrecy! They told me they'd wreck my doll collection if I told!" Sally replied.

"Her Raggedy Annes would've been sent back to her piece by piece. We'd start with the eyes," Christian commented.

"Still, someone should've told me. That was terrifying," I said.

"Being terrified by the dreaded fish eye on your last day of work, that's the way to go out! Great prank!" Salvador says as he slapped hands with Todd.

"Who said anything about the dead eye? I was terrified by his face!" I quipped.

The cast applauded the finality of our playful feud. Todd conceded the final and ultimate defeat amongst my cheering supporters by bowing to me and giving me praise. I laughed heartily and showed my well-earned respect for my opponent by giving him a spirited hug. This was bliss—electric, passionate bliss.

The majority of the cast quickly hopped out of our costumes and into our regular clothes to begin the customary load-out. Sally, however, lingered. It was as if she didn't want the moment to end. She took an absorbent amount of time to take off her makeup and climb out of her wardrobe. When she finally finished getting dressed in her street clothes, she positioned herself in front of one of the glamour mirrors and began to put in her earrings. Through the reflection, she could see the door swing open. In stepped Joey. He approached and stood behind her.

"Great show," Sally said to Joey's reflection.

"Great tour," he responded.

"Yeah, great tour."

Joey looked like he wanted to say something as he watched Sally slide the back onto her second earring. She smiled softly at his reflection, and he smiled back. Then, suddenly, Joey turned her toward him, placed his hands on her face, and kissed her. Pleasantly shocked, she remained silent for a few seconds.

"We've got to stay in touch. Too many flavor combinations we haven't experienced yet," he said.

"I agree," she replied.

Joey then extended his hand and said, "Friends?"

Sally pulled him close, embraced him in one of the most heartfelt hugs I've ever witnessed, and said, "Friends."

***

The final load-out went off without a hitch as we could now get through that hectic action in our sleep. Trent was even seen smiling as he clicked his trusty stopwatch dead when the last item was

shoved into the cargo van. After which he slid his valued trinket back

into its protective case, where I imagined it would remain until the

next tour, and put it in his shirt pocket.

We all took in our last looks of the lush countryside as we

pulled off for home, highly anticipating our return to the concrete

jungle. Our last ride was filled with loud, boisterous chatting,

laughing, finger-pointing, and reminiscing as we traveled down the

dusty afternoon highway.

An infinite sing-along eventually broke out, but was quickly

ceased after the umpteenth song, when Salvador, the driver of the

van, yelled to us and pointed off into the distance. All of us looked in

the direction that he was pointing and immediately began bursting

with joy.

Not too far off in the haze and maze of outstretched

highways and bridges, the festive tip of the Empire State Building

could be seen, glowing magnificently underneath an extremely large

blood moon. We whooped, hollered, applauded, and whistled our

relief and anticipation of returning back to Gotham. Then, all of us, with the exception of Salvador, piled into the backseat on top of one

another and began to have a platonic celebratory orgy.

33

HARLEM, NY

Leroy's apartment looked like Christmas. There was a small spinning strobe in the corner, along with decorative lights, and festive garland draped all over the spacious abode. A bottle of cheap champagne had just been uncorked, and the cast wrap party was underway. Spicy smells filled the air as Salvador was busy employing his culinary skills in the kitchen while Molly diligently worked as his assistant.

Leroy, glow sticks in hand, danced to the techno music that was pumping through several Wi-Fi speakers he'd strategically placed throughout the apartment, his personal collection of tunes being sourced straight from his phone. Nearby, Johnathon was teaching the rest of us how to properly finger our favorite songs on his guitar. "What about 'Stairway to Heaven'?" Christian asked curiously.

"A man after my own heart," Johnathon said. He started playing a few bars then commented, "This was one of the first songs I desperately wanted to learn when I was starting out." I clearly envisioned the many practice hours he'd put in on this piece over the years, as his rendition was beautiful and unflawed. Todd and I, sitting across from each other, shared another uncontrollable glance.

"Ahh, I've always wanted to know how to play this," Christian said as Johnathon continued to strum away. Eventually, Johnathon stopped and began to unstrap himself from his electrical extension.

"Here," Johnathon said.

"No. I couldn't," Christian responded.

"I'll teach you. It's nothin' to it, come on," Johnathon said as he handed Christian the guitar.

"If you can teach me this tonight, I will owe you my life!" Christian exclaimed.

As they began the informal lesson, Todd and I glanced at each other again.

This is it. This is the end. Knew this was coming, was even glad this was coming. Why does this feel so weird, then? Why do I feel so off, especially when I look at him? I should probably leave early.

I excused myself and walked to the kitchen. Todd's eyes remained fixed on me as I left the area, then he told everyone observing the music lesson that he was going to step out for some fresh air, and exited the apartment.

As I entered the kitchen, Salvador and Molly were still firing away. The sizzle and saturating smell of the sausages and vegetables in the skillet tantalized my senses. "What's on the menu tonight?" I asked.

"Patience, my dear, patience. Just believe it will be something that you've never experienced before," Salvador said.

"It's his 'patented' stuffed sausage and peppered linguini. He acts like no one has ever had that before," Molly remarked.

Salvador stopped turning and flipping the sausages and vegetables, looked at Molly and said, "You just had to tell her. You know you can't be the assistant if you give away all the secrets," then resumed shuffling his masterpiece.

"Give me a break. You're no chef," Molly said under her breath.

"I'm no chef? I am a genius in a kitchen. I create magic in here," Salvador said with an air of bravado, to which Molly gave him a look. Salvador threw that look right back at her and said, "Tell the truth."

Molly huffed and puffed, then said, "Oh, all right. Fine." Finally, she turned to me and said, "He really is a genius when it comes to food."

"Really?" I asked.

"Really," Molly confirmed.

"And?" Salvador said.

Molly huffed and puffed again, like she just couldn't deny the truth. "Annnd he really is some kind of magician in here. Things that shouldn't go together taste incredible after he's finished with them. He really has a talent for it," she says as she stroked his arm.

"Why, thank you, sweetheart. Finally, a kind word from you. A bit unusual, but I could get used to it," Salvador said.

"Okay. That's enough," Molly warned sternly.

I smiled at their playful banter then felt a soft tap on my shoulder. It was Todd. "Can I talk to you for a sec?" he asked.

Oh boy. Center yourself, Lamberty. Find your balance.

"Sure," I responded.

We exited the kitchen and stepped into a dimly lit hallway. Our silhouettes positioned themselves across from each other, then leaned back on the walls of the hallway to create the necessary void between us. It was quiet back there, almost as if the activity in the front room had been muted. It was just he and I alone, probably for the final time.

"Wanted to give you this earlier, but couldn't find the right time," Todd said as he pulled a small card-sized envelope out of his pocket.

I laughed and said, "So funny. I got one for you too."

"Are you kidding?" he responded.

"Nope." I reached into my pocket and took out an identical card-sized envelope.

"Did you give anyone else one?" Todd asked.

"Nope. Did you?"

"Nope."

We chuckled at the irony—a nice moment between us. While festive and fun, that night had been incredibly stressful for us in particular. That small crack in the tension was much needed. We both took a necessary breath, and Todd said, "Guess we should exchange."

"Oh yeah, right," I replied.

We gave each other our cards, but we didn't open them.

We shared an intimate moment of silence, then looked into each other's eyes, and I uncontrollably recaptured all the events that took place prior to that final night. I felt the thump, but I thumped back, as I had learned how to. He and I were survivors of war, once prisoners, but somehow, I'd escaped. It was something that we'd shared that I wouldn't ever forget, and I didn't think he would either. At least that's what his eyes were telling me when I looked into them this time. The war was over, but it would be remembered throughout our personal histories forever.

Todd broke the gaze first, then began to say, "I . . . ah . . . I wanted to . . . I wanted to tell you that I—. . ."

Suddenly, Sally rushed into the hallway and interrupted him with, "Hey, y'all, we're about to play 'I Never.' I guarantee you don't want to miss it."

Sally grabbed me by the arm and pulled me out of the hallway. I looked back to catch Todd standing there for a while alone, his unfinished sentence stuck on his tongue. He took in a few final moments of solitude in the dark hallway, then rejoined the group.

***

Hours later, the party was still on full tilt. We danced to the music all while being amazed by Leroy's glow stick–twirling abilities. Todd and I danced in separate groups, but continued to occasionally catch each other's eyes. Eventually, Todd danced his way over to me and said, "Who would've known that Leroy could land spaceships!"

"I'm expecting the Starship *Enterprise* to come crashing through the ceiling any minute now," I responded.

Salvador had just finished wiping down the stove and kitchen counter. With the area spotless, he turned the light off in the kitchen, entered the crowded living room, and yelled to his engaged former castmates, "You guys enjoy the food?" We responded with resounding *whoo*s and hefty applause.

"Bravo!" Sally said.

"Magnifique!" Joey commented.

"The sausages were excellent!" Todd said.

Unable to resist, I said, "Never took you for a sausage lover, Todd. Anything you need to tell me?"

"You wish . . ."

"I just never knew you had such a deep passion for the thick meat!"

"Are you talking about yourself?"

"It takes a special person to love sausage like that."

"Yeah, okay."

"What you don't want is to start craving the sausage. Then you're headed for trouble. Believe me," I said.

"Sound advice from the Sausage Queen," Todd jested.

I thought about it for a second, then sighed and said, "I am the Sausage Queen, aren't I? I can't help it. I'm sorry, I'm just a sucker for the sausage."

"You're a sucker all right," Todd said.

We caught ourselves in our playfulness and enjoyed another much-needed chuckle. Then I looked at him and said sincerely, "I'll miss this."

"So will I. Listen, I was trying to tell you before that I— . . ."

Just then, Molly seemed to arrive out of nowhere and excitedly said, "Anne! Anne, it's time!"

"Time for what?" I asked.

"Remember, we said after dinner, when everyone's together . . ."

"Oh yes! Yes! Uh, Todd?" I said.

"Go ahead. Do what you have to do," he responded.

"We'll pick this up later."

"Sure."

I was whisked away once again, and once again, Todd tried to mentally rejoin the celebration.

***

The party settled to a modest vibe as it eased into the early morning time shift. The clock struck 4:34 a.m., and everyone was still drinking, laughing, and conversing in different parts of the apartment, albeit at a much more relaxed and laid-back pace. I was pretty much ready to go. It had been a long, stressful night, and trying to steal Anne away for two seconds of privacy had become tiresome.

Maybe I'll just text her what I need to say.

In the meantime, Joey, Sally, and I were talking in the dim kitchen, each with a drink in our hands, and I was trying my best to remain interested.

". . . so that's what I mean, man. Art. This guy kept taking out second mortgages on his home just so he could keep making films.

That's the kind of dedication it takes. That kind of sacrifice," Joey said tipsily.

"Not many people are willing to do that, though," I replied.

"Exactly. People don't really want it. They might claim they do, but they have no idea what it takes to do what we do. When they see how much we have to give up and go through, they quickly change their tune," Joey said.

"I knew this guy from back home who traveled to New York to become an actor. He only left a few years before I did. Last week, I saw him panhandling on the train. He looked horrible. You're always right on that edge, you know? A couple of blown auditions and that could've been me," Sally admitted.

"Tell me about it. The month before the tour, I'd completely run out of money," Joey confessed.

Out the corner of my eye, I could see Anne grabbing her purse, putting on her coat, then hugging Leroy.

"If I hadn't gotten this tour, I don't know what I would've done. It's scary. I tell people all the time, don't do this unless you absolutely have to," Joey continued.

I kept watching Anne out of the corner of my eye as she moved on to hug Salvador and Johnathon. She then crossed through the living area to share what looked like sincere dialogue with Molly, then meaningfully embraced her. She then began to approach us as a look of uneasiness washed over her face.

When she arrived, Sally took a look at her and said, "You outta here already?"

"Yeah. Gotta make it all the way to Brooklyn, so . . ." Anne said.

Sally gave her one of her world-famous heartfelt hugs and said, "You take care, sweetheart."

While engrossed in Sally's embrace, Anne replied with, "This isn't the end for us."

"You bet your ass this isn't the end. I expect a phone call at least once a week!"

"Absolutely."

Anne released Sally and hugged Joey. "It was a pleasure listening to your counsel in the Friar's lair everyday," Joey said.

"And it was my pleasure to give it," she responded.

Anne released her embrace, then paused in front of me.

"You," she said, then gave me what I imagine was the most heartfelt hug she'd ever given. I held back, but I still felt the emotion between us, and I'm certain she felt it too.

After we'd released each other, I asked, "How are you getting home?"

"Subway."

"I'll walk you."

"Okay."

"Just let me get my coat."

"Hold it, you're going to the subway? We owe Leroy a bottle of Jack for always having our back during load-in, so we'll come with you guys. Cool?" Joey said.

"Yeah, that's cool," Anne responded.

Fuck.

They all exited the kitchen, with me moving much slower than the others. We all grabbed our coats and exited into the night.

***

The sky was starting to become that controversial soft shade of purple. We night owls know this color well, and it either makes us extremely happy or extremely angry once recognized. I'm generally the latter. Seeing this kind of color in the wee hours of the morning can make one change his/her life if witnessed one too many times. However, that wasn't the case with this night. People were still outside enjoying conversation and the night air without a care in the world. It was typical daybreak in the loving, friendly confines of New York City, specifically, Harlem.

Our foursome walked down the street in a horizontal line, forcing other pedestrians to either scrape against buildings or walk in the street in order to get around us.

Anne and I were at opposite ends of the chatty group. My mind was going a mile a minute; thus, I had very little to offer to the conversation they were having.

"I'd be in heaven if the subway was at the end of my block," Sally said.

"I'd be in heaven if a liquor store was at the end of mine," Joey commented.

"And the truth finally emerges!" Anne said with a laugh.

"Not that I'd be there every day . . ."

"It's just nice to have the convenience . . ." Anne replied.

"Exactly!"

"I understand."

"Whoo boy! Promise me y'all won't ever go into the liquor business together. Would be too much temptation for the both of ya!" Sally said, sparking a laugh from Anne and Joey, as we reached the subway entrance.

Anne turned to the group, shrugged, and said, "Well, guys— . . ."

Joey and Sally cut her off by rushing toward her and giving her a group hug. "Remember, at least once a week!" Sally said.

"Definitely," Anne replied.

"Me too! We'll go get hammered sometime!" Joey said.

"I'm up for that! Anytime!" Anne responded.

"Stop it!" Sally shouted.

"I'm just kidding. You take care of yourself, Ms. Lamberty," Joey said as he broke away from the group embrace.

"You got it."

Sally released Anne too and gave her a small wave goodbye. Joey and Sally looked at me to see if I was going to say anything. Anne also waited. Joey and Sally ratcheted up the pressure by stepping aside, providing me ample space and privacy to deliver my ultimate adieu.

After a few breaths, I finally stepped toward Anne and said, "Well, this is it."

"Yeah. It's gonna feel funny," she said.

"What is?"

"Not seeing you every day."

"Guess I'll have to find someone else to sharpen my verbal sparring skills," I said.

"Anytime you want to go for another round, just let me know."

"You'd really accept my challenge?"

"Of course. You proved to be a worthy opponent," she said.

"I may have been a worthy opponent, but I'm a horrible friend. I have already lost the card you gave me. I put it in the inside pocket of my coat, and now it's gone. Must've slipped out or something when I put it back on. I checked all around the area where I'd left my coat. I even checked all the other coats! Nothing. I'm sorry," I said.

Anne blushed, reached into her pocket, and pulled out the card she initially gave to me!

"I took it back."

"Why?"

"I don't know. I . . . I wrote something I probably shouldn't have."

"Oh. Well, if you don't want me to have it . . ."

"No, no, it's okay," she said as she extended the card toward me. "Here, take it."

"No, if you're not comfortable . . ."

"It's fine. I want you to have it. Take it."

I reluctantly took the card. Anne bowed her head and said, almost to herself, "You should already know what's in that card, because it's the truth."

"Are you sure you want me to have it?" I asked.

"Positive."

"Well, thanks."

Loaded silence sat on us as the soft purple horizon began to turn to a deep shade of pink.

"Guess I better get going," Anne said.

Fuck me!

I couldn't say what I wanted to say. I'd been waiting all night to tell her, and I just couldn't bring myself to say it out loud. I was crushed with disappointment. Nonetheless, I embraced her and held her in my arms one final time. The hug was long and forthright. Joey and Sally could even notice the emotion beneath the genuine gesture as evidenced by them looking at each other and whispering.

I will miss this. I will miss her. Every day.

We lost ourselves in our eternal embrace. Eventually, I took a deep breath and said what I believed was best: "You take care."

"You do the same," she replied as we released each other.

I watched Anne descend the stairs, then disappear into the subway cave, her red scarf whipping in the wind becoming a permanent memory. Eventually, I made my way over to Joey and Sally.

"Y'all must've washed some serious laundry for that kind of goodbye," Sally commented.

"Yeah, you could say that," I responded.

We began to walk away from the subway together. I kind of lagged behind their pace as I wanted a little privacy to open and read the card Anne gave me. I gently pulled the card from its encasing and began to inspect it.

At a certain point during my reading, I abruptly stopped my lazy stroll. I could feel my face and chest tightening as I continued to read. Then I forcibly flipped the card closed and yelled to Joey and Sally, "Hey, guys! I'll catch up to you, okay?" I then took off in a dead sprint toward the subway.

I dodged people and objects on my determined pursuit. I made it to the subway station in no time, fired down the stairs, and hurdled past the turnstiles, much to the chagrin of the booth attendant. I desperately searched up and down the platform with my eyes as the last few passengers were entering a waiting train.

There, at the absolute end of the platform, was my target, Anne, wiping away a few tears as she boarded the train. The moment I saw her, the train doors shut, and the electrical monster began to slowly grind forward on the tracks as Anne took a seat facing away from the window.

I resumed my sprint and began to call out for her: "Anne! Anne!" The loud mechanical screeching from the departing train unfortunately drowned out any auditory. My calls were still too far away as the train began to pick up speed.

I continued to scream for dear life and run down the platform, hungrily hoping and praying that she would hear a smidgen of my voice and be able to recognize it. Fortunately, and unbelievably, I was getting closer.

"Anne! . . . Anne!"

I was like a thoroughbred, galloping with confidence and purpose. My resolve continued to get stronger and stronger as I outpaced the medium trot of the train and gained significant ground on Anne's car. The sound of the screeching train began to get louder.

"Anne!"

I was really close now. Just a few more steps and she'd be in audible range.

"Anne!"

The train grew even louder as it picked up speed, and I began to fall behind its pace. Slowly, I started to realize that this possibility was impossible. As the train was getting away from me, I made one last desperate attempt.

"ANNE! ANNNNNE!"

She finally heard something! I saw her beginning to turn her head in my direction and . . .

She was gone, whisked down the shadowy crevice. I leaned over with my hands on my knees, trying to catch my breath and trying to soothe the deep burn in my lungs. I watched the train's bright lights as they traveled down the shaft and got farther and farther away from me until they were completely enveloped by the darkness.

EPILOGUE

Todd and I have finished lunch, our empty plates having been cleared away long ago. The only thing that remains on the table are a few loose crumbs, an empty bread basket, and water stains from our coaster-less glasses. The dark, damp day outside the café window is beginning to lighten up as our three-hour conversation comes to a close. I, who had been listening to Todd's account of our last night together, am surprised at what Todd just revealed to me.

"I never knew the platforms were that long. Felt like I'd run a mile," Todd says.

"Why didn't you call me afterward?" I ask.

"Couldn't work up the nerve. When I'd read what you'd wrote, it was just . . . whew! I felt like I had to say something to you. After the moment passed, I thought it would be best if I just left it alone, even if it left things . . . I don't know . . ."

"Unfinished."

"Yeah. Unfinished," Todd says.

"I felt the same way. We kind of just left it as it was. It was weird. That whole night was just odd for me. That's one of the reasons why I wanted us to sit down and talk about what happened out there, now that we're out of that situation," I say.

"I'm glad you called because I've been wanting to tell you something since that night. Was trying to tell you, but we kept getting interrupted."

"I know. I remember being so afraid to hear what you had to say. I'm still a little afraid, but I'm sure I can handle it much better now."

"I don't want to cause any problems . . ."

"You won't. Tell me."

Todd takes a breath, then releases. "Well . . . I just wanted to say that whatever happened out there was real for me. Everything I said, everything I wrote, everything I felt, was real. It was the first time I was completely open and honest about everything with someone else, and this wasn't something that was just physical for me. I had a connection with you. An emotional connection. I don't know how to explain it. You're not even my type, for crying out loud! I guess we were just made from compatible chemicals. Combustible chemicals. It killed me when things changed for us. I felt like you were being selfish. It was like you were done with me and there was nothing I could do about it. I felt so stupid for coming on so strong—helpless, dumb. What was even more frustrating was trying to figure out why any of it mattered. Why was this tearing me up inside, and why did I have such strong feelings for someone I met just a few months ago? At some point, I actually thought about quitting the tour. I had it bad. All the while, I knew what you were doing was right, for the both of us, but it still didn't stop the pain. Even with that, I wouldn't trade what we experienced for anything. We had something pure—something visceral, potent. Something rare.

I enjoyed our dance together, my lady, and will gladly reserve a spot for you on my dance card in the next life."

When he stops speaking is when I realize I'm a mess. A snotty, mascara-smeared mess. Todd tenderly kisses my hand, looks up, and realizes as much too. He hands me a napkin from the table, and I do the best I can to clean myself up. I take a deep breath and don't speak until I'm composed. It takes a minute or two.

"Wow. Wow. Thank you. Uh . . . yeah. This is something truly unique," I say.

"How do you mean?"

"I mean, I've never had this happen before. Here we are: we've been completely away from each other for months, and you still have such a strong impact on me. It's still alive, Todd, and yes, it is real. I never wanted to read too much into it and be 'that' person, but I do think we shared something special, a powerful, unspoken draw toward each other. It was uncontrollable. That reason and that reason only is why I had to be selfish. I had to protect myself from destroying what was waiting for me in the real world. I hated having to keep my distance from you. The tour was not fun anymore for me either. I enjoyed doing the work, but after that, there was no more enjoyment, just stress. By no means was I done with you though. Not at all. I just couldn't control my attraction, so I thought it would be best if I tried to avoid you. Every step you took toward me had to be met with resistance on my part because I didn't need to get drawn in again, even though I desperately wanted to. I wanted so much to call you, to talk to you, to hear your voice, to touch you, to be alone with you. It was killing me not to. You were on my mind most of the time when I was avoiding you. I looked forward to seeing you every day. I thought about you at night until I went to sleep, then dreamed of you, then was ecstatic when the dream ended and I woke up because I knew I'd be seeing you soon. It was so strong for me that I couldn't be in the same room with you without feeling these feelings that would've capsized both of us if I'd acted on them. I was in extreme pain too, being away from you, but it was the right thing to do. I wouldn't change a thing either. But believe me when I say that this was as real as it gets for me. What I felt for you has not died and probably never will, and because of that, this will be the last time we'll see each other."

Todd takes a long moment to absorb the tragedy of my words and I can tell that he is struggling. I am dealing with a raging war inside myself as well, so much so that I can't detect exactly what he is going through, but I can tell it is something. Something silent and very real, as real as it is for me.

I continue, "In a way, I'm kind of glad this happened . . . you and me . . . us. It showed me who I am, what's underneath. It was like I was this massive dirty pot with loads of dried-up shit stuck to its walls. You and I, our experience together, was like soap and water. It brought all that caked-up shit in the pot to the surface, and I had to deal with it in order to get clean. I had to deal with me, the real me, and before I met you, I don't think I really knew who I was or what was inside of me. I still don't know it all, still learning about myself every day, but because of our experience, I know more about who I truly am, and who I want to be. I thank you for that. I'm thankful for what we shared, but it has to end. Today it will."

I have to think that Todd was prepared to hear this, but even so, I can almost see my words sear into his chest. My last few sentences have affected even me as the finality of it all lands upon us like a mountain, and we both are visibly shaken. We're both fighting like hell to not break down in front of each other, but we're rapidly losing the battle against the inevitable.

Before he completely shows his hand, Todd musters up enough strength to nod, crack a barely seen smile, and say, "I understand. Let's drink to it." I take a moment to review and approve the full weight of this transaction, then raise my glass. He follows.

"To closure," he says.

"To closure," I respond.

Both of us are on the supreme verge of tears as we clink glasses.

"Goodbye, Anne," he says.

"Goodbye, Todd," I respond as we salute and drink.

Another long, heavy pause persists as we just sit there, looking at each other. Eventually, Todd reaches out and grabs my hand as tears well up in both of our eyes.

"So, next week? Same time, same place?"

Reluctantly, I feel a smile begin to generate that reaches from my gut to my lips.

Goddamn you, Mr. Happy. Goddamn you.